Lust, Money & Murder

Books 1, 2 & 3

Mike Wells

DEDICATION

For Anya, with love

BOOK 1

LUST

PROLOGUE

Italy – Present Day

The man picked her up in Vernazza, a picturesque village perched along the rugged coastline of the Italian Riviera.

From his salt-and-pepper hair, and his lined face, Maria guessed he was in his early 50s. He bought her a drink, then dinner, then a new dress and a pair of pumps and a few other things, spending lavishly on her in the quaint village shops.

There were no pretenses. They went to his plush villa, which afforded a breathtaking view of the sea. When she asked his name, he looked at her with his brooding dark eyes and said, "Are names important, *cara?*"

All she knew was that he was a businessman from Rome. She supposed it didn't matter.

They were soon hungrily making love to each other on the king-sized bed. She hadn't expected such energy out of a man his age—he was insatiable. She often had to fake orgasms with older men, but not with this one.

They spent most of the weekend in the bedroom. In between sexual bouts, they hiked up and down the cobblestone streets of the village, admiring the view and the lovely, narrow houses that were painted in pink, blue and yellow pastels. They gorged themselves on the local cuisine— *cappon magro*, a pyramid made of fresh vegetables and a half dozen different types of fish, and the *torta pasqualina*, a cake made of 18 layers of light pasta and stuffed with *ricotta* cheese.

They spoke very little. Maria didn't care. Words might break the spell, and she didn't want this to end.

On the third day, he felt that he had won the girl's trust.

The experiment he wanted to perform was far too important to delegate to one of his lieutenants. There was much riding on the outcome. He needed to see the results first hand.

But he had to be careful.

When she lay in his arms, spent, he said, "Did you know I am celebrating this weekend, *cara*?" He stroked one of her full, firm breasts. "You are a gift to myself."

She looked up at him with liquid brown eyes. "What do you mean? What are you celebrating?"

He rose naked from the bed and picked up a small leather Gucci bag that was sitting on the coffee table. He knew she was curious about what was inside—he had been carrying it around everywhere they went, keeping it close at all times.

When he opened it, she gave a little gasp.

The satchel was packed with crisp, new U.S. $100 bills.

"So much money," she said in a hush. "Where did it come from?"

"I sold a flat in Portofino, a dilapidated hovel I have been trying to rid myself of for years. I finally found an American gullible enough to buy it, but he insisted on paying part cash. It's only about fifty thousand dollars."

Even though she was trying to hide it, he could see the greed in her 21-year-old eyes. She was a *velina*, a soft hooker who survived on her good looks, roaming up and down the Riviera, living off one rich man after another, staying a few days or weeks in a villa or onboard a yacht until the current sponsor tired of her and threw her out, after which she moved on to the next.

He said, "I was thinking of driving up to San Remo and trying my luck. Have you ever been to the casino there?"

"No," she lied.

"You'd love it—it's the largest casino in Italy. All the richest people gamble there." He also happened to know that the establishment had just updated its currency verifying machines with the latest software.

He motioned to the cash, feigning frustration. "Unfortunately, I left my passport in Rome. There's no way to change this kind of money without one."

"I could change it for you," she blurted, but then checked herself. "I mean, if you want me to." When he didn't react, she said, "I have my passport right here," and reached over to her purse and produced it.

He smiled. He already knew she had a valid passport. He also knew that she had left her home in Naples at the age of 16, and was unknown to anyone in these parts.

Ten minutes later, they were driving up the coast, heading towards San Remo in a metallic blue Porsche cabriolet, the wind blowing through their hair. It was just before sunset. The highway ran up and down the rugged cliffs along the shore. Soon, the sky exploded into a riot of orange and indigo and violet.

Maria was excited, looking forward to a few more days of luxurious meals, plush accommodations, and expensive presents. Maybe he would buy her a diamond bracelet at the casino gift shop. Why not?

When they reached San Remo, he surprised her again. He pulled up in front of the sidewalk that led to the casino entrance and handed her the Gucci bag. "Take that inside and convert all of it to casino chips." He motioned to the other side of the street. "I'm going to have a cup of coffee and catch up on a few business calls I have to make."

Maria was astounded that he was going to let her walk away with all that cash. When she got out of the car, he leaned over and looked up at her and smiled. "Try not to gamble it all away before I get there!"

She walked up the long sidewalk towards the casino. When the uniformed man opened the door for her, she glanced over her shoulder. Her generous friend was just sitting down at one of the tables at the cafe. He waved at her.

Maria was tempted to try and run away with the money. But she wasn't some stupid *puttana*—she knew better than to try and steal from a man like him.

Carrying the Gucci bag in one hand and feeling very chic and powerful, she went inside the busy currency exchange.

There were security cameras above each counter. Then she noticed a sign on the wall:

- WARNING -

ANYONE CAUGHT TRYING TO PASS AS MUCH AS ONE
COUNTERFEIT BANKNOTE ON THESE PREMISES WILL BE
TURNED OVER TO THE POLICE

Of course the money she had to change wasn't fake—she had nothing to worry about.

"Casino chips, please," she told the male clerk, emptying the bag on the counter.

She was disappointed with his reaction—he only looked bored. "Passport?" he said.

Maria handed it over.

He studied the document, then took a few of the bills and studied them, rubbing them between practiced fingers.

Maria was suddenly terrified. What if this money *was* fake? She didn't know the man who had brought her here! He could be a criminal!

With a sinking feeling, she wondered if she was being used to change counterfeit currency.

The clerk began feeding stacks of the notes into a big, complicated-looking machine. It had a red digital display that showed the total amount, the numbers escalating as the bills were swallowed up.

If any of the money was fake, it was too late now. She would be arrested on the spot, just like the sign said. And the man who had supposedly given it to her? Conveniently disappeared.

"Here you are, *signora*," the clerk finally said. He handed her a handsome, leather-crafted carrier that was loaded with casino chips.

Thank God, she thought, greatly relieved. She let out a little laugh as she carried the chips into the casino. It was silly of her to think badly of the man she had just spent the last three days in bed with—he was a nice person, she had known it from the start.

She began playing roulette, betting only €50 at a time.

A few minutes later, her friend showed up.

"Ah, there you are!" he said, rushing over to her. He took the chips and placed a drink in her hand and gave her a warm smile. "Come, *cara*—I will teach you how to play baccarat."

He gambled recklessly that night, delighted with the results of the experiment. Within several hours, he had lost €15,000 worth of chips, but he didn't care. It was a drop in the bucket compared to the amount of money he would make in the coming months. He gave Maria €10,000 in chips to gamble with and sat back and watched her lose it.

By 3 am, she was tipsy, and he was getting tired.

"Let's go back to Vernazza," he said, stopping her before she placed another bet.

"Vernazza?" she said. She looked disappointed. "I thought we would stay here..."

"It's silly to waste money on a hotel room here when I own a beautiful villa so close by."

A guilty look flickered across her face. "I'm sorry I lost all that money..."

"It's nothing," he said. "It was thrilling, wasn't it?"

By the time they were back at the villa, he found his second wind. He drove his lean, hard body into the young girl, bringing her to a series of toe-curling orgasms.

They lay there for a few minutes, and then he suddenly rose from the bed and started putting on his pants. "I'm buzzing with energy—I can't sleep. Let's go for a walk."

"A walk? Now?"

"Come," he said, pulling on her hand. "The fresh air will make you feel better."

"But it's so late..."

He ignored her protests and helped her get dressed, making sure she wore only her own clothes and not anything that he'd bought for her. When she reached for her wristwatch, he grabbed her hand and impatiently said, "For God's sake, *cara*, you're not going to a fashion show!"

It was windy outside, the sky just hinting at the coming dawn. They walked up the hill, along the cliffs.

Vernazza is part of a cluster of five villages known as the *Cinque Terre*. They veered off in the direction of Corniglia, the next closest village, which was only 3 km to the south. The path soon became so narrow that they had to walk single file.

"Be careful, *cara*," he said, letting her move ahead of him. "It's slippery in places."

The sea along this particular stretch of coastline was always rough, the waves breaking over clusters of jagged rocks that were covered with razor-sharp coral. It was not uncommon for hikers to slip and fall down the sheer 200-foot cliff face. Within minutes, their bodies were pulverized into bloody slabs of unidentifiable gristle and bone.

"Isn't the view incredible?" he said, stopping her after the path widened again.

"Yes," Maria said, snuggling her back up against his warm chest. Far below, the waves were exploding over the rocks, the spray filling the air with brine.

He kissed the top of her head, hugging her tightly. It was a shame. She was a beautiful girl—he was already developing a paternal, protective feeling for her.

Even though the fake $100 bills had passed through the casino's verifying machine, they would eventually be detected. She had shown her face on video. Her passport had been in the camera's field of view as well.

He gently turned her around and kissed her again, aggressively, shoving his tongue deeply into her mouth.

When he drew away, her eyes widened—all at once, somehow, she understood everything.

He shoved her into the abyss.

A few minutes later, he placed a call to a number at a sprawling dacha on the outskirts of Moscow.

A deep voice answered on the other end. "*Da?*"

"I have good news, my friend. Our experiment was a smashing success."

CHAPTER 1.1

Pittsburgh, Pennsylvania – 1985

The day Elaine Brogan was born, Patrick Brogan's life underwent a dramatic change. Patrick Brogan was a construction worker, and his existence consisted of a never-ending blur of brick-hauling and muddy work boots and dented hard hats and drunken bar brawls. He hadn't given much thought to the baby that had been coming for the past nine months.

When he gazed down at the spastic little creature he cradled in his arms, his life suddenly took on meaning.

By the time Elaine was four years old, Patrick would carry her up to the tiny wooden deck he had added onto the attic of their run-down Garfield house, holding her in his arms.

"Your great-great-great-great grandmother was an Irish Princess," he whispered, his beard tangled in her blonde hair. "She lived in a beautiful, ancient castle. It had a moat, and a—"

"What's a moap, Daddy?"

"A *moat*. It's a pond that goes all the way around the castle and protects it from attack." He paused. "Princess Alana's daddy, the king, would hold great feasts and celebrations at Brogan Castle. Afterwards, Alana would come out on the balcony, like this one, and all the people would cheer her. 'All hail to the Princess! All hail to the Princess!'" Patrick pointed out into the tiny backyard. "Can you hear them cheering?"

Elaine listened. She *could* hear them! Except they were crying, "All hail Princess Elaine! All hail Princess Elaine!"

"Was Princess Alana very rich, Daddy?"

"*Very* rich, sweetheart. Just like you're going to be one d—"

"Why do you fill her head with that nonsense?"

Kathy Brogan was standing in the doorway, smoking a cigarette, her face haggard from working a 12-hour shift at the supermarket. "You're going to make her think she's better than everybody else," she said.

Patrick looked genuinely surprised. "But she is better than everybody else."

Elaine was six years old when she realized her father was little more than a beer-guzzling manual laborer with an overactive imagination, and that Garfield, where they lived, was one of the worst areas of Pittsburgh. She would never be rich and there had never been any Princess Alana or a Brogan Castle. But she adored her father all the same.

Elaine loved to nuzzle her face into his broad chest when he came in the door from work. He smelled of sawdust and bricks and the outdoors.

She knew he would always be there to protect her.

As a little girl, Elaine felt a special affinity for working the visual puzzles in newspapers and magazines. The ones with two pictures side by side that appeared identical at first glance, with a caption that said: *There are ten differences between the girls in these two photographs. Can you find them?*

Patrick marveled at the speed with which his little tow-haired prodigy could work these puzzles. "The girl on the right doesn't have a bracelet, and there are two straps on her sandal...see how easy it is, Daddy?"

"No," he chuckled. "I don't see how easy it is. How the heck do you do that?" To his wife, he said, "She has an incredible eye for detail. Someday she might become a great artist."

"Uh-huh," Kathy said.

Patrick was forever concerned about his daughter's safety. When she started school, he drove her in his truck each and every morning, and picked her up and took her home each and every afternoon. At the construction sites, no matter how busy he was, he would drop whatever he was doing and say, "I have to go pick up my daughter." These words were always uttered with a great sense of pride.

His bosses put up with him because he was such a diligent worker, and they could not help but admire his fatherly dedication. Patrick was always the first one to arrive on site, and the last one to leave. During the day he worked faster and harder than anyone else.

His employers had no idea that he was the one responsible for the pilfering and theft that plagued the sites for years.

When Elaine was seven, Patrick caught her and the girl next door smoking cigarettes in the back yard.

That night, Patrick said to his wife, "I'm sending Elaine to a private school. I want her out of this shitty neighborhood."

"And how do you plan to pay for it?"

Patrick took a sip of beer, gazing at the TV. "Don't ask."

The Bromley Academy for Girls was housed in a cluster of brick colonial-style buildings nestled on 40 tree-filled acres of land, a half hour drive from Garfield. It was quiet and peaceful there, with plenty of fresh air, a gazebo, a stable, and the ruins of a little country church, complete with a graveyard.

The day of Elaine's interview, Patrick was a nervous wreck. His hair was slicked back, his beard neatly trimmed, and he wore a five-year-old ill-fitting suit he had bought for his mother's funeral. He was afraid that Ms. Prentice, the director of the school, would be an arrogant snob. To his surprise, she turned out to be a pleasant, unassuming little woman with a pug nose and a gentle smile.

"Your daughter is adorable," Ms. Prentice said, perusing Elaine's file, "and her grades and tests scores are outstanding. We would be thrilled to have her here at Bromley."

Patrick breathed a great sigh of relief. He picked up a heavy satchel and began stacking piles of rubber-band bound bills on her desk. "I hope you don't mind if I pay cash."

"I'm sorry, but we only accept checks."

"That's not convenient for me. See, I run a cash business." Patrick Brogan was a big man, with rough-looking hands. He had listed his occupation on the application as "construction site foreman."

"And what kind of business is that?" Ms. Prentice said uneasily.

"Me and my friends have some investments in different things. Video arcade for kids, stuff like that, you know. Cash businesses."

"I see. Still, I'm afraid we can't accept ca—"

"I was noticing that the paint's beginning to peel out there on your gazebo, and some of the pillars are rotten out front." He paused. "Appearance is important, don't you think?"

"Well I—"

"I'd be happy to fix things up around here on Saturdays." Patrick smiled easily. "I'm good at that sort of thing."

The first day at Bromley was a nightmare for Elaine. She made the mistake of telling the girls where she lived. There was a great deal of snobbery. She instantly became "the girl from Garfield" with the construction-worker father. His pickup truck was visible somewhere on the campus practically every Saturday, Patrick in his jeans and T-shirt, somewhere nearby painting or sawing or standing on a ladder and repairing a gutter.

Patrick went out of his way to be friendly and helpful to all the students, knowing how important this was for Elaine. He could speak in a passable Irish brogue, and he would say, "Top a de marnin' to ya, gershas!" or "I saw a leprechaun hidin' in de gerden!" They would all giggle.

Eventually they accepted him, and they accepted Elaine.

As Elaine grew up, Patrick lost all interest in his wife. To Kathy Brogan, it seemed that her only purpose in life had been to bring her husband's beloved "Lainie" into this world.

Kathy found herself more and more jealous of the constant attention he gave their daughter. Kathy was from Beaumont, Texas, and the high point of her life had been when she had been named prom queen at her high school. Her natural blonde hair and model-like figure had always made her the center of attention when men were around.

Kathy hated herself for being jealous of her own daughter, yet the feelings were so intense at times she couldn't control herself. One Sunday night after Patrick had spent the entire weekend with Elaine, she said, "Maybe you would rather little Lainie sleep in our bed and I can sleep in her room?"

Patrick slapped her so hard it knocked her off her feet. Pointing his shaking finger at her as she lay on the floor, her lip bleeding, he said, "You ever say anything like that again, I'll kill you."

Two weeks later, Kathy Brogan ran away to Florida with a 23-year-old check out clerk from the supermarket.

She was never seen or heard from again.

CHAPTER 1.2

"Have you ever done any modeling?" the man asked.

Elaine was 16 years old and had a summer job at a Pittsburgh shopping mall to help save money for college. She was on break, looking at a window display, when he approached her from behind.

When she turned around, he said, "My name is Randy," and shook her hand. He had an easy, disarming manner. A professional-looking camera was hanging around his neck. "I work for the Rising Star Modeling Agency." He gave Elaine a business card. "We're doing scouting for new models right now. You've got a fresh look. You should drop by our office."

When she got off work, Elaine took the bus straight downtown to the Rising Star Modeling Agency. There were dozens of beautiful young girls walking in and out of the sleek offices, which were on the third floor of a fancy office building. The walls were covered with posters of glamorous looking models in designer clothing. She didn't recognize any of them, but she was sure they were top fashion models.

A chain-smoking, middle-aged woman named Ms. Crawford interviewed her. She studied Elaine's face, asked Elaine to turn around.

Elaine was tall, almost 5' 10", and had her mother's figure—modest breasts, a flat stomach, and long, slim legs.

"I think you have a lot of potential. Do you have a comp card?"

"A what?" Elaine said.

The woman sighed as if she were dealing with a total amateur. "A comp card is a piece of paper that has your photos with different poses and tells potential clients all about you—your height, weight, dress size, shoe size. Like this." She showed Elaine one. "No agency will hire you as a model until you have a comp card."

Elaine blushed, embarrassed by her own naïvety. "How do I get a comp card?"

"You start by getting some top quality photos. You can use whatever photographer you want, but I can only recommend Randy. A comp card costs two hundred dollars."

"Two hundred dollars!" Elaine gasped. It was a small fortune to her.

Ms. Crawford sighed. "Look, honey, do you want to be a model or not?"

Elaine emptied her bank account and paid the $200. Posing in different outfits under the bright lights and with all the colorful props was thrilling. Elaine felt a heady rush when she picked up the comp cards. She looked spectacular in all the different photos. Now she was a real model!

She gave the cards to Ms. Crawford and went home, waiting for the phone to ring.

Ms. Crawford did not call. Two days passed, then a week, then ten days.

Elaine finally decided to go talk to Ms. Crawford and see what was wrong.

When she reached the agency, Ms. Crawford was standing next to the open window, smoking, talking on the phone. She seemed to talk forever. Finally, she hung up and looked at Elaine. "Yes, dear?"

"I...I was wondering if there were any modeling jobs for me yet."

"And you are...?"

"Elaine Brogan. I left my comp cards with you almost two weeks ago."

"Oh. Yeah. I thought you looked familiar. You're B list, right?"

"B List...?" Elaine didn't know what she was talking about.

She went over to a file cabinet. "Let's see... Bailey, Bennington, Bernstein...Brogan." She pulled out Elaine's file, glanced at the stack of comp cards, then put it back and shut the drawer. "Everything is in order. Is there anything else?"

"What does 'B List' mean?"

"Means you're untrained. You're not client-ready. Modeling is a highly competitive field, honey." She blew out smoke, looking at Elaine. "It's tough to get work unless you're client-ready."

"How do I become client-ready?"

"Training of course." She handed Elaine a color brochure that showed all the different classes the agency offered. When she saw the price for the whole program, her eyes bugged out. "Two thousand dol—"

"Do you think you could be a successful doctor without any training?"

"Well I—"

"A successful lawyer?"

Elaine didn't speak.

"A successful engineer? Honey, modeling is no different than any other profession."

Elaine felt stupid again.

She left with the brochure.

"Two *thousand* dollars?" Elaine's father said, staring at the paper.

"Modeling is no different than any other profession, Dad. If you want to be a successful doctor, you have to have training. If you want to be a successful lawyer, you—"

"I know all that. But two thousand dollars..."

"You don't think I'm pretty enough to be a model?"

"Of course you're pretty enough."

"Then what is it?"

"It's just that...I was hopin' you'd choose a profession where you'd use your brains."

"It's only a hobby, Dad. I don't expect to do it as a *career* or anything." The truth was, Elaine had fantasies about being a supermodel and having her picture splashed all over the cover of *Vogue* and flying all over the world and being filthy rich. She wasn't keen on the idea of going to college.

Patrick scratched his head, looking at the brochure. "I don't know...seems like this could be a scam to lure a lot of gullible young girls—"

"It's not a scam! Why do you always have to be so suspicious?"

"Lainie..." Patrick sighed. He gazed into his daughter's big blue eyes. He couldn't say no to her. "Is this really that important to you?"

"Yes," she said emphatically.

When he finally agreed, Elaine threw her arms around him and kissed his cheek. "I've got the best father in the whole wide world!"

For Elaine, the rest of the summer was an exhilarating blur of activity. She took classes on how to walk the ramp and catwalk, on hair and skin care, on fitness and diet, and on positive mental attitude. She attended seminars covering what to do in the "green room" and backstage, how to create good portfolio poses, and the use of body language. Outside of the agency, she also signed up for aerobics classes to burn off extra fat.

Her father brought home a ten-foot length of wood and sanded it down so she could practice "walking the beam," for catwalk training. He installed a huge mirror on her bedroom wall to help her refine movements and improve her posture.

Elaine slowly transformed from the proverbial ugly duckling into a swan. She didn't consider herself naturally beautiful, but she learned to make the best use of everything she had. She learned to buy clothes that accentuated her long legs and downplayed her small bust, and to do it on a budget that created a classy impression. She learned to smile more often, and to hold her head high when she was afraid. In general, she became much more aware of her posture and facial expressions and learned to move with much more grace and finesse.

Elaine worked hard, day and night, anxious to complete all the courses as quickly as possible, so she could get her career off to a roaring start.

In mid-August, she finished the last class offered by the agency, *Acting in TV Commercials*. She excitedly took the certificate down the hall to Ms. Crawford.

"All done," Elaine said.

"All done with what?"

"With the acting class," Elaine said, proudly holding up the signed certificate. "I've completed the entire program now."

"Congratulations," Ms. Crawford muttered. With her cigarette dangling from her mouth, she took the paper and turned to the file cabinets. "What's your name again, honey?"

Elaine gritted her teeth. "*Brogan*. Elaine Brogan."

She pulled Elaine's file out, dropped the certificate in with all the others, and shut the drawer.

"We'll call you."

Two long weeks passed. School started. Elaine heard nothing from the agency. She had expected the phone to start ringing off the wall for auditions. But every night when she got home, there were no messages on the answering machine.

She finally took the bus downtown to the agency and went straight to

Ms. Crawford's office. The woman was on the phone, as usual. Elaine impatiently tapped her fingers on the counter until she hung up.

"Can I help you?" Ms. Crawford said, lighting up a cigarette from the fire of the previous one.

"Yes." Elaine mustered up her courage. "I want to know why you're not calling me for any jobs. I've completed the entire training program, and—"

"What's your name, dear?"

Elaine couldn't believe it. "Brogan!" she snapped. "*Elaine* Brogan!"

"Don't get snippy with me, honey. We have hundreds of girls at this agency."

"I'm sorry...I'm just a little upset. You told me that when I finished the training classes, I would be able to get modeling jobs."

"I told you no such thing."

Elaine blinked once. "You said that to be client-ready, I had to have training."

"That's right."

"Well? I've taken every training class you offer."

"Yes, that's right. You've done all the group training. To be client-ready, you also need individual training, one-on-one, with Mr. Eskew."

Elaine fought the anger that was growing inside her. "And how much does that cost? Another two thousand dollars?"

"My, you're the jaded one, aren't you, missy? It so happens that personal training with Mr. Eskew is free."

Elaine was taken aback. "Free?"

"You have to be personally selected by Mr. Eskew."

"Oh. And how does that work?"

"By asking for an interview. Would you like me to schedule one for you?"

"Yes, of course." She added, "Please."

Ms. Crawford went to a desk calendar and opened it. "Let's see...Mr. Eskew has an open slot three weeks from—"

"I want an interview *now*. I don't want to wait three weeks."

Ms. Crawford stared. Elaine's heart was beating hard with anxiety, but she intended to hold her ground. She wasn't going to let herself be pushed around anymore.

The woman ran her pencil down the calendar. "There has been a cancelation for six-thirty tomorrow night—would that suit you?"

"That's perfect," Elaine said.

Elaine turned to leave, then looked back. "Thank you."

Ms. Crawford blew smoke out of the side of her mouth. "The pleasure was all mine."

Ronald Eskew, the owner of the agency, was a handsome man. In his 40s, he had a swarthy complexion, long sideburns, and a droopy mustache. He was always immaculately dressed. The only time Elaine ever glimpsed him was on the elevator or passing through the hall to his office. He was always with a beautiful young girl or two, who were decked out in expensive designer outfits.

For her interview, Elaine wore what she thought was her best outfit, a pair of skintight white jeans that showed off her long legs, and a top that revealed her flat stomach. She spent her last three weeks' pay to have her hair styled and splurged on a professional makeup job, even though she could have done it herself now.

She took the bus to the agency. For some reason, she did not want her father to know what she was doing, so she told him she had to work at the mall. The weather could not have been worse. It was pouring down with rain, the wind blustery. Even with her umbrella she was wet from the knees down when she arrived at Rising Star.

Ms. Crawford let her right in—she didn't have to wait.

"Well, Ms. Brogan, it's a pleasure to meet you," Mr. Eskew said. "Please have a seat."

She sat down on his leather couch. His office smelled of cigar smoke and musky aftershave lotion. He closed the door, then pulled up a chair and turned it backwards, sitting directly across from her. He was so close their knees were almost touching. He wore a lot of gold jewelry. She noticed that he had a Rolex watch.

Taking her comp card from her sweaty hand, he glanced at the front, then the back, then looked her up and down, pausing to admire her figure. His gaze rested on her bare stomach. "You have a fresh look. There's a certain innocence about you that's appealing."

"Thank you."

He set the comp card down on the coffee table, then looked into her eyes. "I know I don't have to tell you how competitive the modeling profession is, Ellen."

"It's Elaine."

"Right. Elaine. To make it in this business, you have to bring out your true self, your uniqueness." He motioned to her. "You know what I mean?"

Elaine nodded.

"The camera picks up what you're thinking, what you're feeling, your...*attitude*. That's really what it's all about. *Attitude*." He moved his hands a lot when he talked.

He glanced back down at her stomach. It seemed like every time he looked there his droopy mustache gave a little twitch.

"With my personal coaching," he went on, "I bring out the model's uniqueness." He peered down at her knee, then reached out and put his hand there. Gazing into her eyes again, he said, "Would you like to receive personal coaching, Elaine?"

"Well..." She wanted to brush his hand away. "I'm not sure I—"

"Would you like to go on photo shoots in the Caribbean? In Paris? In LA?"

"I—"

"To own expensive clothes? To have so much money you can buy whatever you want without giving it a second thought?"

His hand slid up her thigh. Elaine looked down at it, unable to move. She abruptly rose.

"I don't like you touching me," she blurted. "I'm only sixteen."

He looked up at her, frowning with disapproval. "You're acting like you're twelve. Professional models have to be mature."

For a second, Elaine felt an impulse to repress what she was feeling and try to act more "mature," but then she realized it was just more manipulation. Everything was crystal clear to her now.

"This agency is just a scam," she said. "I know what you're doing."

"And what is that?" he said, raising an eyebrow.

"I've seen those other girls—"

"What other girls?"

"The others..." Elaine realized that she had no concrete evidence of anything this slimy man did. "I want my money back. I spent two thousand dollars here, and I want it back!"

"I'm afraid that's out of the question."

"Really? Then I think I'll go to the police and tell them what you just did to me."

"And what was that?" he said, raising his eyebrow again.

"You..." She realized she had very little to say. *He touched my knee.*

"Yes?" he said.

"I'll—I'll tell my *father* what you did. He's six-three and weighs two hundred and fifty pounds. He's a construction worker."

Mr. Eskew's dark complexion lost a little of its color. He watched her for a few seconds.

"There's no reason to make threats," he said, cordially. "At Rising Star, we guarantee satisfaction." He stepped behind his desk and crouched to one of the cabinets. She heard clicking. It sounded like he was opening a safe.

"Two thousand dollars, you said?"

"That's right." Elaine was sure this was some kind of trick. She couldn't believe he would actually refund her money.

He shut the safe and placed two bundles of $100 bills on the desk, then pushed them towards her.

She stared at them.

"Go ahead. Take it."

She picked them up before he could change his mind, putting both bundles in her purse.

"I hope you see now that we are a reputable agency, and that you will tell others so. Just because your personal expectations weren't met, it doesn't mean the same will hold true for other girls."

When Elaine reached the lobby, she saw that it was still pouring with rain outside, and then realized that she had left her umbrella in Mr. Eskew's office. She wasn't about to go back and get it.

She flew out the door and dashed down to the bus stop. By the time she reached the shelter, she was soaked to the skin. But she was grinning ear to ear.

She had gotten all the money back! Every last dollar!

Her father would be proud of her. He had been right all along. He would have the satisfaction of saying "I told you so," but at least she got the money back.

As she waited for the bus, she began to worry.   Something was bothering her. It felt too easy. She glanced up and down the rainy street. What if Mr. Eskew called some thug to intercept her and steal the money back?

Making sure no one was watching, she took the bundles from her purse and slid them into the front pockets of her jeans.

The bus soon arrived. Elaine took a seat in the back and worried all the way home, glancing out the rear window every so often, afraid someone might be following along in a car.

When she reached her stop, she asked the driver to wait for a second while she stepped out and checked the road behind the bus, but no car was following.

She quickly made her way home. She didn't live in the kind of neighborhood where it was safe to carry more than $10 around in your purse. But then, nobody expected her to have any money, and everyone on her block was terrified of Patrick Brogan.

Elaine found her father in his usual position, sitting in front of the TV set, a beer in his hand.

"How was your day, sweetheart?"   He looked more closely at her. "You're soaked, Lainie!   You better change clothes."

Elaine pulled the two damp bundles from her pockets and deposited them on the coffee table in front of him.

"What's this?" he said, sitting up.

"All the money we spent at Rising Star, Dad. Every penny." She leaned over and put her arms around his neck and kissed him. "You were right."

"About what?"

"It's a scam. All they do is...well, I'd rather not say. The point is, I got the money back."

Her father looked at the two stacks of bills in amazement.

"I want you to put it in the bank, for college," she said.

Patrick gazed at his daughter with admiration in his eyes. "You've grown up, honey, you know that?"

In her bedroom, when Elaine took off her wet jeans, she shuddered, remembering Mr. Eskew putting his hand on her leg. Then she noticed that there were two grayish stains on the white material over the pockets, where the two bundles of bills had been.

Even the man's money is dirty, she thought, as she put the jeans in the laundry hamper.

She hoped the stains would come out.

The following evening, when Elaine and her father were eating dinner, there was a knock at the door.

"I'll get it," she said, rising from the table. She went to the front door and cracked it open, leaving the chain in place. The first thing she saw was the flashing of blue light on the houses across the street.

"Is this the Brogan residence?" a man in a gray suit asked.

"Yes."

He flashed some kind of badge with a star on it. "U.S. Secret Service. Open the door, ma'am."

Stunned, Elaine unchained the door and pulled it back. There were not one, but two men in gray suits.

"Does Patrick Brogan live here?" one said.

"Well...yes." She swallowed, having a very bad feeling. "Dad," she called, but he was already stepping up behind her.

"What's going on?" he said nervously.

"Patrick Brogan?"

"Yes..."

"Did you deposit some cash this morning at the First National Bank branch over on Penn?"

"Well...yeah, I did, but—"

Handcuffs snapped around his wrists. "You're under arrest for passing counterfeit currency."

The other man said, "You have the right to remain silent. Anything you say can and will be used against you in a court of law. You have the right to an attorney..."

CHAPTER 1.3

Under federal law, Patrick Brogan had committed a Class C felony, punishable by up to 12 years in prison and a fine of as much as $250,000.

Bail was set at $500,000. He was interrogated repeatedly by local police, the Secret Service, and the FBI, but he refused to disclose where the $2,000 in counterfeit money had come from.

A few days later, he was charged with a second crime—theft. His fingerprints had been run through the criminal database and matched a latent print taken at a crime scene two years ago, a construction site where he had worked.

Elaine's father was looking at a combined sentence of 25 years.

Elaine was sick with grief. She did not know what to do. Tormented by guilt, she went to the police station and tried to tell them that she had gotten the counterfeit money from the modeling agency, but they brushed her off as a distraught family member trying to protect her father.

He refused any visitors. He wouldn't speak to an attorney, not even a court-assigned one.

Six days after he was arrested, Elaine was finally allowed to see her father.

She sat down at the visiting window and waited, struggling with her emotions. A guard brought Patrick Brogan in and pointed. "Number Seven."

Her father walked slowly down the opposite side of the visiting booths, wearing orange prison coveralls.

"Daddy," she gushed, pressing her hands against the glass.

His lips trembling, he said, "I can't stand for you to see me like this," in a strained voice. He wouldn't even look up at her.

"Please don't be ashamed," she said, tears running down her cheeks. "Look at me, Daddy."

He finally raised his eyes. They were shadowed with dark rings, and his skin looked sallow. He had only been in jail a week, and he seemed like he had lost at least twenty pounds.

"Tell them where you got the money," she begged.

"I'm not dragging you into this, baby."

"Please, Daddy! They're going to put you in jail for twenty—"

"It won't make no difference." Patrick reached up and pressed his hands to hers against the glass. "What I done was for you, honey. For your future. I don't ever want you to feel bad about it. Ever."

The truth was, knowing that her father had been robbing construction sites to put her through Bromley all these years made her feel ill. Somehow she had known the money was coming from shady activity all along, but she had made herself believe his stories about his video arcade businesses he and his friends owned.

He lowered his voice to a whisper. "You have to keep your mouth shut about that counterfeit money, sweetheart. Don't never tell a soul. Promise me."

"But—"

"Promise me, Elaine."

"I— I promise."

"Time's up," the guard said gruffly, stepping behind him.

Elaine pressed her hands harder against the glass, desperately wishing she could touch him. She had a terrible feeling that this would be the last time she would see her father.

"I love you, Daddy!"

The guard guided him out of sight.

Elaine had no idea what would happen to her now. She knew her days at Bromley were numbered. She drove her father's old pickup truck to school by herself every day in a state of utter despair. She avoided Ms. Prentice, as if delaying any contact with the woman would help.

It's all my fault, Elaine thought. *If I hadn't gotten mixed up with that stupid modeling agency, none of this would have happened.* She wanted to destroy Ronald Eskew, but she could not think of a way to do it without defying her father's wishes.

Three days after she had visited him in jail, a student aid came to her world history class and asked her to come to the office.

Elaine knew what was about to happen. As she walked down the hallway, she wondered how Ms. Prentice would feel knowing that her tuition all these years had come from the sale of stolen property. She shuddered at the thought.

When she entered the office, Ms. Prentice was sitting at her desk. Her eyes were red and puffy. A wadded-up handkerchief was in her hand.

"What's wrong?" Elaine said, a feeling of dread descending over her.

Ms. Prentice moved from behind her desk, gazing sympathetically at Elaine, sniffling.

"What is it?" Elaine said.

"Your father..." Ms. Prentice held both Elaine's hands tightly. "He killed himself this morning."

Elaine drove the truck home in a robot-like stupor.

The words *He killed himself this morning* kept reverberating in her ears. But they didn't have any meaning. They were just random noises.

She glanced around the inside of the truck, at the fuzzy dice that hung from the rearview, at his leather work gloves, at the faded picture of herself at age eight in a cowboy suit, clipped to the sun visor.

I knew I would never see him again, she thought, remembering the feeling she'd had at the jail. She laughed hysterically, her lower lip trembling. Then she began gasping for breath and almost ran off the road.

When she pulled into the driveway at the house, she was only partially aware of what she was doing. She felt like she was in a dream, a nightmare, and that she was viewing herself from above.

She watched herself unlock the front door. She watched herself walk through the small living room and go down the steps into the basement. She watched herself open the bottom drawer of her father's beat-up metal desk and pull out the .38 revolver.

Under her father's orders, she had never touched the gun before, but it didn't look very complicated to operate. She found the button that released the cylinders. Her fingers spun them around slowly—there were bullets in all six of the chambers.

She put the gun in her purse, ascended the stairs, and went back out to the truck.

It was all Ronald Eskew's fault.

The sleazy bastard was going to pay.

As Elaine drove downtown, she visualized the scene. *You killed my father*, she would say, ramming the gun into his chest. No, under his neck. Into his Adam's apple. She would make him beg for his own life, get down on his knees and blubber like a baby. She would make him regret the day he was born. She would make him tell her where the counterfeit money had come from. When she was satisfied that she had completely broken him, she would call the police and hold him there until they arrived.

It was just getting dark when she pulled up to the main entrance of the office building where the Rising Star Modeling Agency was located.

She parked and got out, not bothering to lock the door.

When she stepped into the lobby, the security guard stood up and said, "You're not allowed to park there, miss..."

She was already heading towards the elevator.

"Hey, wait! You can't just—"

She stepped onto the elevator and pressed 3.

"Hold it!" the guard said, but before he could get there, the doors closed.

When the lift reached the third floor, she stepped off the elevator, her heartbeat thumping in her ears, yet sounding far, far away. She reached the agency's front door and twisted the handle.

It was locked. Then she noticed that the office lights weren't on.

Elaine frowned—it wasn't even six o'clock yet. Where the hell were they all?

The stairway doors burst open and the security guard trotted towards her. "What do you think you're d—?"

He stopped, glanced at the door, then back at Elaine. "They're gone."

"What do you mean?" Elaine said.

"Gone. Packed up their tent and moved away."

Elaine peered through the window into the darkened offices. All the desks were still there, the file cabinets, chairs...but there was trash scattered around on the floor.

"They didn't leave a forwarding address, nothing," the guard said. "Skipped out on the last sixth months of their lease." He looked at her sympathetically. "Did they owe you money, too?"

Elaine was dumbfounded. They had left, they had all left! Ronald Eskew must have known that her father had been arrested.

She turned and walked back down the corridor in a daze.

CHAPTER 1.4

Elaine was able to stay on at the Bromley Academy.

Ms. Prentice arranged for a full scholarship, which included room and board on campus. All the students grieved over the death of her father, and showed nothing but kindness towards Elaine.

She buried herself in her studies, hiding herself from her pain. She could not escape the deep-seated hatred that welled inside her for Ronald Eskew, or whatever the man's real name was. It grew inside her like a cancer.

One day, in the 11th grade, she and her best friend, Kaitlin, were in the guidance counselor's office, filling out their careers forms. Elaine noticed a magazine with an article titled *Careers in the Secret Service*. She read the part about the Anti-Counterfeiting Division.

She decided then and there that she was going to become a Secret Service agent, and that she was going to track down Ronald Eskew and punish him for what he had done.

The article said that to qualify for the Secret Service, you needed a college degree and that competition was fierce. It also said that if you were fluent in a foreign language and/or had some special education relevant to currency production, such as in intaglio printing, your chances of becoming an agent were much higher.

Intaglio printing, Elaine thought. She had no idea what that was, but she had always liked art and graphic design.

She didn't mention her plans to Kaitlin, or to anyone else. It was her secret.

In her senior year, Elaine applied to all the top colleges in the Northeastern U.S. that had strong graphic design departments and mentioned intaglio printing in their course catalogs. Ms. Prentice and her teachers wrote her glowing letters of recommendation.

Elaine was thrilled to be accepted at the prestigious Rhode Island School of Design and Architecture, with a full scholarship.

Kaitlin was accepted at Northwestern University in Chicago, also with a full scholarship. She planned to study economics.

When they both graduated from Bromley, they had a teary goodbye, and they promised to stay in touch.

CHAPTER 1.5

When Elaine arrived on the RISD campus, she felt strange. It was like suddenly being set free. Life back at Bromley had been fairly strict, even senior year, with her comings and goings from her living quarters tightly controlled. And fairly isolated, the school located out in the countryside 30 minutes from Pittsburgh.

Now, she found herself in a coed dormitory with very little in the way of supervision, and living in the middle of an urban area, in Providence, Rhode Island.

The strangest thing was attending classes with boys. Elaine hadn't been to school with boys since the second grade, and she felt shy and awkward around them. She became tongue-tied whenever they talked to her.

She tried to ignore the problem by throwing herself into her studies, which wasn't difficult—college was so exciting and different compared to high school, especially at a design school. She loved her studio courses—Drawing, 2-D and 3D—and did very well in them.

But her insecurity with the opposite sex persisted, and she finally decided that she needed to do something about it. She thought that being a virgin was the main problem. If she had sex with a boy, then she would feel more comfortable around them.

Her assigned roommate, Ashley Page, was one of her more experienced classmates. She was the complete opposite of Elaine—a short, curvaceous, curly-haired artist from Brooklyn.

"We've got to get you laid, girl," Ashley said frankly, when Elaine felt comfortable enough to talk openly with her. "What kind of guys do you like?"

"I don't know," Elaine said. "Strong, but kind." Like her father.

"Strong, but kind," Ashley said. "Hm. That eliminates about ninety-eight percent of the male population. What about looks? Tall, beefy, slim? Blonde, dark? Blue eyes—"

"I don't know, Ashley. Does it matter? I just need somebody to get the job done."

Ashley laughed. "Boy, you are jaded."

Elaine had long given up on the idea that the process of losing her virginity would be a romantic event. It was simply a barrier she wanted to break—both literally and figuratively. She thought it would not only make her feel more comfortable with boys, but would make her feel like she was a complete, fully functioning female.

Ashley told Elaine that her best bet was to go to the athletic center at Brown University, which was available to RISD students. "Who knows, you might get lucky and end up marrying a rich Ivy League type."

"Yeah, sure. They'll be very impressed when they find out I'm from a ghetto in Pittsburgh."

"Better than Brooklyn," Ashley said.

"You haven't been there."

Elaine took Ashley's advice and signed up for a Tae Kwon Do class at the Brown athletic center. There, she met several young men, though only one of them was a Brown student. The others were from RISD.

Elaine's first three sexual encounters were like the fairy tale of Goldilocks and the Three Bears. The first one was too hot, the second one was too cold, and the third was just right...or at least, she thought so at first.

Too Hot was the one from Brown, a sophomore philosophy major. He had a shuddering orgasm the instant the tip of his rubber-clad manhood touched her vagina.

"Isn't—isn't it supposed to last longer than that?" Elaine said.

His face flushed, he quickly pulled his pants back on. "Who do you think I am, Superman?" He told her to get out of his room.

Too Cold simply couldn't get his machinery working. He was a rather shy graphics design major she met while she was working out on a stationary bicycle. Elaine had to make the first move, asking him how to work the machine. They went back to his dorm room and started making out on his bed. He quickly got an erection, but by the time he had fumbled with a condom and clumsily tried to put himself inside her, he was soft as dough. They tried again, three times. He finally became so humiliated he made up an excuse about being stressed about an upcoming test and asked her to leave.

Just Right gave Elaine her first satisfying sexual experience, but he was an oddball from the start. A good five inches shorter than Elaine, he was on the RISD hockey team, The Nads. He had a thick, muscular physique and a hairy chest, which Elaine found exciting. They met in the Tae Kwon

Do class and made plans to meet at a bar.

She found him sitting in a booth, waiting for her, watching a basketball game on the big screen TV. As soon as she sat down, she noticed a prominent tenting in his jeans that, to her amazement, persisted the entire time they talked. He spoke of nothing but hockey and how he hoped to become a professional, that RISD was just a "backup plan" in case he couldn't make it.

"Let's get out of here," he finally said, and took hold of her hand as they left the bar. She expected him to take her to his dorm room, but instead, he led her across the street and directly into another bar. They had another drink, and talked, continued to watch the game on TV, talked, and then he took her to another bar. And another. And another.

She kept stealing glances at his crotch, and felt like saying, *Don't you get it? You don't have to impress me and chat me up all night. I'm a sure thing.* But she didn't want to scare him off.

She finally figured out what was going on about the time they went to the third bar. He always hung back when they entered, letting her walk ahead of him, by herself, to sit at the bar alone a few minutes. He always had an excuse—he had to use the restroom, needed to buy a pack of cigarettes from the machine—whatever. Then he would join her, stepping up to her and saying "Hey, beautiful," as if she was a total stranger to him. He wanted everyone in the bar to see him approach the pretty blonde who had just come in, who all the other guys were eying, and then—effortlessly—pick her up. It was a competitive, alpha male type thing.

Weird but understandable, Elaine supposed. He was too sexy to abandon on that basis...and that lump was too promising, especially after the Brown philosophy major.

Finally she could stand it no longer. "Want to go back to my room?" she whispered, holding onto his thick arm.

"We'll go to mine."

When they arrived, he locked the door and immediately turned on the TV. Another stupid basketball game was on. "You want a beer?" he said.

"No," she said dreamily. She turned down the volume on the TV set. "I just want to be with you." The truth was, she just wanted to get this over with.

They sat down on the bed and he kissed her, giving lots of tongue. When he pulled down his pants, his erection popped out and eagerly bounced up and down. It was short and thick, just like he was. But she wasn't complaining—at least it was hard. Hopefully it wouldn't explode at the slightest contact with any part of the female anatomy.

He expertly laid her down on the bed and plunged himself inside her, breaking her hymen with the first powerful thrust—at last. Within a moment or two, he brought her to her first externally-generated orgasm. He made love with a machine-like rhythm, his manhood maintaining a constant turgidity. He just kept going and going and going. She kept her eyes closed the entire time, and after a while she thought he seemed distracted, as if his mind were elsewhere.

He suddenly began thrusting harder. "Go, Rodriguez, go!" he yelled.

For a second, she thought Rodriguez was his pet name for his own penis. Then she opened her eyes and saw only the bottom of his chin.

He was still watching the basketball game on TV.

"Shoot!" he bellowed. "What are you waiting for, dumbass?"

"I...can we..." Elaine tried to wriggle out from under him.

"What's the matter?" he said, looking down at her.

"I've had enough." She rolled off the bed.

He looked at her a moment, then gave a shrug and bobbed his way into the bathroom. Elaine took advantage of the opportunity to quickly get dressed. When she reached under his bed for her shoe, she glimpsed a little blue pill on the floor.

She moved closer, squinting at the label.

VIAGRA.

That explains a lot, Elaine thought. *He must be pickled in the stuff.*

He came out of the bathroom, still naked and still erect, the bloody condom dangling from his finger.

She looked away.

"You've never done it before?"

"No," Elaine said, putting on her other shoe. *And I'm certainly not going to do it again with you.*

When Elaine told Ashley what had happened, she started laughing. Then Elaine started laughing, too. They both laughed so hard they cried. "Go, Rodriguez, go!" Ashley kept repeating, in between fits of hysteria, pounding the mattress of her bed.

When they finally composed themselves, Ashley looked somberly at Elaine. "So, how was it, overall?"

Elaine shrugged. "Okay, I guess."

"Well, that's good. Did you come?"

Elaine blushed. "A couple of times."

"That's great!"

"Yeah. Overall, I think sex is overrated."

Once Elaine lost her virginity and no longer felt like a leper, she concentrated on her studies again. It actually did make her more comfortable around boys. But she didn't pay them much attention. Romance could come later—she was on a "mission." She did not tell Ashley or anyone else the real reason she was at RISD, that it was part of a grand strategy to get a job at the Secret Service. Like most of the other RISD students, Ashley was a gifted artist. She and everyone else were so passionate about what they were doing that Elaine felt terribly cold and calculating at times, like someone who was using RISD merely as a means to an end.

Still, she was determined to avenge her father's death. Nothing could stop her from that. Deep down, she simply didn't feel like she could move forward in life until justice was done. She was going to track down Ronald Eskew, legally, and punish him.

To increase her chances of getting a job at the Secret Service, she took a second major in Russian. She had learned that much of the international currency counterfeiting activity occurred in Eastern Europe and the countries that made up the former Soviet Union. Even though Russian was difficult, it was the common language among those countries, and she figured that it was the best choice. She took the Russian classes at Brown. She enjoyed hanging out with the students there, as they were quite different from the arty, RISD types.

The four years at RISD went by amazingly fast for Elaine. She and Kaitlin kept in touch with each other, as they had promised they would. The first couple of years, they communicated using Facebook on almost a daily basis. But then, they slowly drifted apart, especially after junior year, when Kaitlin met this incredibly hunky law student at Northwestern named Matthew and moved in with him.

Elaine roomed the entire four years with Ashley, but like Kaitlin, Ashley eventually found a serious boyfriend, another design student at RISD, a year ahead of them. After that, Ashley spent most nights with him.

Cupid never shot his arrows Elaine's way. Every now and then she would see some young man that gave her goose bumps at a distance, but when she engaged in physical contact, it was always a disappointment. Like "Mr. Rodriguez," as she and Ashley referred to the young man who deflowered her, Elaine inevitably found the good-looking ones too vain and self-centered. And like the Brown philosophy major, the intellectually stimulating ones all seemed unsure of themselves in bed.

In May of her senior year, Elaine got a call from Kaitlin, telling her that she and Matthew were getting married. Elaine flew to Chicago for the wedding, which was held in a beautiful park on the edge of Lake Michigan.

When Elaine came back to Rhode Island, she cried her eyes out.

She told herself that love could not be forced, that she had no choice but to wait patiently—or impatiently—for it to come her way.

CHAPTER 1.6

One afternoon Elaine came back from her intaglio printing class and Ashley was in the room, a rare occurrence these days. She was sitting at her drawing table and turned around to look at Elaine.

"What the hell have you done?" she asked, staring.

Elaine frowned. "What's wrong?"

"A few minutes ago, some 'government agency' called and started asking questions about you."

"What did they say, exactly?" Elaine's heart was already pounding.

"All kinds of personal stuff—if you were honest, if you ever stole things, if you did drugs..."

Elaine was grinning ear to ear.

Ashley stared. "This makes you happy? Am I missing something?"

"I applied for a job with the Secret Service."

"You applied for...*what?*"

"A job at the Secret Service. It's not so strange, Ashley," Elaine added, a little defensively. She had known Ashley wouldn't understand. Like most everyone else at RISD, Ashley was applying for jobs at the fashion houses and design firms in New York, Boston, LA and Chicago. Elaine had applied for most of the same jobs—she and Ashley had filled out a lot of the applications together.

"The Secret Service hires a lot of people who have experience in graphic design and printing," Elaine explained.

"I'm sure you're right, but...jeez, Elaine. The Secret *Service?*"

"It was just a whim, Ashley. I thought I would just send in an application and see what happened. Why not?"

She did not tell Ashley that the application was 34 pages long and that she had slaved over it for an entire month. Elaine had filled out most of it online, and had made sure no printed portions were around for curious eyes to see. The hardest part was the Knowledge, Skills and Abilities (KSA) essays. They were supposed to show the applicant's "ability to deal with people, take responsibility, and make independent decisions."

Before Ashley left for her next class, she looked at Elaine a long moment. "You're a strange bird, Ms. Brogan." She gave Elaine a warm hug. "But I love ya. I hope you get the job, if that's what you really want."

"It's what I want, Ashley. And thanks for the support."

The Secret Service called two days later and scheduled an interview for the following Monday at 2 pm, at the field office in Providence.

Elaine was euphoric at first, but the feeling soon faded. She realized that on some level she'd hoped she wouldn't get this far. The multi-stage process she was about to voluntarily engage in was intimidating, to say the least.

If she passed the interview, she would have to take the TEA, or Treasury Enforcement Agent Exam. From what Elaine could gather, the TEA was a bit like the SAT test, but for people who wanted to become Secret Service agents. It had three parts—Part A, verbal reasoning; Part B, arithmetic reasoning; and Part C, problems for investigation. There were commercial study guides available for it. She was studying for finals right now. She dreaded the thought.

Then, if she was clever enough to pass the TEA, she would be invited back to the local field office for another interview. This somber event went under the imposing name of "Factor V." A panel of three senior Secret Service agents grilled you for 90 minutes to make for a fun-filled afternoon.

If you passed the Factor V, then came the lie detector test, an intensive physical exam, and an equally intensive psychological exam.

Only if you jumped all these hurdles would the Secret Service get serious about hiring you as a Special Agent. All the jobs in the Service required a Top Secret security clearance, so you had to undergo a thorough background check that left no stone unturned. Every address you had ever lived was verified and investigated. In-depth interviews were conducted with your friends, neighbors, coworkers, classmates, teachers, former employers, and anybody else you had ever known. This was to evaluate your honesty, judgment, reputation, financial responsibility, and of course your overall character. Then, and only then, would the Hiring Panel meet and make a final decision about you.

What bothered Elaine most was the psychological exam. By that point, they would know all about her father's arrest for passing counterfeit currency. Elaine was wise enough to know that no law enforcement agency would ever hire anyone who had a vigilante mentality, someone who wanted to settle a personal grudge against a criminal. Elaine knew from the beginning that she had to hide her heartfelt desire to avenge her father's death and create the impression that applying for the Secret Service was an idea that only recently occurred to her.

This was the main reason she had applied for all the "normal" jobs with Ashley. The truth was, she had no interest in any of them.

The only job she was interested in was being a Special Agent in the Secret Service.

Elaine did well in the interviews, passed the TEA by a wide margin, and passed the physical exam and the lie detector test. There was one tense moment when she was taking the lie detector test and the questioner said, "Did you have any knowledge of your father's illegal activities?" Elaine had answered "No." She half-expected the needles on the machine to swing wildly off the scale, but she didn't notice any change. Her answer was truthful, but she thought she had known from a very early age, at least unconsciously, that her father was doing something illegal to pay for her education at Bromley. Apparently the machine did not notice.

By the time the psychological exam finally rolled around, Elaine had graduated from RISD and was living in a microscopic apartment in Providence. She increased her hours at the cafe to support herself. She'd had a couple of job offers, one in New York and one in Boston, but turned them both down, banking on being accepted into the Secret Service. She knew it was crazy to put all her eggs in one basket, but she just couldn't get excited about working for a graphic design firm. The farther along she progressed in the Secret Service employment process, the more determined she became to get the job. It was a challenge.

When she sat down in the comfortable chair in the psychologist's office, she was surprisingly calm.

His name was Dr. Steiner. He was in his 50s, with a snow-white goatee and penetrating blue eyes. He looked like the type of man who didn't miss a trick.

He started with the usual psychological tests with Elaine—Rorschach ink blot, free association, freehand drawing—and then started asking questions about Elaine's childhood.

"I see here that your father was arrested for passing counterfeit currency and construction site theft." He looked up at Elaine. "How do you feel about that?"

She tried to remain relaxed. "Of course I was very upset. I was only sixteen. I had no idea that my father was involved in any kind of—"

"I didn't ask you how you felt about it *then*, Ms. Brogan. I'm asking how you feel about it now."

"Oh." The man was apparently too smart to fall for that approach. "I'm not sure what you mean. Can you be more specific?"

Steiner motioned to her. "Do you feel angry about it? Sad? Ashamed? Vindictive? You and your father must have been very close." He looked at the file. "It says here your mother left when you were...ten?"

"That's right." Elaine could feel sweat trickling down her back. She had prepared a dozen different answers to this question, but she didn't know which one to use. "My father was not a sophisticated man, Dr. Steiner. He only had a ninth grade education. Now that I have some distance on my growing up, I feel genuinely sorry for him. I know he was doing the best he could."

Dr. Steiner nodded. "You're not angry with him, then?"

"Not anymore. At first I was mad at him for killing himself and leaving me all alone. But I've come to terms with it now. He just couldn't cope."

"The police report says he never revealed where he got the counterfeit money." Steiner looked up at her. "Do you have any idea where it came from?"

"No," Elaine lied. "I always assumed he got it from whoever was buying the stolen construction site materials." She shrugged. "Honestly, I never gave that part of it much thought—I'm sure he didn't know the money was counterfeit, no matter where it came from."

"I see." Steiner studied her for a long moment. "So, your desire to become a Special Agent has nothing whatsoever to do with your father's arrest..."

This was the $64,000 question. "Well, I wouldn't go that far. Of course my father's arrest made me dislike counterfeiters a little more than other types of criminals. I'm basically a very moral person. I applied for this job because I think it will be satisfying to help protect the United States against criminal activities of all kinds."

What a bunch of hogwash, Elaine thought.

She waited anxiously as Dr. Steiner looked back at the file. He flipped through a couple of pages, scratched his beard, thinking, then closed it. "That will be all, Ms. Brogan. Thank you for your time."

Elaine rose from the chair uncertainly. The interview had seemed too short. She wondered if she had blown it with her morality pitch. "So...did I pass?"

"We'll let you know."

CHAPTER 1.7

When Elaine received the official letter informing her that she had been accepted into the Secret Service, she let out a whoop and did cartwheels through her little apartment.

She called Ashley and Kaitlin and told them the fantastic news.

Ashley still couldn't understand why Elaine wanted the job, and she could tell Kaitlin thought it was a little weird, but they both congratulated her.

A month later, Elaine began to wonder if she had made a mistake. The qualifying process had been bad enough, but the Secret Service training course was like going from the frying pan into the fire. It was one of the most challenging and stressful experiences Elaine had ever been through.

The first part of the course was conducted at the Federal Law Enforcement Training Center in Glynco, Georgia. For 10 weeks she and 47 other new hires received an intensive education in criminal law and investigative techniques. It was mostly "book learning," as her father would have called it, something at which Elaine excelled.

The going got tough during the second part of the course. The 17-week intensive for Special Agents was held at the Secret Service James J. Rowley Training Center, in Laurel, Maryland. There were no signs indicating the facility's existence, except for GOVERNMENT PROPERTY—KEEP OUT postings around the fenced in, 500-acre perimeter. The center boasted six miles of roadways, 31 buildings, including the simulated downtown area of a city, underground bunkers, obstacle courses, a firing range, a high-speed driving course, and a simulated airport and helipad, including perfect mock-ups of Air Force One and Marine One, the president's airplane and helicopter, respectively.

The training was intense. Even though Elaine's knowledge of intaglio printing had slated her to work in the Anti-Counterfeiting Division, she was required to pass the same stringent requirements as any other Secret Service agent, including those who protected the President of the United States.

"By mid-term, half of you will have dropped out," the leather-faced instructor barked the first day, "and the other half will sorely wish you had." He glared out at the trainees, his eyes mere slits. "Those of you who survive until the very end will know how to protect this country against terrorists, threats against critical infrastructures, including our financial system." He chuckled. "You'll also learn how to kill a potential assassin three different ways before his body hits the ground."

One of the things Elaine quickly learned to loathe were the simulated attacks on presidential motorcades, on a just-landed presidential airplane or chopper, or on buildings where the highest government officials were being protected. The attacks would begin with "flash-bang" bombs, simulating sudden, unexpected gunfire. Computer-controlled cardboard cutouts of people would jump up in windows and on the street, some wielding various deadly weapons, and others who were merely innocent civilians holding a wallet or a telephone, caught up in the havoc. Agents had to react with split-second precision, without thinking, knowing exactly what to do in each and every scenario.

If there was one motto that the Secret Service lived by, it was:

Expect the unexpected.

A key part of the training involved replacing instinctual human responses—such as flinching at the sound of a gunshot—with practiced responses that were designed to neutralize the attacker and protect the intended target from harm.

Of course, firearms and marksmanship training was fundamental. Elaine had never liked guns, and the first time she held a pistol in her hand, she flashed back to the day her father committed suicide and she carried his gun to the Rising Star Modeling Agency offices, intent on teaching Ronald Eskew a lesson.

Elaine struggled to achieve the high marksmanship standards that the Secret Service demanded. At night, she tossed and turned, the instructor's voices still in her ears. *Come to the ready position! Lock the slide to the rear. Decock—reholster with one hand. Check the chamber and magazine well. Check, check, check twice!*

It seemed that Elaine's ears rang all the time with the sounds of gunshots, even though she wore ear protection. The pungent odor of gunpowder permeated her hair and clothes.

She had to qualify on a .357 caliber pistol and a shotgun, and be functionally familiar with virtually all other weapons known to man. There was a gun vault on site where they were shown a wide range of weapons, including those made from the latest technological advances, such as cellphone guns. She had to learn how to shoot in the darkness, from a moving vehicle and how to accurately hit moving targets from a variety of positions. She had to learn to draw her gun in a split second, to click off the safety, and to fire with pinpoint accuracy.

The training device Elaine dreaded most was The Dunker. The horrid contraption sat in a huge swimming pool that was in simulated sea crashes of Air Force One and Marine One. Strapped into the seats near an instructor who posed as the President, the machine was slammed into ice cold water at a random angle. Underwater, often upside down, you had to orient yourself and then release your safety belt and rescue the "President," who was unconscious. You had to swim him safely to the surface and protect him from harm. Like many of the students, the first time Elaine was dunked, she inhaled half a lung full of water. She was sure she was going to drown.

The Dunker alone caused six students to drop out of the program.

By the end of the fourth week in Laurel, Elaine was telling herself that if she had any sense, she ought to drop out, too, that she should abandon this crazy idea of being a Secret Service agent. She could use her RISD degree to get a mundane job at a copy shop designing stationery and business cards. But then, in her mind's eye, she would see Ronald Eskew's sleazy face, and she would find new resolve.

Elaine's worst nightmare came in the form of her martial arts instructor. All the instructors used pseudonyms. This particular woman called herself Luna Faye.

Luna Tic, Elaine thought, would have been more appropriate.

Luna was a jet black, 5 foot 10 inch tower of power. She had a face like a viper, with triangular jaws and beady eyes. Her voice was an octave lower than Elaine's. She sported a man's figure, her trunk-like legs tapered up to a stocky torso. Her breasts like two flattened cupcakes riding on 50 pounds of chest muscle.

Elaine was about the only trainee who looked, dressed, and acted like a woman, or who at least tried to. This seemed to infuriate Luna.

The first day, in front of all the other trainees, Luna gently raised Elaine's arm by the wrist. "Your nails are *so* beautiful," she cooed in her husky voice. "Do you do them yourself, or do you have them done at a salon?"

There was a lot of laughter.

Despite Luna's ridicule, Elaine actually did well in the course, at least in terms of learning the basic martial arts moves. All her aerobics and swimming and running she did at RISD kept her in great shape, and she easily mastered difficult moves that made other students sore for days, such as some of the more challenging Tae Kwon Do kicks.

Elaine's problem was that after spending so many years in sports facilities, she had developed a habit of gazing at her own reflection in the wall mirrors to make sure she was moving correctly. And, if the truth be told, to see if she looked good.

Luna picked up on this the third day. "You just can't stop watchin' your pretty self in that mirror, can you, honey?"

All the other trainees laughed.

Every time Elaine glanced at herself in the mirror, even for a split second, Luna mercilessly took her down. "This ain't no fashion show, baby-doll. You take your eyes off your assailant, you dead, and so is the person you're supposed to be protecting."

The second week of training, as Elaine dragged herself off the mat for what must have been the tenth time, Luna said, "You look at yourself so much in that damn mirror, I'm gonna start callin' you Alice. Alice through the lookin' glass."

All the students got a kick out of this.

"Can't we do the training somewhere else?" Elaine suggested. "Maybe outside?"

"Outside?" Luna snickered. "Why, baby-doll, you'd just admire your pretty self in the window reflections."

There was more laughter.

Elaine wanted to strangle the woman, but she also knew that Luna was right. When acting as a Special Agent in a protection role, she had no business looking at anything but the face, hands, and feet of an assailant. She found that glancing at her reflection was an incredibly difficult habit to break.

Luna only exacerbated the problem, constantly baiting Elaine during the training sessions with comments like, "Your hair's out of place," or

"Your thong's showing."

Every session with Luna became a living hell.

Elaine began to worry that her "Alice" habit was her Achilles' heel, the weak point that would knock her out of the training program and out of the Secret Service for good. The day before her final review in Luna's martial arts class, Elaine ran into the big woman on the way to the obstacle course.

"Why don't you just throw in the towel right now, Alice? You ain't gonna make it."

"I'm not quitting," Elaine said.

"You can't shoot worth a damn, you're lousy on the obstacle course. My grandmother can drive a car better than you, and she's been dead twenty years. There's no way in hell you'll pass my review tomorrow."

"I'm not quitting."

Luna shrugged. "Face it, honey, you're too much of a girly-girl for this kind of work. Why don't you just get a job at some department store cosmetics counter and save yourself the humiliation?"

Elaine brushed passed her.

Luna looked on, snickering. "If you go on like this, I'm warning you—you might chip your nail polish."

Elaine did not sleep more than two hours that night, worrying about Luna's martial arts review.

Luna made Elaine wait until the very end of the session and watch everyone else get their reviews. Six of the students failed and had to take the "walk of shame" back to the main building to turn in their equipment and officially drop out of the program.

"Now, who's left?" Luna said, looking around.

Elaine slowly raised her hand.

Luna said, with a sigh, "Okay, Alice, come on," as if Elaine's failing the test was merely a formality.

Elaine put in her mouth guard and Luna started circling her.

"Your lipstick's smeared," Luna said, taking a light jab at her. "Don't you want to check it in the mirror, Alice?"

Elaine kept her eyes locked on Luna's viper-like face. *Don't even blink,* she willed herself.

"Your mascara's running," Luna said.

Ignore the bitch. If you don't pass this test, you're out of the Secret Service.

"Come on, Alice," Luna jeered. "Don't you want to check your pretty doll-face in that lookin' glass?"

At that instant, one of the students cackled.

Luna's eyes cut in that direction.

Elaine's right leg shot up. It was a perfectly executed snap kick. It connected solidly with Luna's jaw. The big woman's head jerked up, and then her heavy frame went down hard, hitting the mat with such force she let out a loud "ugh!"

Elaine leaped on top of her, twisted her arms behind as required for cuffing.

All the other students were stunned. No one had ever knocked Luna down before.

Luna quickly rolled over and got to her feet, wiping her mouth with her hand. She looked at her fingers. They were smeared with blood.

Elaine backed away, terrified.

The room was so quiet that all she could hear was the sound of her own shallow breathing.

Luna glared at Elaine for a long moment, and then her lips pulled into a crimson smile. "Well done, girl. Looks like there's hope for you after all."

From that day forward, it seemed like the rest of the training was downhill for Elaine. She was filled with elation, thankful that she hadn't given in to the temptation to quit halfway through, like some of the others. She and Luna became close. Elaine was thankful that she had faced such a formidable instructor and had passed all the tests. Her father would have been proud.

When the 15th week of training finally began, Elaine was excited—this was when the anti-counterfeiting modules began.

The instructor for the first day was a man who simply used the pseudonym "Judd." Rumor was that he was an official from the highest echelons of the Secret Service Anti-Counterfeiting Division, perhaps even the director of the entire unit.

When the balding man entered the room, everyone stopped talking. Even though he was thin and walked with a cane, there was an intensity about him that was intimidating. He had a shock of red hair and a ruddy complexion. He seemed ill-tempered before he even opened his mouth.

Silently, he appraised the 32 students in Elaine's class. He did not look impressed.

"Who can tell me what intaglio printing is?" He said this so abruptly that some of the students jumped.

Elaine glanced around—the trainees who had made it this far in the program were all cream of the crop, and were quick to volunteer answers. No one said a word.

"Not a single one of you knows?" Judd said, jingling the change in his pocket.

Elaine didn't want her class to look like a bunch of dummies. She raised her hand.

Judd looked over at her and nodded.

"Intaglio printing is a special process that uses an etched or engraved plate. The plate is smeared with ink and wiped clean, and the ink left in the recesses makes the actual image on the printed material."

Judd raised an eyebrow. "That's absolutely correct."

He turned back to the center of the room. "And what's unique about any document that is printed using the intaglio process?"

Again, the entire class was mute. At the risk of looking like a know-it-all, she raised her hand again.

Judd again nodded to her.

"The ink surfaces on intaglio-printed documents are slightly raised on the front and indented on the back. You can feel this with your fingers when you touch them."

"Correct," Judd said. He opened the thick notebook that contained the module materials. "Now, why is it that intaglio printing is particularly effective against counterfeiters?"

Elaine thought he glanced at her, but she wasn't sure.

"Several reasons," Elaine said. "First, an intaglio printing press costs ten times as much as an offset printing press. Second, intaglio plates themselves cost *hundreds* of times more. Third, intaglio printing yields very fine levels of detail that—"

"Are you finished?" he said, staring at her as if she had just shat upon the classroom floor.

Elaine's face flushed. "I thought you—"

"Nobody likes a smart-ass. See me after class."

He turned to the rest of the students and said, "Today we will discuss the intaglio printing process in great detail..."

Judd did not look at Elaine again for the rest of the lecture, which lasted all morning—an eternity for her. She wanted to crawl under her chair and disappear. She was mortified at making such a fool of herself in front of her peers—she felt so humiliated now that she really did want to quit. If this monster was typical of the people who worked in the Anti-Counterfeiting Division, she wanted nothing to do with them. Had she gone through all this misery just to end up working for obnoxious assholes?

After a while, she found her hurt transforming into anger. How dare he chew her out like that in front of all her colleagues, and then tell her to see him after class, like some troublemaker in elementary school!

By the time the students had finished filing out of the room, Elaine had made up her mind. She didn't care who this "Judd" was or how high up he worked. She was going to put the old bastard in his place.

She approached him just as he was gathering up his things.

"I think you owe me an apology," she said boldly. "You had no right to attack me like that in front of the whole class. I was just trying to answer the que..."

He was smiling at her.

"What?" she said, flustered.

"I'm sorry I had to do that to you, but you wouldn't want everyone to think you're the teacher's pet, would you? The only reason I bother to come over and give this Mickey Mouse lecture is on the small chance of discovering a diamond in the rough, like you." He pulled out a business card and handed it to her. "When you get fed up working for the Secret Service, young lady, you give me a call. You're just the type of person we like to have at Treasury."

She looked down at the card. It simply said "Gene Lassiter," with a phone number printed underneath.

He picked up his satchel, smiled again, and gripping his cane, hobbled out of the room.

CHAPTER 1.8

The day Elaine graduated and was officially a United States Secret Service Special Agent, she felt like she was walking on air. When she received the gold, five-pointed star that was attached to her badge, there were tears in her eyes.

It did not matter to her that there was a note in her file from the head of the academy that said that due to her low marksmanship scores, she was "not recommended for protective services duty."

She had made it!

She and the rest of the new agents met at a D.C. bar and got utterly smashed.

Luna Faye showed up. She was wearing a stunning black halter-neck dress that showed off her toned shoulders and chest.

"You look fabulous!" Elaine gushed, giving her a big hug. She truly meant it.

"You inspired me, honey," Luna said modestly, holding out her hands palms-down so Elaine could see her manicure.

"French? Very stylish, Luna."

"I don't know if it's worth thirty bucks."

"It is."

Luna smiled. "You know I had to throw everything I had at you to see if you could take it."

"I know," Elaine said, wiping away a tear. "I'm glad you did."

Luna appraised her evenly. "It's only gonna get tougher, girl. This is only the beginning." She glanced around and lowered her voice so no one else could hear. "I'm not talking about only toughies you might have to face on the outside. I'm talking about on the inside, too. The Service is a damn competitive organization. You'll end up working for at least one first-class asshole, maybe more. You'll have to survive on a lot more than your looks and charm."

Elaine nodded. "I understand."

"Good." Luna's face relaxed into a smile. "Anyway, baby-doll, congratulations!" She gave Elaine another warm hug. "I'm so damn proud of you I could pop!"

CHAPTER 1.9

On the Monday when Elaine arrived in Great Falls, Montana the temperature was a nose-numbing five below zero. The city, with a population of only 60,000, was flat as a pancake. There was no skyline. The tallest building, where the new Secret Service office was located, was the U.S. Bank "Tower" —a staggering seven stories high.

When Elaine had received the notification letter informing her that she was assigned to the Secret Service field office in Great Falls, Montana, she tried to keep her chin up. She had known she would be sent to the least desirable location in the country, that it was standard practice for all new Special Agents.

Shivering as she locked her beat-up Toyota, she told herself she could stand living in Great Falls for a year or two, and to make the best of it. *Look at the bright side,* she thought. *It's a small town. People will be a lot friendlier than in Pittsburgh.*

"You can't park your fuckin' car there, lady."

Elaine turned around—there was a blubbery man shoveling snow off the sidewalk, a cigar jutting from his mouth. "What's the matter with you, can't you read?" he said, pointing at the NO PARKING sign.

Well, she thought, *'most' people were probably more friendly than in Pittsburgh.* She moved her car down one space.

For her first day at work, she had bought a new navy blue business suit and had her hair styled. When the dumpy receptionist ushered Elaine into the office of the SAIC-—the Special Agent In Charge—the man slowly rose from his desk, staring at her.

"Ms. Brogan?" he said. His eyes moving down to her legs, her shoes, then back up to her face.

"Nice to meet you," she said, shaking his hand.

"I didn't know you were..." The receptionist was standing there, watching him ogle Elaine. He glanced at her, his face red. "Thank you, Susan. That will be all."

Susan left, giving him a dirty look.

The SAIC's name was Bill Saunders. He began making nervous small talk, telling Elaine about the new-fangled office, which had only been established in Great Falls a year ago. He was about 35 years old, had a pot belly, was nearly bald, and what little hair he had left was speckled with dandruff. Elaine noticed that he was wearing a wedding band, which she thought was a good thing—the excitement she sensed in him had raised alarm bells in her mind.

He outlined her responsibilities, and mentioned that there would be a lot more training on "corporate stuff," such as Ethics, Diversity, and Interpersonal Awareness.

Near the end of the meeting, Elaine asked, "Will there be time for me to work on some of my own cases?"

"Your 'own' cases? How do you mean?"

Elaine shrugged. "Cases that originate from my own leads, maybe cases in other states."

"Trying to get out of Great Falls already?" he said, smiling.

"No, I just—"

"I don't see why you can't work on outside cases. As long as you get your required work done, do your DOPS."

"My—DOPS?"

"Daily Operation Summaries."

"Oh."

"Anyway, as long as you get your required work done, I don't see it as a problem."

Elaine spent the first few weeks settling in. There was only one other field agent working out of the new office, Ken, a man who had been with the Service only two years. A former Chicago police detective, he had a lot of experience and he spent much of his time working alone. Most of the activity in the Great Falls office concerned financial fraud, counterfeit checks, and Internet account hacking. Great Falls, Montana, was not the center of the world's illegal currency counterfeiting activity. Or the center of anything else, it seemed.

Bill Saunders seemed to make constant excuses to go into Elaine's office and talk to her, or call her into his. When he had to pick up a file or get his coffee cup, he would move uncomfortably close to her, sometimes "accidentally" brushing up against her. She noticed that he often discreetly inhaled when he did this, as if savoring the smell of her perfume.

One evening they were going over a list of banks in Montana that had been receiving a certain type of fake check, Bill reached over and took her hand.

"Elaine," he said, his voice wavering, "I have to tell you something."

"Don't," she said, pulling her hand away. She had been expecting this ever since the first day. She glanced at his open office door, afraid Susan would hear them.

"Susan's gone, and Ken is up in Billings tonight."

"I don't care," Elaine said, standing. She had been sitting beside him at his credenza. She put several feet of distance between them.

His face went red, and his scalp went even redder. "Elaine, I can't stand it. Ever since you came to work here—"

"Bill, don't do this. Please?"

"You don't feel attracted to me?"

"That's not the point, Bill. You're my boss."

"So what?"

Elaine opened her mouth, but closed it again, not wanting to sound like a newbie reciting rules from the Secret Service employee manual. "You're married."

"Not really."

She motioned to the wedding band on his finger. "I suppose you're going to tell me that's a Secret Agent Decoder Ring?"

He chuckled. "Joan and I are finished. We're getting a divorce."

Sure you are, Elaine thought.

Bill noted her expression. "Look, I'll take the ring off, if that makes you feel better." He did so, putting it in his desk drawer. "I won't even wear it home."

"Bill..."

"What?" he said, reaching for her waist.

"I'm not going to do this," she said, moving farther away. "I refuse to mess up my career."

"Mess up? What are you talking about? This can only be good for your career."

"You know better than that, Bill." She searched for excuses. "If we started something and then it fell apart, it would be bad. Really bad."

His expression grew cold. "What about after I get my divorce?"

Even if she had been attracted to him, and he really did get a divorce, she wouldn't allow herself to become involved with her boss, not at a place like the Secret Service. But if she told him that, she didn't know what he might do. She didn't have much experience with men, but her instincts told her to tread very carefully with this one.

"Well," she said, "of course if you were di... single, things would be different." His face brightened at this. "Now can we please put this aside and get back to work?"

"Sure thing," he said.

For the next few weeks, Elaine diligently went about her duties, hoping that Bill's infatuation would pass. She stopped wearing perfume and tried to dress down, hoping that would help.

She often came in early and spent an hour or two working on what she now thought of as the "Ronald Eskew" case. She ran the name through all the criminal databases but came up with zilch. She was sure that Ronald Eskew was an alias the man had only used for his sleazy Rising Star Modeling Agency scam.

Elaine wished she could travel back in time to the day she confronted Ronald Eskew in his office. If only she had thought to pick up something with his fingerprints on it. Of course, at that moment, she could not have known what was about to happen to her, and to her father.

She began doing detailed searches of all the modeling agencies that had been started in the year following the closure—or disappearance— of Rising Star. There were over 50 agencies that had started during that time in the USA. One by one, she began painstakingly investigating them.

One day when Elaine and Bill were working together in his office, going over the details of a new bank check fraud case, Bill suddenly grabbed her and kissed her.

"Stop it," she said, struggling against him. He pushed her back on his desk and hungrily pressed his mouth against hers. She could feel his erection pressing against her thigh. Before she knew it, his hand went under her skirt, his fingers rubbing her vulva.

"Bill!" she gasped, roughly pushing him away.

He backed off, breathing hard.

"This is not *acceptable*. Do you understand?"

He blinked, wiping his mouth. "I understand."

"You do?"

"Yes. You may go back to your office."

When Elaine went home that day, she had a bad feeling about what had taken place. She didn't sleep at all that night. The next morning, she went to a downtown cafe and had breakfast, dreading the thought of confronting him again. Things would be awkward, at best.

When she got to the office, he was already there. She passed his door.

"Good morning, Elaine," he said evenly.

"Good morning," she said, backtracking.

He was sitting at his desk, his arms crossed.

With a warm smile on his face, he said, "What the hell do you think you're doing?"

"Excuse me?"

His face was red, but not with embarrassment. "Do you think the law enforcement computers are here for your personal amusement?"

He tapped on a printout on his desk. "Would you mind telling me who Ronald Eskew is?"

"Bill...I asked you if it was all right for me to work on my own cases, and you said it was."

"Did I?"

"Yes. The first day I was here. You said..." Now she noticed another look in his eye.

"Abuse of law enforcement databases is a serious violation of your security clearance. I could fire you for that."

Elaine swallowed. So this is how Bill Saunders dealt with his bruised male ego. She remembered Luna's words. *You'll end up working for at least one first-class asshole, maybe more.*

"Bill," she said, willing herself to stay calm, "please don't fire me. I won't use the databases anymore." She decided it was better to put herself at his mercy than to confront him about the real reason he was doing this.

He gazed at her for a moment with obvious resentment. "Well, you've been doing a halfway decent job here. What I'm going to do is recommend a transfer."

Elaine was taken aback. "A transfer? To where?"

"You'll find out soon enough. I'll put in the request this morning."

He picked up his pen and cut his gaze from her. "That will be all."

Elaine was furious, in a quandary about what to do. She was tempted to fly to Washington and file a formal sexual harassment complaint, but she thought the better of it—doing that so early in her career would probably just get her known as a troublemaker. Nobody would want her then. Besides, she had no proof of anything, including Bill's permission to use the confidential databases. It would come down to her word against his.

She tried to tell herself that a transfer was a good thing. Just about anywhere was better than Great Falls, Montana.

CHAPTER 1.10

"*Bulgaria?*" Elaine said, staring at the confidential transmission in her hand.

Bill smiled.

"You bastard," she said under her breath.

His expression darkened. "I'm going to pretend I didn't hear that."

Elaine just stood there, glaring.

"I had nothing to do with where they chose to transfer you," Bill said. "I simply told them that I thought your talents were being wasted here—" he looked distastefully down at her legs "—and I think they are. Maybe in Bulgaria you'll find a situation that's more *acceptable* to you."

He turned back to the papers on his desk. "You'll leave tomorrow. Summarize everything you're working on and have it on my desk by five o'clock today."

That evening, Elaine stayed late, packing up her personal things in the office, putting them in boxes. Bill would go over it all with a fine-tooth comb and send it on to Bulgaria.

She felt as bitter as the weather outside.

Just as she was about to leave, she sat back down at her stark desk. She looked at the dark computer screen, hesitated, then turned it on and logged into the system. *The damage has been done*, she thought.

She opened up the criminal databases and continued her work on the Ronald Eskew case.

After only an hour, she stumbled on something exciting.

There was a modeling agency that was started in Dayton, Ohio only two months after Rising Star disappeared. It was only open eight months, then closed. According to city records, the owner had been R. E. Crawford.

Crawford—that was the name his assistant had used.

What about Robert E. Crawford?

Elaine typed the name into the FBI criminal database, waiting on pins and needles.

After a moment, it came back with a match.

Ronald E. Crawford, a.k.a. Robert A. Eskew, a.k.a. Steven B. Hayes, a.k.a, Edward T. Cane, a.k.a... The list went on.

She opened up the rest of the file.

Her heart gave a thump as the man's mug shots appeared, front and side views, holding a number.

It was him! He still had the droopy mustache, and a beard as well.

She skimmed through the file, her heart beating faster and faster. *Wanted for direct mail fraud, computer phishing, passing bad checks, currency counterfeiting...*a dozen white-collar crimes.

Elaine frowned, confused, scrolling back and forth through the long file. Where was he now? He'd obviously been arrested, because there were mug shots.

Ah, there it was. Five years ago...

Convicted on three counts of direct mail fraud, Decatur, Illinois. He was sentenced to two years in an Illinois minimum security prison.

And then what?

The file seemed to end there.

Then she noticed the last line.

September, 17th, 2006. Deceased.

Deceased? she thought numbly. The man is *dead?*

That couldn't be...

With a growing sense of disappointment, she clicked on some more buttons. She finally found the death certificate.

Cause of death: heart failure. It is the opinion of the examining physician that the deceased passed away peacefully in his sleep.

Elaine left Montana in a daze.

As she gazed out the airplane window, watching Great Falls sink away, it felt as if the rug of life had been yanked out from under her.

...passed away peacefully in his sleep.

It wasn't possible! The loathsome man who was responsible for her father's death, had *passed away peacefully in his sleep.*

The bastard! The lucky, despicable bastard!

Only during the last few hours did Elaine fully realize that everything she had done since her father committed suicide—every major decision she had made, and every action as a result of those decisions—was driven by her desire to get even with Ronald Eskew.

And now the man was dead!

It just wasn't fair. The greatest irony was that he had died long before she had even finished college.

Elaine felt every emotion imaginable, and she felt nothing. She had turned down two perfectly good jobs, had gone through that hellish process to join the Secret Service—and for what?

She was the captain of a rudderless ship.

When the plane landed in Chicago, instead of changing planes for the flight to Washington, D.C., she bought a ticket to Pittsburgh. She had not been home since she'd graduated from Bromley. Something told her it was time she came to terms with her past.

She rented a car at the Pittsburgh Airport and found herself driving to her old house in Garfield. A thousand memories flooded her mind as she drove down Penn Avenue, passing familiar landmarks— the little market where she used to shop, the laundry, bus stop where she had walked a thousand times back and forth to her house.

As she slowly rolled by the tiny, humble dwelling itself, it looked even tinier and humbler than she had ever remembered it, and the neighborhood much more run-down. She could see the balcony her father had built onto the back, the paint peeling. She could see herself as a little girl, held in her father's arms.

Your great-great-great-great grandmother was an Irish Princess. She lived in a beautiful castle. It had a moat, and a —

What's a moap, Daddy?

She felt a sharp pang in her heart and sped away.

A few minutes later, she pulled up to the Bromley Academy for Girls. She went inside to the main office. Ms. Prentice had long retired and had been replaced by a new, young director. There was a security guard on duty at the front desk, also a new touch. Even he was a stranger.

"Can I help you?" he said.

"I'm a Bromley grad," Elaine said. "I'm just going to walk around the grounds, if it's ok..."

"Knock yourself out."

Elaine went back to the rental car and, from the trunk, retrieved a small pot of chrysanthemums. She trudged through the snow around to the back of the main building, past the soccer field, across the hill, until she reached the remains of the church. Ms. Prentice had arranged for her father's body to be buried there, in the old graveyard. The school had paid for everything.

Elaine squatted in front of the simple headstone and brushed away the snow.

IN MEMORY OF PATRICK KEEGAN BROGAN, A WONDERFUL FATHER AND GREAT FRIEND OF THE BROMLEY ACADEMY FOR GIRLS

Elaine stared at the words cut into the slab, tears coursing down her face. She placed the pot at the foot of the marker. Suddenly she fell forward, weeping, overwhelmed by a feeling of loneliness and despair.

"I wish I could talk to you Daddy," she gasped, pressing her hands and face against the cold marble. "I don't know what to do."

She wept for a few minutes, and then became aware of a crunching sound behind her in the snow. She turned around. Two girls about 12 years old on horseback, in their riding helmets, were moving along the side of the graveyard.

Elaine wiped her eyes and waved. The girls waved back.

She thought of Kaitlin, and how they had grown apart.

When Elaine went back to the car, her grief faded into a sweet sorrow. She would cope, somehow. She was a Brogan. *We're made of the tough Irish stock*, she could hear her father saying. She would go to goddam Bulgaria and see what happened.

If things didn't improve, she would quit the Secret Service.

CHAPTER 1.11

Sofia, Bulgaria turned out to be a pleasant surprise. The city had a distinctly European flavor, with balconied buildings overlooking tree-lined, cobblestone boulevards that rattled with slow-moving trams. The summer air was filled with the smell of flowers and the sounds of laughter and romantic accordion music. There was simplicity to the Bulgarian people and the way they lived, that Elaine found charming and down-to-earth.

In the center of the city, the men and women were better dressed than in the States, the men in suits and the women in stylish skirts or dresses, most wearing high heels. When they walked in couples, the woman would often take the man's arm the old fashioned way.

The males, with their dark eyes and swarthy looks, were handsome enough, but their attitude towards females left much to be desired. In some parts of the country, girls as young as 14 were still auctioned off at fairs to the highest bidder.

Still, Sofia was a thrilling place for Elaine to find herself. A helluva lot more interesting than Great Falls, Montana.

The day she arrived, she was met at the airport by a Bulgarian driver from the office and formally escorted to an apartment in the center. The flat had been rented for her on a weekly basis until she could find permanent accommodations. It was lovely, with antique furniture and ten-foot ceilings, and overlooked a quiet, tree-shaded square.

When she arrived at the Secret Service office, a stocky receptionist said, "We've been expecting you," in accented English. She motioned down the hall. "The SAIC's office is the last one at the end of the hall."

Elaine didn't know a thing about the SAIC except that his name was Nick LaGrange. She went down the corridor and stopped at the door marked with his name.

There was a tall, broad-shouldered man bent over a desk cluttered with papers, stained coffee cups, and other debris. He was counting out money from an envelope, muttering to himself, and scribbling on a piece of paper. Elaine couldn't see his face—he had long, unkempt brown hair that obscured it. He was wearing faded, holey jeans, hiking boots, and a cracked leather flight jacket over a wrinkled-looking linen shirt.

He looked up, brushing the hair out of his face. He saw Elaine and gave a warm smile. "Hi there."

He was the most handsome man she had ever laid eyes on.

"I'm Nick LaGrange," he said, offering her his strong-looking hand. "You must be Elaine?"

"Yes," she finally said. She didn't want to let it go.

"I'm about to go on an undercover assignment. You wanna come along, get the feel of the place?"

Elaine glanced uncertainly down at her business suit.

"Don't worry, you're dressed just right for this assignment." He paused. "Got your service pistol with you?"

"Yes, of course." Elaine started to open her satchel.

"Leave it here." With a faint smile, he said, "I read the note in your file."

Five minutes later, they were climbing into an old cherry red Mustang that was parked in a garage near the office. Nick put the key into the ignition and the engine thundered to life.

"Bought this in New York, shipped it to the UK, and drove it all the way here from London," he said proudly, as he pulled out of the garage. "An original Boss 429. '68 model." He glanced at her. "You're probably not much into muscle cars..."

"No," Elaine admitted. She was still a little offended by the comment he had made about the note in her file.

They drove through the center of Sofia, with Nick honking, and pulling around trams and clusters of pedestrians. Steering with his knees, he pulled out a bag of tobacco and started rolling a cigarette. He slipped the perfectly rolled smoke between his lips and lit it.

He smiled when he saw her watching. "Had a lot of experience in college. Want me to roll one for you?"

"No, thanks," she said, grinning. This guy was a real character.

As they continued on through the city, she noticed that everyone stared at the vintage American automobile as it rolled by.

"Isn't this car a little conspicuous for a Secret Service agent?" she said.

Nick laughed. "There are no secrets in this place, Elaine. Everybody knows everybody else. And Americans stick out here like sore thumbs." He turned a corner and waved at some man who was standing on a corner, smoking a cigar. "Any Bulgarian can spot a *chuzhenetz*—a foreigner— at a hundred yards. They can tell by the way you dress, walk, move, the shape of your face, and a hundred other cues. You have to be careful here, too. In Bulgaria, a foreigner spells only one thing—M-O-N-E-Y."

"How long have you been here?"

"Five years. Five long years. Before that, Warsaw. Before that, Paris."

"You like being abroad, then?"

"I like being as far from headquarters and their goddam DOPS as possible."

He made a sharp left, into a square. He pulled into a parking space along the street.

"What exactly is this undercover assignment?" Elaine said nervously.

Nick finished his cigarette and tossed the butt out the window. "Ever heard of the Turkey Roll?"

"No."

"Sounds like a sandwich, doesn't it? It's a con they pull around here."

They got out of the car and walked across the street. There was a huge Byzantine-style church at the far end of the square, with glittering gold domes and curving, turquoise roofs.

"That's the Alexander Nevsky Cathedral," Nick said. "Probably the biggest tourist attraction here."

Nick suddenly took Elaine's hand. "For this to work, we need to look like a couple," he said, in a low voice.

She wondered if he was just saying that as an excuse to hold her hand. *Wishful thinking*, Elaine thought.

After they had walked only a few feet, a man appeared from nowhere and cut directly in front of Elaine. He stooped to pick something up from the sidewalk, this all happened so abruptly that Elaine almost stumbled into him. He picked up a thick roll of American $100 bills.

For an instant, Elaine felt angry— if the man hadn't cut in front of her, she would have found it herself.

He looked up at Elaine, then at Nick.

"Yours?" he said, holding up the money.

Now Elaine realized maybe this was the con. The Turkey Roll.

Nick glanced at her, then said to the man, "Yes, it's my money." When he reached for it, the man quickly stepped away.

He said, "We split it—fifty-fifty. Okay?"

Nick looked at Elaine again. "Well…"

"Let's go over there," the man whispered, pointing behind a building.

He led them around the corner.

Elaine glanced nervously around, afraid of what might happen next. She didn't like this situation, being in a strange country, mixed up with criminals, and unarmed.

The man pulled the rubber band off the money and quickly started counting it out. *Edin, dvama, trima, chitirima…*

There were 30 crisp $100 bills in the roll, or $3,000.

He handed half of them to Nick, then glanced past Elaine, his eyes widening. He turned and scurried away, running along the side of the building.

Two men trotted up to them from the opposite direction. One was in a rumpled suit, the other in a dirty-looking jogging outfit. The latter pointed at Nick, babbling in Bulgarian.

The well-dressed one flashed a police badge at them. "This man—he say you stole his money."

Nick glanced nervously at Elaine. "I don't know what you're talking about. I didn't steal any money."

"Empty your pockets!"

Nick hesitated.

"You want go to jail?"

Nick reluctantly reached into his jacket pockets and turned them inside out. Then, from his jeans' pockets, he pulled out his car keys, his wallet, and a cigarette lighter. "See?"

"There!" the other man said, pointing at the little watch pocket in Nick's jeans.

Nick sighed and pulled out the roll of money. "Look, it was just laying on the sidewalk. I didn't steal it from anyone."

"*Da!*" the other man said, snatching it from Nick's hand. He unrolled the bills, then frowned, looking back at Nick. "*To ne vsichko e tuk!*"

"He say you take some of his money," the cop said.

"I didn't take any of it," Nick said. He motioned to the back of the building. "Some other guy picked up the roll and gave me half."

"Other guy?" the cop said, looking around. "What other guy? I see no other guy."

Nick glanced at Elaine.

"You want go to jail?" the cop said again. He squinted at Elaine. "You want *both* go to jail? Bulgarian prison very bad. Not like in America."

Nick glanced around, then opened his wallet. "Look, I'll give you all the money I have..." He pulled out a few hundred dollar bills, and another few hundred Euro notes.

The cop looked at Elaine.

"I don't have any money," she said, her throat dry. She sure hoped this was the con that Nick had been talking about, and not something else.

The cop asked the other man a question. The man glared at Nick. "Okay," he finally said, and pocketed all the money. He turned and walked back around the corner, muttering to himself.

Pointing at Nick, the cop said, "You should be careful. Bulgaria very dangerous for foreigners."

He walked off in the other direction.

As they were alone again, Nick looked knowingly at Elaine. His lips curled into a smile.

"He wasn't a real cop..."

"Nope," Nick said.

"I don't get it—what was this all about?"

"This," Nick said, reaching into his back pocket. He produced a single $100 bill. "This came off that roll of money—all of it was probably counterfeit. A couple of undercover cops—real cops—will keep tabs on those guys until we find out."

As soon as they were inside the Mustang and headed back to the office, Elaine said. "You should have let me bring my gun. I'm not incompetent."

"Did I say you were incompetent?"

"No, but..." She was angry with herself for wanting to impress him, but she couldn't help it. "You make me feel incompetent. I'm not a helpless girl."

"Don't get feminist on me, okay? I don't pay a lot of attention to rules, but when it comes to important things, I play by the book. Something happens to you, and I'm responsible." He glanced at her. "Is that all right with you?"

"Well, yes, of course it is. I just don't want you to think I'm inept."

"The Secret Service must have thought you had other assets that made up for your weakness in marksmanship." He glanced at her legs.

"Thanks a lot," she muttered.

"I didn't mean that. I meant, for example, intaglio printing." He looked curiously at her. "Your file said you know a lot about that."

"I ought to know something about it. I majored in it."

Nick looked surprised. "Where the hell can you major in intaglio printing?"

"RISD. That's the Rhode Island School of—"

"I know what it stands for. That's a damn good school."

She gave a modest shrug. "I guess so." Of course it was a good school—it was one of the best design schools in the USA.

Nick said, "Your intaglio printing knowledge could be very useful here. The main crime we deal with in this office is counterfeiting. But I'm sure you know that already."

They rode along in silence for a few minutes. Even though Elaine felt a bit frustrated with how he was acting towards her, she had a very good feeling being with Nick LaGrange. His open, honest, and confident manner was very attractive.

As they passed a group of rough-looking men on a corner, her thoughts turned to the con artists they had just been involved with. "That's a clever scam those guys pull," she said. "For a split second, I was mad when the first man cut in front of me and looked like he'd picked up that big roll of money. I thought I should have found it instead of him."

"Yeah. I always get the same feeling, even though I know it's a con." He smiled at her. "We're all greedy, Elaine. It's human nature."

When they got back to the office, Nick cleared off some debris from one of his guest chairs and offered her a seat.

"So, what do you think of this bill?" he said, handing Elaine the $100 note. He also handed her a magnifying glass.

The look in his eye told her this was a test.

She carefully rubbed the bill between her thumb and forefinger. It had been printed with an intaglio press, as she could feel the ridges in the paper. She squinted at it through the magnifier, inspecting the finer details.

After a moment, Nick said, "Want a genuine note for comparison?"

"Don't need one," Elaine murmured, peering at the front side of the bill. "This is definitely a fake."

Nick raised an eyebrow. "How do you know?"

"For one thing, the color-shifting ink isn't quite right. It changes from black to gold but the—"

"Yeah, good. And?"

"And the lines on Jefferson's face aren't spaced the same, especially around the jaw line. Plus, the microprinting isn't quite as sharp as it should be." Elaine paused. "Still, it's a well-done counterfeiting job."

Nick smiled. "Not bad, Elaine. Not bad at all. Usually we have to send bills this good back to the States to know for sure."

He picked up the phone and punched in a number. While he waited, he opened his drawer and pulled out a stack of $100 bills that was an inch thick. "See what you think of these."

CHAPTER 1.12

The more Elaine worked with Nick LaGrange, the more she liked him.

He was so exciting to be around, always passionate about whatever he was working on, and so confident in himself and the abilities of everyone around him, including her own. Elaine felt completely safe with him, as if he radiated a sort of magical, protective energy that warded off evil.

She also enjoyed her job. She found she had a natural talent for recognizing fake banknotes, something Nick had seen right off. He gave her tasks that helped her further develop her skill at counterfeit detection, such as making detailed lists of all the major differences she could find each time a new type of fake banknote surfaced in the region. It seemed that in this particular Secret Service field office, you could create your own job, which was a nice change from the rigid position in Great Falls.

For Elaine, identifying counterfeits was easy, like working those picture-puzzles that she loved so much as a little girl. *There are ten differences between the girls in these two photographs. Can you find them?*

Soon, Nick was funneling all the fakes found by the other agents in the office to Elaine for scrutiny. With time and a lot of practice, she was able to distinguish fakes so quickly that agents at nearby Secret Service field offices— in Moscow, Bucharest, Frankfurt and Rome—began sending her suspicious banknotes to check for fast turnaround. Sending paper money to Washington to be verified through official channels was slow and required a lot of paperwork. By making this unnecessary, she began to develop a reputation for speed and reliability, even gained a little fame around the region.

A few weeks after she had gotten settled, Nick came excitedly into her office, a piece of paper in his hand.

"Remember the fake we picked up from that undercover operation the first day you were here?"

"Yes..."

"Turns out it matches a couple of others that have surfaced around Eastern Europe. I just got this report from Treasury, and it says these notes may be coming from a genuine KBA Giori printing press."

That was a bit of a shock. KBA Giori was a company in Germany that made all the intaglio presses used to print U.S. dollars. The machines were manufactured under top secret contract for the American government. From what Elaine knew, the factory in Wurzburg had tighter security than the Pentagon.

"How's that possible?" Elaine said.

"Well, I'm sure you know Giori makes basically the same machines for virtually every country in the world."

"Yes..."

Nick shrugged. "Some third world country could have sold one of their machines to a criminal ring. Every Giori press is accounted for, except for one that never made it to Chile about five years ago. Nobody ever figured out what happened to that one." Nick paused. "This is *big*, Elaine. Maybe the biggest case I've ever worked on. My god, if someone actually has their hands on a genuine KBA Giori machine like the ones we have at the Bureau of Engraving and Printing, and figure how to use it right, they could make a perfect counterfeit, one that's so good even the Treasury Department wouldn't be able to tell the difference."

"But there were a lot of mistakes in the one I checked."

"Yeah, but from what I've been told, other notes they've found are better. Whoever has this machine is on a learning curve, figuring out how to use it as they go along."

"Can you get me scans of those other notes? I'd like to see them."

"I'll see what I can do," Nick said. "Once they go to Treasury, getting them back is like pulling teeth."

At the end of the month, when Elaine was doing paperwork, she asked if she could see Nick's DOPS to get a better feel for how the Sofia office worked.

He frowned at her. Gesturing around his messy office, he said, "You think I do DOPS?"

"I just assumed—"

"I'd rather spend an afternoon at the dentist than fill out those summaries. I'd rather be tied up and forced to listen to the President's State of the Union address. I'd rather have bamboo shoots—"

"But don't you have to do DOPS?"

"Well, yeah. Everybody has to do them. Every once in a while my boss in D.C. calls up and chews me out. I lock myself in here for a few hours and make stuff up, fill out as many as I can. It's pure torture."

"I'll be happy to do your DOPS, Nick."

"You'll do my DOPS?"

"Yes, I can do them when I do my own. I don't mind doing DOPS—they make me feel organized."

He pointed at her. "You're on, girl!" He nodded slowly, thinking about it. "Yes. Perfect! I can tell my boss we 'synchronize our DOPS.' He would like that." Nick grinned at her. "Sounds kinda kinky, doesn't it?"

Elaine blushed.

Elaine soon found that she looked forward to every moment she spent with Nick, and that she felt empty when he was out of the office or away on an assignment.

The highpoint of her week was when Nick would come into her office and say, "Let's synchronize our DOPS."

They would pack up their papers and go to an Ethiopian cafe across the street that served delicious coffee, and Elaine would sit there and write all of Nick's DOPS, with him catering to her every need. He would buy her a double cappuccino and make it just the way she liked it—with one spoon of white sugar stirred in, and a half spoon of demerara sprinkled across the froth. *Lovingly* sprinkled over the froth, she liked to think.

Nick would hover around her. "Can I get you a muffin? A fresh-squeezed orange juice? A thousand dollars in cash?"

They talked a lot during this hour-long ritual and got to know each other better. She didn't know how Nick felt about it, Elaine relished every second of it.

After three months of working in Bulgaria, she finally admitted it to herself. She was falling madly, hopelessly, unstoppably in love with Nick LaGrange.

CHAPTER 1.13

Nick seemed to know everyone in Sofia, and he took Elaine with him to "make his rounds" at a variety of the city's seediest clubs and bars, which she found deliciously intriguing. At least at first.

It was clear that Nick had lots of casual girlfriends, the type that hung around bars and lived off the generosity of men they met there, particularly "rich" foreigners.

The third night they were out, two young ladies who clearly knew Nick stopped at their table. One of them had a pageboy haircut, with jet black bangs cut straight across her dark eyes. The other had a thick blonde braid that came down to the crack of her butt, the features of which were so clearly outlined by tight black spandex she could have worked as a live model in an anatomy class.

"Come party with us, Neekie!" the brunette said, her pouty mouth glistening with bright red lipstick, tugging on his leather jacket.

"Can't you see I'm with a colleague?" Nick said, his face flushed. The way Nick said it, Elaine felt like a piece of office equipment.

The blonde glanced saucily at Elaine with her dark eyes. "You can breeng your colleague, Neekie. We no mind."

When he finally got rid of them, he glanced sheepishly at Elaine. "I just hang around with them to keep my ear close to the ground. You pick up a lot of stuff that way."

"I hope it responds to penicillin," Elaine said.

Nick smiled.

The younger Bulgarian women dressed to the nines, in short skirts, high heels, and low-cut blouses. They paid great attention to their hair, makeup, and their hands and feet—half of them wore fake fingernails and had eyelash extensions. It seemed to Elaine all the girls in Sofia were in a life-or-death competition with each other to see who could be the sexiest. There were so many beautiful women that Elaine felt positively plain and ordinary in her boring gray business suits and sensible flats.

One night when she, Nick, and two other agents—both married men—were out at a bar, Elaine made this observation to Nick when a girl walked by with a skirt so short you could see her frilly black stocking tops.

"Life is tough here, Elaine," he said. "It's not like in the States, where you have all those systems in place to protect women and give them equal opportunities and all that. Here, women need men to survive, and there aren't enough good men to go around." Nick shrugged. "To get a good man, they have to take full advantage of all their assets."

"And I'll bet you take full advantage of their assets," Elaine said.

Nick glanced at the other two agents and grinned. "Well, you know what they say. 'When in Rome...'"

Elaine wanted to strangle him.

CHAPTER 1.14

By December of that year, Elaine was so bogged down in checking the suspect $100 bills sent in from other offices that she had no time for anything else. Her office walls were covered with huge sheets of paper with hundreds of banknote serial numbers, linked together like huge family trees, showing when and where each note had been found, and the geographical interconnections between them. This helped other agents track down the origin of the counterfeit bills and locate the illegal printing presses. Elaine's detective work had been partly responsible for two big busts already, one in Romania and another in Chechnya.

"You and I make a great team, Elaine, "Nick often said. "You track 'em down and I bust 'em."

As the Christmas holidays approached, Elaine began to feel depressed— the Christmas season had made her feel down ever since her father died, as she had no family to spend the holidays with.

A week before the break began, Nick came in with a new set of suspect notes for her to check, his leather jacket dusted with snow.

"So, what are you doing for the holidays?" she asked casually. She hoped he might stay around Sofia, and maybe they could spend some time together.

"Oh, probably I'll go down to Minorca for a little R&R. That's what I usually do."

A little R&R. She wondered which one—or two—of his bar girls he was taking with him.

"And you?" Nick said, smiling politely.

"Oh, I'm thinking of taking a trip with a friend to Rome or Paris." The vague "friend" part was a lie, an effort to make him jealous. *A pathetic effort,* she thought.

"Sounds good," he said, unfazed. "But I'd head south if I were you. The winters here are murder."

When he turned around, Elaine felt like throwing her glass paperweight at him. But she didn't want him to leave.

"Nick?" she said.

"Yeah?"

"What about those two bills we sent to Treasury that came from the genuine Giori press?

"Oh, those?" he said. "I don't know what happened, you know how they are. I'll ask again."

After he left, she had the distinct feeling he was being evasive.

She ended up spending the holidays in Paris. She visited the Louvre, the Eiffel Tower, Versailles, and took a riverboat ride on the Seine.

And she was miserable.

CHAPTER 1.15

When Elaine returned to Sofia, her obsession with Nick deepened. When he brushed his arm against her, electricity shot through her whole body. When he left her phone messages, she would play them over and over again in the privacy of her office or living room, where she could relish the sound of his voice. Her emotional state would swing wildly to one extreme or another based on the slightest inflection or look in his eye. She longed for him to take her hand, like he had the first day she had arrived in Sofia.

Elaine could only imagine the shock he would experience if he knew the emotional turmoil he was causing inside her.

She felt like a schoolgirl endlessly pining over a boy who was utterly unaware of her existence.

She hated herself for it, yet she seemed powerless to do anything about it.

You want Nick so badly simply because you can't have him, she thought, trying to talk herself out of how she felt. *He's out of your reach, and that makes him all the more attractive. If he was easily available, you wouldn't be interested.*

She didn't believe a word of it.

One day she came into Nick's office and he was so engrossed with something on his computer screen that he didn't seem to notice.

"Nick?" she said.

"What?" he muttered distractedly.

She gradually came closer, looking over his shoulder. She almost expected to see pornography on the screen.

"Ever been to the Provence region of France?" he said. He was scrolling through a series of small countryside villas.

"No," Elaine said. "It looks lovely. Are you thinking of taking a vacation there?"

"Yeah. A permanent one."

"What do you mean?"

"I mean I'm retiring. And soon."

Elaine was taken aback. "Aren't you a little young to retire?"

"Oh, I'll keep working at something. But something that's not life-threatening." He glanced over at her. "I've got plenty of money socked away," he said. "That old Mustang is the only thing I own."

Elaine often thought about what Nick had said during the next couple of days, wondering how he had so much money "socked away" that he could retire in his 30s.

One night she had a wonderful dream. She was eating dinner with Nick in a huge, rustic kitchen. The windows were open, the breeze blowing through the room. Fresh vegetables were spread over the table. Outside, she could see rolling, golden hills and poplar trees, like in a Van Gogh painting.

Two children were sitting at the table, a boy and a girl, and both were speaking French. The boy favored Nick. The girl had strawberry blonde hair.

There was a knock at the door. Suddenly, the feel and texture of the dream changed. For a second, she was back in her little house in Garfield.

"I'll get it," she said, getting up from the table.

As she walked through the hallway, she was filled with terror. The Secret Service was there, and they were going to arrest Nick, and take him away, and destroy her beautiful family and her idyllic life with him.

When her hand touched the doorknob, it was cold as ice. Swallowing, she twisted it and pulled the door open.

The two girls that had approached Nick at the bar in Sofia were standing there, the brunette with the pageboy haircut, and the blonde with the braid down her back and the skintight pants.

"Is Neekie here?" the dark one said, her lipstick-smeared mouth grinning lewdly. "Can he come party with us?"

Elaine awoke with a start.

She finally decided to call Ashley and spill her guts. She needed to talk to someone about her obsession—keeping all her feelings bottled up inside was making her crazy.

Ashley was good at giving advice about the opposite sex—ever since Elaine had lost her virginity to "Mr. Rodriguez," Ashley had been a kind of mentor to her, at least in the romance department.

"You've got to let him know how you feel," she said.

"How?" Elaine said, shivering. She was standing in a phone booth in a Sofia suburb, and it was about 10 degrees outside. She wouldn't have dared talked to Ashley about this on her cellphone or from the phone in her office or apartment.

"If I make a pass at him and he's not interested, I'll be so humiliated, I won't be able to look him in the eye again. I'll have to transfer to some other field office. And I like it here—I *love* it here!"

"You love *him* there," Ashley said.

Elaine didn't say anything. There was no need.

"Look, Elaine, I'm not talking about 'making a pass' at him. I'm talking about subtle hints. You're a woman, you know how to do it."

"I've given him every subtle hint in the book, Ashley. He doesn't respond to any of them."

Ashley was quiet a moment. Elaine knew what she was thinking. *Well, maybe the man just ain't interested.*

Ashley said, "Look, it's probably the boss-subordinate thing. Does he know about the bastard in Great Falls?"

Ashley was the only one Elaine had told about Bill Saunders. "I don't think so. How could he know?"

"Don't ask me, I'm not a secret agent."

"Ashley, we're not 'secret agents,' we enforce the law, like the FBI."

"Whatever." Ashley had never understood Elaine's career choice. "The point is, if he does know about the bastard in Great Falls, then he's probably scared shitless to make a move towards you. He's afraid you'll fly off the handle and get him fired for sexual harassment."

Elaine had considered this already. "I don't think that's it. This guy isn't into following rules, Ashley. That's one of the things that makes him so attractive—he's a rebel, he does whatever the hell he wants."

"Yeah, those types are exciting."

Elaine sighed. "I just think that if he was really interested in me that he would take the risk."

Well, there you have it, she could hear Ashley thinking.

"Look, Lainie, if you're that crazy about this guy, you should just come out and tell him. You know what they say. 'It is better to have loved and lost, than not to have loved—"

"Come on, don't feed me clichés!"

"Well, you call me for advice, and then when I give it to you, you reject it. What exactly are you wanting me to tell you?"

"I'm sorry. I'm just so upset about this. You've been a big help, really. I—I just need to think some more."

"You've done enough thinking already—you're just driving yourself batty. It's bad for your self-esteem."

"Yeah," Elaine sighed, hugging herself and shivering again. "Listen, I'm freezing my butt off, Ashley, I've got to hang up. I appreciate all your advice, and please, *please* don't breathe word of this to anyone."

"As if I'm going to share it with all my secret agent friends."

Two hours later, Nick came into Elaine's office.

"How would you like to go on an undercover assignment with me to Belarus?"

It was as if he had overheard the entire telephone conversation. Of course, Elaine knew such a thing was impossible.

"Sure," she said, trying to hide her excitement. "What's the assignment?"

Nick explained it to her. He suspected that there was a small counterfeiting operation there and couldn't get any cooperation from the Belarusian authorities, so he wanted to go investigate himself. "It would only be for a couple of days," he added casually.

"That's fine," she said, struggling to hide her exhilaration. She wondered if he would want them to pose as a couple again. She actually felt herself becoming sexually aroused at the thought of holing up with him for a few days in a hotel in Belarus. Who knew what might happen?

"You'll need a fake passport, of course," he said. "What country do you want to be from? Are you any good at any particular accent?"

"Might yeh be gettin' me a passport from Ayerland, so? Some say I do an Ayerish brogue that ain't half bad."

Nick burst out laughing. "That's awesome! Are you Irish, or part Irish?"

"My great-great-great-great grandmother was an Irish Princess. She lived in a beautiful castle."

Actually, what Elaine said was, "My father used to wander around muttering in an Irish brogue for fun. Brogan is an Irish name, but I don't think he ever actually knew any real Irish people."

"Oh. Well, I know some people who can make an Irish passport. These ex-Soviet block countries love the IRA."

When they flew to Minsk, the Belarusian capital, Nick traveled on a fake British passport and listed his occupation on the landing form as "Engineer." He told her to write "Accountant" on hers. Her passport was a diplomatic issue, supposedly granted by the Irish Department of Agriculture, Fisheries, and Food.

"We've been married five years, we live in London, I work for British Petroleum. We have no kids. We're here on vacation. Got it?"

"Yes."

Elaine was so excited she could hardly contain herself. When they stepped out of the taxi and approached the hotel lobby, she mustered up the courage to take Nick's hand.

He quickly let go, frowning at her.

"I thought we were supposed to be married," she said, a little hurt.

"We are. Five *years*, Elaine. No married couple holds hands after five *years*."

When they actually went to the hotel room Nick had reserved, Elaine was even more disappointed. She had hoped it would only have one large bed. Instead, it not only had two separate beds, but they were in separate rooms. It was a suite designed for a family, with one bedroom for the parents and one bedroom for the kids. There were even separate bathrooms.

She was disappointed that he would never get to see her in the new peignoir that she had spent half her salary on.

"I thought this would give you more privacy," Nick said, as he took his suitcase into the smaller of the two rooms.

"Thanks," Elaine muttered.

She went into the other bedroom and glumly unpacked her suitcase.

A few minutes later, Nick appeared at her door.

"I'm going out, see what I can stir up."

"You don't want me to—"

"No, you need to stay here. Be ready to check out any bills I bring back—we'll have to move fast."

The three days they spent in Belarus were miserable for Elaine. Nick made her stay in the room like a prisoner. He went out and tracked down suspect $100 bills, brought them back for her to check, and then went out again, leaving her alone nearly the entire time. The only reason he wanted her with him was so that he could quickly determine if the bills he tracked down were fake, and to tie them to other notes that had surfaced elsewhere in Eastern Europe.

On the third day, when Nick was preparing to leave again, she said, "I'm getting awfully tired of room service, Nick. Can't we at least go out to dinner?"

"Can't do it," he said.

"Why not?" she said angrily.

"Because it's too dangerous here. I'm almost sure I was followed today." He paused, looking at her sympathetically. "If anything happened to you..."

"What?"

He looked away, brushing the hair out of his face. "It's my responsibility to keep you safe, that's all."

He left without saying anything else.

Nick did not return until early the next morning. He looked haggard, with two days of stubble on his face. There was a small gym bag over his shoulder. With a sigh, he slung it onto the coffee table and unzipped it.

It was packed with bundles of dirty-looking Belarusian rubles, held together with bright yellow rubber bands.

He silently unzipped his own suitcase, opened up a false bottom, and began carefully packing the money into it.

"Do you mind explaining where that came from?" Elaine said.

"A false bribe," he muttered. "I posed as a corrupt Interpol agent to get closer to the source of those counterfeits that I think are coming out of Russia." He glanced up at her. "I think we're getting close to the source of those, Elaine. That could be a big bust, a real feather in our cap."

He finished packing in the bills and closed his suitcase. "It's only about $10,000, but it will come in handy for my undercover operations. " He glanced at her again. "I don't want to report it as coming from here, it's too much to explain and too much paperwork. I'll convert it to American dollars and say the money was found during an undercover operation in Sofia—we can recycle it much easier that way."

When they got back to Sofia, Elaine seriously considered asking for a transfer to another Secret Service office. Her one-year anniversary was almost up. Technically, it was possible.

Why should I keep torturing myself? she thought. Working side by side with a man she was madly in love with, but who would not return her feelings? It was masochistic.

Finally, Elaine could stand it no longer. Two days before her one-year anniversary, she downloaded the Request for Transfer form on her computer and started filling it out.

When she reached the blank that said, Reason for Transfer Request, she hesitated, her fingers hovering over the keyboard.

Can't take this anymore—have the hots for my boss, and it's driving me insane.

"Morning, Elaine."

She looked up sharply. Nick was standing in her doorway, smiling at her.

She quickly minimized the window on her screen. "Good morning."

"Are you free Friday night?"

"Why?" she said guardedly.

"I thought we'd go out and celebrate your anniversary."

"I—" She feigned surprise. "Has it been a year already?"

"Sure has." Nick grinned. "Time flies when you're having fun."

Elaine watched him a moment, standing there in his jeans and leather jacket, his hair disheveled. He looked like he just tumbled out of bed with one of his bar girls.

She wanted to strangle him.

With a sigh, she said, "Nick, I really don't want to go out with you and your..."

He looked puzzled. "My...what?"

"Groupies."

"My *groupies*?" He laughed. "Is that how you think of them?"

Elaine didn't answer. He stood there a long time, gazing at her. "If I didn't know better," he said, "I'd think you were jealous."

"Don't be ridiculous," she said, blushing. She opened the window on her screen. He couldn't see what she was doing, so it didn't matter.

He said, "The only reason those girls like me is because I spend money on them."

Elaine ignored him, filling in another field on the transfer application.

"I've got a present for you," he said.

She looked up at him. Smiling, he reached into his pocket and took out a small cardboard box. It was about the size of jewelry box for a ring.

Keep dreaming, she thought, but her heart beat a little faster as he set it on her desk in front of her. "Just a memento of your first day in Bulgaria."

All she could remember about the first day here was how good her hand felt in his. Hiding her bitterness, she opened up the box.

Inside was a little plastic turkey, with funny little legs hanging down. Nick picked it up, wound the knob on the side, and let it go. It waddled crazily around the desktop, making an awful grinding noise.

They both started laughing.

"The Turkey Roll," Elaine said.

"Bet you'll never forget that day, will you?"

No, Elaine thought, *but not for the reasons you think*.

He just stood there and they both watched the little toy wind down until it fell over on its side.

"Well?" he said.

"Well what?"

"About Friday night. Do you want to go to dinner, or not? I made reservations at Maison Godet. It'll just be you and me." He smiled. "No groupies allowed."

Maison Godet was the best restaurant in Sofia, an, intimate, romantic setting.

No way was she going to set herself up for another letdown.

"What time?" she said.

"About seven? Pick you up at your place."

After he walked away, she looked after him, thinking that the dinner would be a good chance to tell him that she was requesting a transfer.

When Friday night rolled around, Elaine took the afternoon off. It wasn't so she could get ready for her evening out with Nick. She wasn't about to do anything special to prepare—she just wanted to relax for a few hours, maybe take a nap so she wouldn't get sleepy if they had wine at dinner.

No way will I do anything out of the ordinary to try and look prettier, she thought, as she sat in the Salon de Pierre, having her hair and nails done. *No way will I spend my good money to try and impress him,* she thought, as she paid the clerk in the boutique for the soft, flowing cashmere dress that picked up the blue in her eyes. *No way will I get my hopes up just to have him cruelly dash them again,* she thought, admiring her new outfit and hairstyle in the mirror, her heart pounding madly at the thought of what might happen if he walked her up to her apartment to say goodnight.

I'm a bloody fool, she thought, as she touched up her lips in the bathroom. *I'm the biggest bloody fool that's ever walked this earth.*

"You look nice," Nick said simply, when he picked her up.

"Thank you," she said. "So do you."

Nick was wearing slacks and a sports coat over a sweater, which was about as dressed up as he ever got, except when someone from Washington visited.

When they were seated at the restaurant, Nick said, "You seem a little distracted. Are you all right?"

"I'm fine. It's just been a long week."

"Yeah. For me, too."

He started talking animatedly about one of his cases. "I think we're going to bust the operation wide open." It was a counterfeiting operation in Russia, but the printing operation was located somewhere else. Nick suspected it was in Croatia, but he wasn't sure. "Without your help identifying the fakes, this would have taken months longer. We wouldn't be nearly as far along."

"I'm glad," she said.

Despite her determination not to enjoy herself, she had a wonderful evening with Nick, as always. She had never felt more comfortable with any man in her life. The Russians had a word that described it perfectly— *rodnoi*. A warm, close, family-like feeling.

That's exactly how she felt with Nick. Like they were meant to be together, always, forever.

By the time they were eating dessert, Elaine started to feel annoyed with herself for letting her infatuation run so wild. She had a wonderful job, and Nick was a fantastic boss who truly appreciated her skills. And the best friend anyone could ever have! Why was she about to screw everything up just because the man didn't have any romantic interest in her? She felt selfish and stupid and immature. She ought to just delete the Request for Transfer and, once and for all, fix it firmly in her mind that Nick was a *coworker*, and that was all he would ever be. Period.

"You want to go have a drink somewhere?" Nick said, when they got back in his Mustang.

Elaine glanced at her watch—it was almost eleven.

"Come on," he said, with a boyish grin. "We'll go to a place none of my groupies can afford."

She smiled, but on the inside, she wasn't laughing. It amazed her how fast her feelings could flip-flop. How could he be so cold and start talking about his damn groupies? She sorely regretted ever calling them that. And how could he not know how she felt about him? He had to be an absolute moron if he couldn't tell. But then, men were pretty blind sometimes.

"I'd rather go home, Nick. I'm tired." She opened the car door.

"Ok. I'll walk you up."

"You don't need to do that, Nick."

"Yes I do."

When they went inside the building and got on the elevator, Nick looked a little uncomfortable. He kept stealing glances at her, but she avoided eye contact.

They stepped off the elevator and she unlocked the door to her apartment. She turned to him and smiled. "Thanks for dinner, it was really nice."

"Glad you enjoyed it." Before she could turn away, he touched her chin. "Are you mad at me about something? I haven't done anything to offend you, have I?"

No, she thought, looking up into his brown eyes. *That's just the problem, Nick. You never do anything to offend me.*

"I'm just a little tired, that's all."

"Oh. Well, if I ever do offend you, you'll tell me, right? I don't think I could stand it if I ever hurt your feelings or anything."

"Why's that, Nick?" she said, now looking directly into his eyes.

"I...I don't know. You're just...too nice a person."

They both just stood there, gawking at each other.

"I wanted to tell you how much I've enjoyed working with you this past year, Elaine. I'm not very good at saying this kind of thing...but you've really brightened up things around here. For me, I mean."

"I'm glad," Elaine said. "I like working with you, too, Nick."

There was another awkward silence.

"Well," Nick said, "I'll see you Monday, then." He hesitated just an instant, looking past her, into her apartment.

"See you Monday," she said.

He just stood there, looking into her eyes.

Time seemed to have completely stopped.

Suddenly, he grabbed her and passionately started kissing her.

The next instant, they were falling all over each other, knocking over furniture. Nick kicked the door shut with his foot and pushed her down on the couch.

Elaine found herself tumbling down a long, deep, delicious tunnel of ecstasy. Nothing else in the universe existed except her and Nick. He tore off her clothes and devoured her, his lips and tongue exploring every inch of her body.

"Why didn't you tell me?" he whispered, sometime in the middle of the night.

"I didn't think you liked me."

"My god, I'm crazy about you, I have been since the first day you walked into my life!"

When Elaine finally drifted off to sleep in his arms, her worst fear was when they awoke, under the sober bright light of morning, Nick would be all fidgety and awkward, regret what they had done, and tell her that it was a "slip", that they should just go back to being coworkers and friends.

But that didn't happen.

The next morning, he held her close to him, stroking her hair and her face, looking into her eyes.

They made love again, and then finally got up and dressed. He was going to Russia for a one day undercover operation and wouldn't be back until late Sunday night.

She hugged him tightly. She didn't want to let go of him. She was afraid that if she did, she would lose him.

"I won't see you again until Monday morning," he said, gently pulling himself back so he could look at her face.

"What are we going to do, Nick?"

"What do you mean?"

"At work. It's going to be awkward, isn't it?"

"How so?"

"Everyone will know. You can't hide something like this from people. They sense it."

Nick shrugged. "I don't give a shit."

Elaine stayed in bed long after he left, in a euphoric afterglow like nothing she had ever experienced, smelling his manly scent on the pillows, still hearing his voice, feeling his touch. It was all like a dream—she couldn't believe it had actually happened.

She'd harbored a fear, partially instilled by Ashley, that if it did actually ever happen, it would be a letdown, that the real thing would never live up to her fantasies. But it turned out to be quite the opposite. Making love with Nick was even better than she had imagined, partially because she had never slept with someone for whom she had such strong feelings. Sex with Nick wasn't complicated, it was easy and effortless—she would do anything to please him, and he seemed to have the same attitude towards her.

At about 10:30 am, her cellphone started ringing. Elaine was still in bed. She was in such a dreamy, exhilarated state that she was almost unaware of the sound until she realized it might be Nick calling her.

She pulled the blanket around herself and retrieved her cellphone from her purse.

The display said UNKNOWN CALLER.

"Hello?" she said, her voice still husky with lust.

"Hey, smart-ass."

Elaine frowned. "Excuse me?"

"It is you, isn't it?" a raspy male voice said. "The smart-ass who was in my anti-counterfeiting class at Laurel a while back?"

The memories of the training class at the Secret Service Academy slowly came back. It was Judd, or whatever his real name was, the instructor from the Treasury Department. Gene Lassiter. That was his name.

"Yes, it's me," Elaine said, sitting up in the bed.

"How come you never called me? Being sent to Bulgaria ought to be enough to get you fed up with working for the Secret Service."

"It's—it's not bad." She glanced over at the mussed up bedcovers. "I like it here." *Especially now.*

His voice changed tone. "I hate to tell you this, but you're in trouble. Serious trouble."

She sat up even straighter, suddenly afraid. She wondered if he could already know she had slept with Nick. "What do you mean?" she said cautiously.

"We shouldn't talk about this on the phone. All I can tell you at this point is that the SAIC there is about to be arrested. You need to get the hell out of that office, and fast."

Elaine was having a difficult time taking all this in. "Arrested for what?"

"It's better not to talk about this on the phone." He paused. "On Tuesday I'll be in Berlin, on business. Can you meet me there for a chat?"

"Well...yes, I guess so." Elaine's mind was racing, trying to come to grips with what Nick might be doing to get himself arrested. And why Gene Lassiter would be warning her about it.

He said, "Tell your office you have some personal business in Berlin on Tuesday, a sick relative or something, and that you'll just be out one day. Make absolutely sure no one knows anything else. Especially the SAIC. Is that clear?"

"Yes. Yes, sir."

The line went dead.

CHAPTER 1.16

Elaine spent the rest of the weekend in a state of despair. She couldn't believe that Nick was doing anything wrong. But then she remembered their trip to Belarus, and the $10,000 worth of Belarusian rubles he had smuggled back in his suitcase. He had asked her not to report it, saying that he would convert it to dollars and say that it had been found in Sofia. When they had gotten together for Elaine to fill out their DOPS, the money had not been mentioned. Nor had she heard it mentioned since.

On Monday morning, Elaine made sure she arrived at work before he did so she could make her reservations without calling too much attention to it. Nick would find out, of course—he had to approve any requests for personal leave.

At about 10:30 am, he appeared at her office door. "Hi," he said simply. He gazed at her, smiling, his eyes saying more than words ever could. He lowered his voice a little. "How are you?"

"Fine." She tried to behave as warmly towards him as possible. "How was Russia?"

"Made a lot of progress this time." He opened his jacket and handed her a small bundle of $100 bills. "Check these out and see if any of them match the old ones."

"Fine."

He just stood there, watching her. Looking over his shoulder, he stepped closer and took her hand. He kissed it tenderly, gazing into her eyes. "You sure you're okay with what happened between us?"

"Yes." Her face flushed.

"I know it's a little awkward..."

"Nick, I have to go to Germany tomorrow."

"Germany?" he said, puzzled. "Why?"

"A friend of mine from college—Heather—who moved there with her boyfriend. He walked out on her last night." Elaine felt horrible lying to Nick. But she told herself this was for the best—she would go talk to Gene Lassiter and straighten this out. Lassiter obviously was on the wrong track about Nick. Surely Nick hadn't taken those Belarusian rubles as a real bribe. "Heather's a basket case right now. I told her I would come see her." Elaine added, "It will just be for one day."

"Oh." Nick nodded. Elaine thought she saw a flicker of suspicion cross his face, but she wasn't sure. "Well, I'll see you when—Wednesday?"

"Yes, Wednesday."

"What about dinner Wednesday night...?"

"I'd love that."

He gave her hand a warm squeeze. "See you Wednesday, then."

CHAPTER 1.17

The meeting took place at the Ritz-Carlton, in downtown Berlin. Elaine found Gene Lassiter sitting at a booth in the bar, two beers in front of him.

He gave her a warm welcome and said, "I hope you like beer. Nobody does beer like the Germans."

Elaine wasn't interested in beer—she was interested in finding out exactly what Nick was being investigated for—but she took a sip, tensely biding her time.

The aging man just sat there, smiling at her, one hand over the other on top of his gold-tipped cane. It was cast in the shape of a horse's head.

"You've got quite a reputation," he said.

Elaine grew even tenser. "What do you mean?"

"Identifying the fake currency. Word gets around."

"Oh," she said, relieved. She was afraid that he somehow knew she had slept with Nick. She told herself to stop being so paranoid.

"It's a gift," Lassiter went on, "being able to spot fakes with the naked eye, without using a lot of fancy equipment. I knew you were talented back when I had you in that class at Laurel."

"Well, I ought to be halfway good at it by now," Elaine said modestly. "That's about all I've been doing during the past twelve months." She wished he would tell her about the trouble he thought Nick was in.

"You know, just three weeks ago, I was about to call you and offer you a job at Treasury. To join a special new project I'm working on." There was a twinkle in his eye. "When I started checking you out, that's when I discovered that the SAIC at your office is under internal investigation."

"Nick LaGrange?" Elaine said, just to make absolutely sure they were talking about the same person.

"Yes. LaGrange."

"What's he being investigated for?"

"Are you aware of a case that concerns counterfeits from a genuine KBA Giori machine?"

"Yes. Nick has mentioned it from time to time."

"What did he tell you, exactly?"

This information wasn't classified, so there was no harm in sharing it. "He said there's a possibility that the Russians, or someone in Eastern

Europe, have a KBA Giori intaglio press. He's working the case himself."

"That's pretty much right," Lassiter said. The old man slowly twirled his cane between his fingers. "So, you haven't had any involvement in that case..."

"No."

"That's damn lucky for you," Lassiter said.

"Why? What exactly do you think Nick has done?"

"From what I can gather, he's burning the candle at both ends."

"You mean, taking bribes?"

"Exactly. To throw the rest of the Secret Service and Interpol off track."

"I don't believe it," Elaine said.

"You better believe it. LaGrange is going to do hard prison time for this, Elaine. What he's doing amounts to treason. He'll get twenty years in a maximum security penitentiary. If you've had any material involvement in his activities, you may get dragged down with him."

Elaine swallowed. Technically, she had falsified her DOPS to cover Nick's tracks.

Lassiter was studying her face. "How close are you and LaGrange, anyway?"

"Not very," Elaine said, a little too quickly. "I mean, we're good friends. But that's all." Damn it! Of course they could only be good friends, in Lassiter's eyes—Nick was her boss!

Lassiter sipped his beer, regarding her as if he was a little unsure of her answers. "The bottom line is, we need you at Treasury on a very interesting and exciting project, one that has to do with stopping these criminals who have the Giori press. It's a project where you can really put this talent for identifying fakes to spectacular use." He paused, raising an eyebrow. "Are you interested?"

Elaine thought it over. Why did this have to happen to her and Nick? Only three days after she'd slept with him?

"We'll give you a twenty percent raise," Lassiter added.

"I won't do anything against Nick," Elaine said.

"I'm not asking you to. But you need to get out of Bulgaria and wash your hands of this. And we really need you on this new project. You pull this off, it will be a fantastic achievement for you."

On the inside, Elaine was experiencing a riot of conflicting emotions, everything from outrage to grief. She was angry that she was being put in such a horrible position. But it wasn't Lassiter's fault.

"Do you want to think about it?" Lassiter said.

"If Nick really is guilty, I don't want to stay in Bulgaria, Mr. Lassiter."

"Gene," he said, smiling. "Call me Gene."

CHAPTER 1.18

Elaine flew back to Bulgaria feeling incredibly distraught. She didn't know how she would face Nick again. She was overwhelmed with guilt. She was betraying him. But now she was fairly sure he was guilty, and she wasn't about to go to jail for him.

But she had to be absolutely sure.

When she arrived in Sofia, she spent the entire evening packing up everything in her apartment. Then, at 5 a.m., she went into work, long before anyone else would be there except the guard at the front entrance.

After she made absolutely sure the space was empty, she donned a pair of latex gloves and went into Nick's office. He never locked his door, nor did he ever lock his messy desk or cabinets. Yet, the very bottom drawer of his large file cabinet was locked.

She pulled out her locksmith tools and, after fumbling around for almost five minutes, finally got it open. Buried in the very back of the drawer, hidden under a sweater that stunk of tobacco, was a cardboard box.

Please don't let there be any money in this, she thought, as she opened the flaps.

Her heart sank.

There it was, staring her in the face. The $10,000 worth of Belarusian rubles Nick had taken from Bulgaria. She recognized the yellow rubber bands that were still around each bundle. He had never converted it to American dollars, never recycled it into the account used for undercover operations.

"Bastard," she whispered, staring down at the damning evidence. Now she felt betrayed. She had falsified her DOPS, and his, too.

She shut the drawer, relocked it, and went back to her office.

Nick came in about the usual time. She was busy packing up the personal items from her office.

He stepped inside her door and said, with a grin, "Let's go synchronize our DOPS." The grin faded as he looked around at the empty bookshelves and the cardboard boxes. "What—what's going on?"

"I have to go to Washington," she muttered.

He looked back at the boxes. "What do you mean, you 'have' to go to Washington?"

"I—I'm being transferred." She avoided his eyes.

"Transferred...what the hell are you talking about?"

"Word spread about me being able to check counterfeits fast, and they want me for a new project they're working on at Treasury."

He looked dumbfounded, then suspicious. She avoided his gaze.

"What the hell happened in Germany?" he said. "Who were you meeting with there?"

"I can't tell you, that," she said, pulling some file folders from her drawer. Before she and Lassiter had parted, he told her that absolutely, under no circumstances, was she to reveal anything to Nick. The cover story was that her skills in counterfeit recognition were needed for a new project in Washington, that her supervisor there was a secret, and that it would be in violation of her security clearance to reveal anything else. Her paperwork that transferred her from the Secret Service to the Treasury Department would be sent overnight. Prepaid tickets to D.C. would be waiting for her at the Sofia Airport.

Nick stepped behind her desk and grabbed her wrist. "What the hell is happening, Elaine?"

"Let go of me!" she said, yanking her arm free.

One of the other agents was passing the door. He stopped and looked into the office. When he saw Nick's contorted face, he quickly continued on.

Nick just stood there, breathing hard. "In case you've forgotten, I'm the SAIC of this office. I'm asking you an official question. Who were you meeting with in—"

"I don't work here anymore," Elaine said, her throat dry. "I work for Treasury now."

Nick looked like she'd slapped him across the face. "What's the matter with you? Didn't the other night mean *anything* to you?"

"I—I just have to leave, Nick." She was fighting tears. "I have no choice. Please don't ask me anything else."

"You *have* to leave? This isn't the damn U. S. army, Elaine. You don't *have* to do anything." He paused, his expression pained. "Is it another man?"

She couldn't do this to him, security clearance or no security clearance.

"Nick...you are about to be arrested."

BOOK 2

MONEY

CHAPTER 2.1

"Arrested?" Nick LaGrange said, baffled. "You must be kidding. What on earth would I be arrested for?"

Elaine was breathing hard. She had to force herself to hold her voice to a whisper. "For that money you've got hidden in the bottom drawer of your file cabinet! For starters."

Nick stared at her with disbelief. "You've been *snooping* around my office?"

"You left me no choice," she muttered and began packing again. "I can't believe you would make me lie on our reports to cover yourself."

"And I can't believe you would take someone else's word over mine! Who told you that I was about to be arrested?"

Elaine didn't answer.

"That money...I just haven't gotten around to changing it yet, that's all. I..."

Elaine would not look at him

"Fine," he said. "Run away to fucking Washington! I don't give a damn."

He turned, and looked back and said, "You know the real reason you're running away? You're afraid to get close to people."

Nick stomped out of the office.

Elaine hoped that the trip to Washington would make her feel better. "Out of sight, out of mind." But it didn't. She felt terrible about what had happened between her and Nick.

You know the real reason you're running away? You're afraid to get close to people.

That was nonsense. The reason she was "running away" was that he was a criminal, just as bad as the men they were supposedly trying to put in jail. Why did she have to get involved with a dishonest man? Nick was just like her father...a good heart, but a corrupt soul.

She ordered three cocktails on the plane and drank herself into a sick, troubled sleep.

Gene Lassiter personally met Elaine at Dulles Airport. They rode to the Treasury Department in an armored SUV, driven by a Secret Service agent. She had no idea what the new project was that Lassiter wanted her to work on. She hoped that it was as exciting as he said it was—anything to take her mind off Nick.

Elaine was awed as she and Lassiter got out of the SUV and walked up the steps between the Treasury Building's impressive granite pillars. It was hard to believe that she would be working in this historic structure, right across the street from the White House.

During the drive over, Gene Lassiter had told her that he was in charge of all the "covert features" built into American paper money that help keep it from being counterfeited.

After she was given a security badge, he led her up to the third floor, to his office. He occupied one of the coveted "semi-preserved" suites.

The office boasted a spectacular view of the White House. The windows were fitted with walnut cornices ornamented in gold leaf. A gilded chandelier hung from the ceiling, which was painted with allegorical murals of "Treasury" and "Justice." Lassiter told her that the space appeared more or less the same as it did in the 1860s. The only thing that did not look like an antique was a wall map of the world that had different colored pins pushed into it, mostly in Europe.

"Your office is very impressive," Elaine said politely, as if it even mattered.

He smiled and motioned to her with his cane. "Spend about forty years working here for the crappy government salary they pay you, putting up with all the bureaucratic bullshit they throw at you, slaving away, and they might give you one, too, about a year before you retire."

Elaine would have smiled, but there was real bitterness in his voice. Still, at least he was an honest man. Unlike some people she knew.

He offered her a seat in a comfortable leather chair, then hobbled on his cane to his antique desk and sat down, grimacing as he did so. His aging frame looked emaciated, his three-piece suit hanging from his limbs. Elaine noticed that there were tremors in his hands.

He opened the desk drawer and popped a couple of tablets into his mouth. "Parkinson's Disease," he explained, swallowing the tablets dry.

He motioned to her. "So, I imagine you're pretty curious about this new project I want you to work on..."

"To say the least," Elaine said.

"You've been checking a lot of these fakes. As I'm sure you noticed, whoever is making them is getting better and better at it."

"Yes, I noticed." She decided to focus her mind on the task at hand. "From what I know, the Giori printing presses are very complicated—there's a learning curve to master using them correctly."

"That's right. But it looks like the criminals recently made a major breakthrough."

"How's that?"

Lassiter pointed to the map on his wall with the pins in it. "Three weeks ago, in San Remo, Italy, a young woman took fifty thousand fake U.S. dollars into a casino and changed it into chips. All of the money—we're talking five hundred of the counterfeit banknotes—passed right through the verifier at the casino's currency exchange, completely undetected."

"How were the fakes discovered?" Elaine said, fascinated.

"Someone at the casino's home office in Marseilles examined a few of the notes very carefully. He noticed some fine discrepancies and sent one to the Secret Service for verification."

"And the girl?"

Lassiter shrugged. "Gone missing. Some Italian hooker. She's probably dead now." He looked evenly at Elaine. "You realize what all this means?"

"Yes. It means banks and currency exchanges can't tell these fakes from real U.S. currency."

"Exactly. Which as you can imagine, is a goddam serious problem."

"I'll say."

"The Secret Service's solution is to try and physically track down the Giori machine. If you ask me, that entire approach is wrong, and it's wasting valuable time. Nick LaGrange has thrown a further wrench into the works. Who knows where the goddam machine is hidden or how long it could take to find it? It could be sitting in the finance ministry of some government that's hostile to the United States—in the Middle East, South America, Asia...anywhere!"

"True," Elaine said.

"From my point of view a much smarter and more efficient approach would simply be to update the software in the currency verifying machines all over the world so that they detect the bills from *that* particular printing press and keep those fakes out of circulation. It's just a matter of sending out updated detection software, which is easy. The problem with this phantom Giori press would be solved like that!" He snapped his fingers. "Game over."

"It sounds like a good plan."

"I'm glad you think so," he said, smiling. "Because you're the one in charge of it."

"Me?" she said, taken aback.

"Yes, you. Who else knows more about these particular fakes than you do? You've been studying their details for a year now, and you've seen more of them than anyone else. You have a strong background in intaglio printing, plus—"

"But I've never done anything like this before."

"I'll be personally supervising you. You'll have access to all the resources you need, I'll see to it. Our top programmer, our top covert feature designer, and the engineers at KBA Giori, in Wurzburg, if you need them."

Elaine was flabbergasted.

"But still—"

"Besides," he said, "I don't trust anyone else to take this on." He motioned to the walls as if they had ears. "Everyone around here has got too much political baggage. I want someone from the outside, someone I can trust."

"I—I don't know what to say."

"Don't say anything, Elaine. Just get to work."

The old man turned sideways in his chair, to a huge safe that was built into the wall. After entering a code into a keypad, he leaned forward and dialed in a combination, blocking her view so she could not see. He opened the safe and pulled out a plastic bag and pushed it across his desk to her.

It was full of $100 bills. There were sticky notes attached to all of them.

"That bag contains every fake that has surfaced anywhere in the world and has been traced to the Giori machine. Time, date, and place found.

Some of them you've checked already."

Elaine looked at them—there were several hundred banknotes.

"What you need to do is go through every one of those bills and find the common defects they have compared to real American currency. Defects that you think will be most likely to remain in the bills no matter how much the criminals fine-tune the printing process and plates. Then, you'll work with the software folks here to find a way to detect those defects with currency verifying machines, and then we'll send out the software updates to all the global banks to end this goddam problem once and for all. Is that clear?"

"Yes," Elaine said. It was a tremendous amount of work. It would take months.

"You can set up shop in the office next to mine," he said, indicating a door to the right. "It's unoccupied at the moment. Whatever equipment you need—microscopes, scanners, or whatever—we'll have it all brought up here." He motioned to the bills. "Every night, those will be locked up in my safe, along with all the notes and other materials from the project until you're finished. I want this kept absolutely top secret."

Elaine nodded.

He folded his trembling hands on his desk. "Any questions?"

CHAPTER 2.2

Elaine dove into the project, working days, nights, and weekends. To be close to the office and to prevent her from "wasting time" looking for an apartment, Lassiter rented a modest suite for her at a hotel a few metro stations away. Elaine never went there except to collapse into the bed or wake up and shower.

Lassiter drove her relentlessly. A perfectionist with little patience for mistakes, he was not an easy man to work for.

Her office on the third floor of the Treasury Building soon looked like the quarters of some demented terrorist determined to bring down the American financial system. It was packed with strange-looking equipment, the ornate walls covered with her family-tree style interconnection diagrams and greatly magnified sections of fake $100 notes. One day there were so many half-full coffee cups lying around that it reminded her—painfully—of Nick's office.

She was a neat and orderly person, but there was no time to tidy it up.

"You can clean up the mess later," Lassiter would scold, "when this goddam project is finished."

Her days became an endless blur. All the data was kept on a secure data key the size of a salt shaker, which they appropriately called, "the salt shaker." Coming into work, Lassiter taking the bills and salt shaker out of his safe, going to her office, endlessly comparing the notes to each other with all her technological aids, going back to Lassiter's office each evening, returning the fake bills and the salt shaker to the safe, and going back to the hotel. Her vision seemed blurry most of the time, her eyes bloodshot, her neck and back aching from bending to look through microscope lenses all day. She welcomed the exhaustion.

She worked Monday through Saturday. On Sundays, she took the day off.

She slept all day and treated herself to room service.

Otherwise, she survived on a diet of caffeine and fast food. She lost five pounds the first month.

She thought of Nick often. By the end of October, she still hadn't said a word to Lassiter about him—she was afraid to speak of Nick. Lassiter had given her strict orders not to have any further contact with him, or anyone else in the Secret Service. Elaine was registered at the hotel under a false name provided by Lassiter, and he had given her a new secure cellphone and number to use. She was sure the old man had taken these precautions so that Nick could not contact her, but he never said as much. She had a distinct feeling that he knew there had been more than a friendship between the two of them.

A week before Thanksgiving, Elaine finally got the nerve to ask him about Nick. Lassiter was in her office. He was sitting at her light table, with his back to her, peering through a loupe, going over some of the common defects she had found in the fakes.

"LaGrange?" he said, not moving his head. "I heard he was arrested a few weeks ago."

Elaine felt a sharp pang in her chest. "Is he...in jail?"

Lassiter turned around and glanced at her. "From what I understand, he's being held by Interpol in Brussels. When they're done interrogating him, he'll be sent to one of the CIA centers and then...I don't know. He'll eventually face a civil trial here in the States."

"So I guess they caught him accepting a bribe or something..."

"I suppose," Lassiter said vaguely. "I only know he was arrested."

Elaine felt sick. An image flashed before her—her father, standing on the other side of the glass in the prison visitor's room, his face sallow, dark circles under his eyes. Nick would probably be in captivity the rest of his life, unless he could somehow escape.

She told herself she would put Nick LaGrange out of her mind, once and for all.

Gene Lassiter entered the lobby of the hotel about 3 pm, as he did each and every day.

"Anything for me?" he said to the manager on duty.

"Another one of these," the man said, discreetly handing over an envelope.

Written across the front in handwriting that Lassiter recognized were the words DELIVER TO ROOM 628. PERSONAL AND CONFIDENTIAL.

It was the third one that had been received.

Later that night, Lassiter sat down in the den of his comfortable Georgetown home, the fire crackling in front of him. Leaning his cane against the couch, he pulled the envelope from his suit pocket. He tore it open and he began to read.

Dear Elaine...

There was only one heartfelt-written paragraph, and then Nick's signature.

How touching, Lassiter thought.

He tossed it into the fire.

Sipping his brandy, he watched the flames transform it into smoke and ashes.

CHAPTER 2.3

By the beginning of December, Elaine had found 75 different printing defects the fake notes had in common. All of the discrepancies were microscopic and could not be seen with the naked eye. Finding them was a frustrating process, as new fake notes rolled in every few days, most of them continuing to be found in Russia and Eastern Europe. Often, the defects common to all the previous notes disappeared in the newer notes. The criminals continued to learn, steadily improving the quality of their counterfeits.

Christmas and New Year's Day came and went.

In mid January, Elaine had narrowed down the defect list to ten errors, ten that currency verifying machines could easily detect if the software were upgraded. Lassiter called in several experts, including an engineer from KBA Giori. A great debate ensued as to which of the ten errors were most likely to persist as the criminals increased the quality of the banknotes.

Finally, after a week of heated discussion, the three key defects were settled on. 1) a missing spot in one of the zeros in the "100" symbols microprinted along the security thread, 2) on the front side of the note, an error in the shape of the blob of light reflected in the pupil of Ben Franklin's eye, and 3) on the back of the note, an out-of-position D—off by only one engraving line—in the phrase IN GOD WE TRUST.

Elaine immediately began working with Treasury's top programmer to modify the verification software to search for bills with these three errors and reject the banknote if one or more of them were present.

By the end of January, software was perfected and thoroughly tested. The 300-odd counterfeits collected were run over and over through a verifying machine with the new software, and it caught every one of them. Flawlessly.

The programmer spent two weeks cleverly disguising this new code so that if the criminals ever got hold of it, it would take years to figure out the three defects it was searching for.

When the software was ready and deemed perfect, Lassiter took Elaine out to Citronelle for a celebration. It was considered by many to be the best restaurant in Washington.

"Elaine, you did an absolutely fantastic job on this project," he said, toasting her jovially with champagne. "You can look forward to a long and fruitful career at Treasury."

"Thank you," she said wearily.

He chuckled with satisfaction. "I would give anything to see the look on these bastards' faces when they casually drop off another load of their damn fakes at their local bank, and the machines kick it all back and set off alarms. They're going to shit their pants. They'll spend the next few months scratching their heads, trying to figure out what happened."

Elaine smiled and sipped her champagne, but she was so exhausted, and still so keyed up from the climactic last few weeks, that she couldn't really enjoy herself.

Lassiter looked at her sympathetically. "Young lady, when I get back from my trip, I want you to take an entire month off. Go to Aruba or Cancun or somewhere and do nothing but lie in the sun and drink pina coladas all day." He pointed at her. "That's an order."

Elaine nodded vaguely.

And who am I supposed to share this wonderful vacation with? she thought.

A worldwide release of the new software was scheduled to begin March 1st. However, as Russia was the country that was suffering most because of the counterfeits, Lassiter's plan was to introduce the software there, first, as a "field test" to make absolutely sure there were no glitches. Lassiter's latest theory was that one of the most powerful Moscow Mafia groups had somehow acquired one of the Giori machines from an impoverished third world country.

Lassiter was due to leave on February 14th, Valentine's Day. His plan was to fly to Moscow, meet with the Bank of Russia, test the software, and then take a week off in Germany, where he had relatives. He wanted Elaine to remain in Washington until the test was complete, just in case.

Elaine came into work earlier than usual to see him off. When she arrived at his office, she was alarmed when she found him slumped over on the leather couch. His face looked pale. His cane lay in the middle of the floor.

"What's wrong?" she said, rushing over to him.

"I'm...I'm not feeling very well." His hands were shaking more than usual. He coughed a couple of times. "Would you get my pills, Elaine? They're in my desk."

Elaine quickly went to the desk and opened the top drawer, but she didn't see a pill vial.

"The side drawer," he gasped

She opened the left-hand side.

"No, the other side."

Elaine finally found the vial and twisted the top off for him.

"Thank you," he whispered. He popped two tablets in his mouth, his lower lip trembling. He closed his eyes, breathing through his mouth.

"Should I call a doctor?"

"No, no," he said, raising his head, peering at her through half-closed lids. "I'll be all right in just a minute." He glanced at his watch, then struggled to sit up. "My flight leaves in—"

"You can't go to Russia like this! Don't even think about it."

"They're expecting this software tomorrow." He took a few more breaths. "It would be very bad, politically, to delay this test—"

"I'll go in your place," Elaine blurted. As soon as she uttered those words, she regretted them—he might think she wanted to steal his glory.

Lassiter looked at her for a moment, then glanced over at his packed suitcase. "I couldn't ask you to do that."

"I'll be happy do it, Gene. You can't possibly travel like this."

"You're as exhausted as I am—"

"I'm not *that* exhausted."

He gazed longingly at his suitcase.

"Damn it, Gene, I'm not going to let you commit suicide!"

CHAPTER 2.4

As there wasn't time for the Treasury Department to arrange travel to Russia for her, Lassiter told her to go down to the street to a travel agency and buy a business class ticket to Moscow with her credit card, one way, and that the return ticket would be delivered to her hotel room once she arrived. He told her he would call the Secret Service office in Moscow and tell them of the change in plans, to put his hotel reservation in her name, and to meet her at the Sheremetyevo Airport and give her "first class treatment" the entire time she was in Russia.

Lassiter put the software on an ordinary, password protected data key, which she attached to her key chain.

She would only be away for three days, so took her satchel and smallest suitcase. As she often worked late, she kept the small suitcase in her office. In it were a business suit, a change of underwear, and some cosmetics.

Also in the suitcase were a couple of things that Lassiter did not know about. One was the fake Irish diplomatic passport Nick had made for her, which had $3,000 in cash tucked inside it—her own "emergency" money. The other was something else she had been given by Nick when they had gone to Belarus on the undercover assignment to carry in her suitcase. It was a silencer-equipped .357 pistol made especially for the U.S. Government by Sig Sauer. The gun was disassembled into three small pieces and hidden inside various mundane items—a can of hair spray, a hair brush, and a blow dryer, and it would pass through any airport security scanner. Nick had never asked for it back.

Lassiter had not told her to arm herself, but the software she was carrying was so important she thought it was a good idea.

One other thing she kept in the suitcase—the most cherished item she owned—was the silly little wind-up turkey that Nick had given her as her one-year anniversary present. As she rearranged the items in her suitcase, she clutched it lovingly in her hand, then carefully put it in one of the pockets.

By the time the taxi dropped her off at Dulles Airport, she was a nervous wreck, but she was also excited.

She was looking forward to seeing the results of her last six month's efforts.

The Bank of Russia would certainly be impressed.

CHAPTER 2.5

Moscow, Russia

"Ladies and gentlemen, please put your tray tables up and seats into the upright position in preparation for our landing at the Sheremetyevo Airport..."

Elaine peered out the window. It was very early morning, but still dark outside. She could make out the farmland below, covered in snow. She could even see some of the so-called "dachas" dotting the countryside, massive brick mansions standing half-finished and abandoned. She remembered Nick telling her about them, leaning over her, looking out the window, his cheek almost touching hers.

The Russian Mafia built those things after the Soviet Union collapsed. Then the gang wars started, and they killed each other off before the dachas were even finished.

Elaine told herself not to think of Nick. She said a silent prayer for him, hoping that wherever he was, he was all right.

The big aircraft soon landed and rolled to a stop at the gate. When the stewardess opened the door, Elaine was one of the first passengers to deplane. She knew there would be a big line at Passport Control and wanted to get through it as soon as possible so as not to keep the Secret Service agents waiting for her.

As she stepped out into the gate area, there were two men in gray suits and trench coats watching everyone who walked by. She could spot the Secret Service image a mile off. She was surprised—she hadn't expected them to meet her right here at the gate. That really was VIP treatment.

The eyes of one of the men locked on her face.

She stepped up and offered her hand. "Elaine Brogan. Thanks for meeting me, guys."

The man grabbed her wrist and the other one took hold of her arm. "U.S. Secret Service. Come along quietly, please."

"What are you—wait a minute—"

"Move along," the man on the left said, his arm tightening. "We don't want any trouble."

"My name is Elaine *Brogan*. Aren't you with the Secret Service?"

"Yes, ma'am."

They were moving her towards a door on the corridor marked

AUTHORIZED PERSONNEL ONLY. Struggling against their grip, she said, "You're supposed to meet me and take me to my hotel."

The two men exchanged glances, and one of them chuckled. "You're going to a hotel, all right. One with bars on all the windows." He keyed in a code and then they forced her through the door. They continued down a corridor.

Elaine was suddenly panic-stricken. *They must have gotten me confused with someone else.*

They took her through a door marked *DOPROC*. She was well versed in Russian, and she knew that word: Interrogation.

Elaine was terrified.

The windowless room had a long, scarred rectangular table with a few metal folding chairs surrounding it. Some empty coffee cups and ragged looking Russian newspapers were scattered about.

"You're in deep shit," one of them said. He was taller and older than the other one, and had a pockmarked face.

"Hand it over," the younger man said.

Elaine looked at them, bewildered. "Hand *what* over?"

"Look, we know you took it, so you can stop the innocent act. You can voluntarily give it to us, or we'll strip search you."

"And that won't be fun," the other man said, with a smile. "At least, not for you."

Elaine swallowed, looking from one face to another. What in the world was happening to her? This didn't make any sense.

"Look, my name is Elaine Brogan, and I work for—"

"Give me your bags," the pockmarked man said, and wrenched both away from her. He dumped out the contents of both her handbag and suitcase onto the table.

"You're really screwing up," she said, trying to maintain her composure. "I'll have you both fired."

When it was evident that whatever they were looking for was not in the bags, both men looked back at her.

"I told you you were making a mistake," Elaine snapped. "Now would one of you kindly call your office and—"

"Strip, lady."

Elaine recoiled. "I *beg* your pardon?"

The pockmark-faced man nodded to the younger one. "Give me your knife." He looked at Elaine as he slowly drew out the blade, the silver glinting in fluorescent lights.

Elaine was paralyzed with fear. These two were out of control. They could do whatever they wanted with her in this interrogation room—there were no cameras that she could see, no two-way mirrors.

The man picked up her suitcase and opened it wide. She winced as the knife cut through the lining.

"You're going to pay for that suitcase," she said, her mouth dry.

Her eyes widened as the man withdrew a sleek black cylinder. It was the "salt shaker," the high capacity data key for the project she had just finished. It contained all the data—the 14 common mistakes in the counterfeits, hundreds of super high resolution scans of the fake banknotes, the three crucial errors that the new software would look for. In short, all the research data that had been used to create the software updates.

Elaine's heart went into her throat.

"You're under arrest," he said flatly. "Gene Lassiter told us this was missing from his safe yesterday afternoon. You can look forward to twenty years in a federal penitentiary, with no chance of parole."

The other man produced a plastic EVIDENCE bag and he dropped it in, and he started writing on the label.

"Somebody planted that there!"

"Sure, lady."

"I'm being framed!"

"Uh-huh."

The room was spinning. Elaine's mind raced from one thought to another. Somebody had set her up. Gene Lassiter. It had to be Lassiter! No one else had the combination to his safe...

Then she remembered what had taken place in his office yesterday, when he was slumped on his couch.

Would you get me my pills, Elaine? They're in my desk.

She had opened every one of his desk drawers! Her fingerprints were all over them.

She pulled her phone from her pocket. She had to call someone—Nick?

The pockmarked man snatched it from her hand. "You're not making any calls." He set it down on the corner of the table, far out of her reach.

The two men stepped over to the other side of the room out of earshot, talking to each other in low voices. This couldn't be...how could Lassiter have done this to her?

Elaine was only dimly aware of the men's conversation—she felt like her ears were filled with cotton, and the voices were far away.

"...the extradition papers..."

"...hold her at the American Embassy while..."

"...they'll want to fly her back to D.C. on a diplomatic jet for formal charging..."

This can't be happening, she thought dazedly. *This can't be happening.*

The two men walked over to the door. "Keep your ass in that chair," the one with the evidence bag said, pointing at her. They both went outside and pulled the door shut behind them.

A sense of unreality swept over her. Elaine gaped at her open suitcase, all her personal items scattered around the table.

You'll spend the next twenty years in a federal penitentiary, with no chance of parole.

She saw herself wearing numbered orange coveralls, standing in line holding a metal food tray, shuffling around with shackles on her wrists and ankles...

Just like her father.

Elaine's eyes were drawn to a clock on the wall. She watched the red needle of the second hand slowly move around the face. Twenty *years* in prison. She suddenly stood up, her vision blurred. There was a sink in the corner. She rushed over to it and vomited.

As she wiped her mouth, she realized how quiet it was in the room. And then she looked at the can of hair spray, the hair brush...she could assemble her gun. Maybe she could escape.

Then she again noticed how quiet the room was. Suddenly, she heard men's voices out in the corridor. They were laughing, speaking Russian.

She looked over at the door. The handle turned.

Elaine quickly sat back down.

Several huge Russian men sauntered into the room. They were all wearing blue Aeroflot coveralls, with photo ID badges clipped to their pockets. Each man held a steaming paper cup in his hand. They stopped talking when they saw Elaine.

"*Kto ti?*" one of them said, staring. *Who are you?*

"Who are you?"

One of them turned and muttered, "*Americanka,*" to the others. The whole group sipped their coffee, watching her.

"I think you should not be here," another man said, in thickly accented English. "This secure area of airport."

"*Puskai ostayotcia, ona ochen krasivaya*" another said. *Let her stay, she's very beautiful.*

The men all chuckled good-naturedly. They just stood there, drinking their coffee, smiling at her.

Elaine glanced at the open door. The sign that had said DOPROC had disappeared.

"Where am I?" she said, standing up.

They glanced at each other, puzzled.

"You are in the Aeroflot baggage handler recreation room." The man smiled. "Would you like some coffee?"

Elaine madly threw all her things back into her suitcase, then banged out through the door that opened onto the main concourse, her mind racing.

The two men weren't with the Secret Service—they were with the Russian Mafia! She'd been tricked and let them get away with the data key.

Lassiter had used her to transport the data key out of the United States. He must have sold it to the Russian Mafia.

It was unbelievable to her, but it was the only logical explanation.

She had to get it back. It was the only way she could stop herself from being framed. If she could recover it, she could take it back to Washington and go to the highest authorities—to the Executive Treasurer, or the Director of the Secret Service. She could explain everything that had happened—surely they would believe her.

As she ran down the concourse toward Passport Control, she mentally recounted everything that had happened yesterday in Lassiter's office. A demonstration at the Bank of Russia? For all she knew, there was no demonstration—the project was so top secret the only information she ever received was directly from Lassiter's mouth. Furthermore, she had no evidence that he had told her he was going to Russia, or that she had agreed to go in his place! She had bought the plane ticket herself, with her own credit card—a one-way ticket!

My god, she thought—I looked as if I fled the USA with no intention of ever coming back!

When Elaine reached the sprawling Passport Control area, she found it packed with hundreds of weary travelers, waiting in endless queues. The two Russian thieves had probably left the airport some other way. It would be a miracle if she could get that data key back now...

Far ahead, Elaine could see the staffed booths: RUSSIAN PASSPORTS, EU PASSPORTS, ALL OTHER PASSPORTS. At the very far side of the room, she spotted another booth: DIPLOMATIC PASSPORTS/VIP SERVICE. There was no queue in front of it.

Elaine dashed in that direction and fished out her fake Irish diplomatic passport from the hidden slot in her suitcase. When she slid it under the window of the booth, the uniformed male Russian officer opened it and peered at it as she stood there, catching her breath.

O'NEILL, SHANNON, the name read. The seal of the Irish Department of Agriculture, Fisheries and Food was clearly visible on the pale gray paper.

"And how long vil you be in Russia?" the officer asked slowly, rolling the r in Russia.

"Just a wee time, a few days," Elaine said, turning on her Irish accent. She glanced beyond the partition, into Baggage Claim. *Come on*, she thought. *Hurry up!*

The officer looked closely at Elaine's face, then peered at the passport again. Finally, he picked up a heavy stamp and *ka-thumped* it on one of the open pages. "Enjoy your stay."

Elaine rushed from the booth and entered the baggage area, then headed straight down the hallway marked GREEN LINE – NOTHING TO DECLARE, rolling her suitcase along behind her. When she emerged into the airport lobby, there were throngs of people huddled around the exit from Customs—men, women, children, many holding bouquets, their eyes anxiously scanning the arriving passengers for their loved ones.

Elaine pushed ahead, tripping over people and luggage, frantically searching for the two men who had conned her. She was immediately accosted by a gaggle of leather-clad taxi drivers.

"Cheap taxi to center!"

"Very low price—"

"One hundred dollars—"

"New Mercedes, very comfortable—"

"Get out of my way," Elaine snapped, plowing through them.

She followed the signs to ground transportation. When she stepped out onto the sidewalk, she was struck by a blast of cold air that chilled her to the bone—the temperature was well below zero. It was still dark outside, and the parking lot was covered with snow.

Elaine desperately scanned the lot for the men, peering into the windows of the passing vehicles.

They're probably long gone by now, she thought, terror-stricken. *What I am going to do?*

She desperately tried to think of someone who could help her, but the only person that came to mind was Nick. And he was in jail somewhere.

Then, across the parking lot, she spotted the man with the pockmarked face. He was unlocking the door of a large black SUV. The other man was not with him.

"Taxi?" a voice said from behind her.

Elaine whirled around, afraid it was the second man. But it was only a taxi driver, in the usual Russian taxi driver outfit—a cheap-looking brown faux leather jacket, a plaid scarf, and a black driver's cap. He looked harmless—big, but with stooped over shoulders. He had sad eyes that reminded her of a basset hound's.

"I give very good price to center," he said, vapor pluming from his mouth. "Ninety dollars. My car not so good—" he pointed to a little beat-up Lada that was splattered with brown slush,"— but price very good."

The black SUV was pulling away now.

"Fine, let's go," she said, moving towards his car.

The big man moved surprisingly fast for his size. He rushed over to the Lada and opened the passenger door for her, throwing the front seat forward. She climbed into the back of the cramped little Russian-made vehicle.

He got in and started the engine. "Which hotel?"

"See that black SUV?" Elaine said, pointing.

"Jeep?"

"Yes, jeep." She had forgotten that's what Russians called all SUVs. "Follow the jeep."

As he pulled away, Elaine nervously glanced around the inside of the car, taking everything in, sizing him up. Attached to the dashboard was a square icon of Mary Magdalene. Next to it was a clipboard with color flyers for nightclubs, photos of scantily clad women on the front. In the compartment below, a dog-eared road atlas and a couple of short fishing poles, the type used for ice fishing.

She didn't think he was anything other than what he appeared to be, an independent taxi driver.

The SUV was picking up speed. It soon disappeared around the ramp that led to the highway.

"Don't lose it," Elaine said, her voice trembling.

The driver glanced at Elaine again. "If you will simply say which hotel —"

"I don't know which hotel!" Elaine tried to think of a reasonable sounding explanation. "That's my friend, I don't know where he's going. Okay?"

"Okay," the driver said, looking skeptical.

Elaine was too preoccupied with recovering the data key to think up excuses for a taxi driver. She checked out the back window to make sure they were not being followed. The road was clear behind them.

They soon caught up with the SUV.

"Hang back," Elaine said.

"*Shto?*" the driver said.

"Stay behind the jeep, but don't lose it." Elaine wasn't sure if he understood. "*Panyatno?*"

"*Panyatno,*" he said, glancing at her again in the rearview. He knew something strange was going on.

Elaine was frantically trying to think of a way to stop the SUV. She didn't have much time, she had to act *now*. She considered calling the Moscow Secret Service field office and trying to explain what had happened, but it was too risky. Lassiter might have already called them, telling them she had stolen the data key. At this point, she couldn't trust anyone.

Elaine opened her suitcase and began assembling the Sig Sauer, keeping it out of the driver's sight. At least she still had the gun.

They came to a cloverleaf—the SUV took the ramp that said MOSCOW – CENTRE.

The driver kept looking at Elaine in the rearview—he had heard the clicking of the pistol as she snapped it together.

118

Suddenly, he pulled a cellphone from his pocket and began punching in a number with his thumb.

"*Ne zvonite telefon,*" Elaine said, alarmed.

He gazed at her through the mirror, hesitating, his finger poised over the keypad.

She pressed the gun barrel against the back of his neck. "I said no telephone calls. Put the goddam phone down in the passenger seat."

He quickly tossed the device over into the other seat and raised both his hands in the air. He stared at her through the rearview, the basset hound eyes wide and frightened.

"Keep steering!" she said, as the car started to veer into the other lane.

He put his hands back on the wheel, but he looked so nervous Elaine was afraid he would panic. She pulled out her Treasury Department badge and held it up so he could see it through the rearview. Speaking Russian slowly and carefully, she said, "I am a special police agent from America. I will not harm you. Just do your job and follow that jeep." She paused, then added, "If you do well, I will give you a big tip."

He looked even more frightened.

Elaine was confused...then realized that she had used the wrong word for "tip," which was a variant of the Russian word for tea. She had told him that if he did a good job, she would give him a big tea kettle.

"I meant extra money," she said, rubbing her fingers together. "*Dengi.* Understand?"

"Ah." He gave a nervous smile. "Extra money good." He watched her for a moment through the mirror. "It is very exciting for me to help American FBI. I like exciting life. My life very borink."

He thinks I'm an FBI agent, Elaine thought. *Let him think that.*

"My name is Dmitry. What is your name?"

"Janet," she lied, saying the first name that came into her head.

"Janyet. This is nice American name."

Now they were in heavy traffic and were coming to the first stoplights they had encountered since leaving the airport. If she waited much longer, the man in the jeep might meet someone else, and then it might be impossible to get the key back. She considered jumping out of the car, running up to the SUV, and trying to catch the driver by surprise. She could smash the window open and put the gun to his neck...but the windows might be bulletproof—the Russian Mafia was famous for its heavily armored vehicles. On top of that, dozens of people in other cars would see her. If someone called the police, no telling what would happen.

"I help you, Janyet," Dmitry said, breaking into Elaine's thoughts. "If you want."

She studied his face as he gazed up at her through the rearview. She wasn't sure she could trust him. Pushing the barrel a little harder into his neck, she said, "Who were you going to call on your phone?"

He raised his hands innocently. "I only call my wife. She worry when I working all night." He looked ahead at the SUV again, shaking his head. "I hate Mafia! I *honest* taxi driver," he said emphatically, pronouncing the "h" in honest. "Mafia no let me go inside airport, take all my customers." He paused. "I have daughter. She study at Moscow State University to be doctor." There was great pride in his voice. "I wish American FBI come and kill all Mafia, like on television!"

"That's a task for your police," Elaine muttered.

"Our police?" He gave a big belly laugh. "Our police, Mafia, same thing." Dmitry raised both his big paws in the air. "All one big Mafia."

"Do you really want to help me?" she asked.

"*Da*, Janyet. I already say I want help you." He paused. "For little extra money, of course..."

"Then listen very carefully..."

When she finished explaining her plan, Dmitry's face turned pale.

"Janyet...this very dangerous. If I do what you say, this man in jeep will kill me."

"He won't kill you. He's not interested in you, Dmitry. Trust me. He'll tell you to go away."

Dmitry swallowed, staring through the windshield at the SUV. It was only 100 feet ahead of them now. They had just crossed the Moscow River. The traffic had thickened. The sky was showing the first violet hues of dawn.

"You ask too much, Janyet."

"I thought you told me you wanted some excitement in your life?"

Dmitry, winced, looking like he sorely regretted those words.

"I'll pay you well," Elaine said, remembering the cash she had with her. "Very well."

She could see temptation in his eyes. Making the sign of the cross over his chest, he pressed on the accelerator and closed in on the SUV.

Elaine rolled down the back window, raising the pistol. The frigid wind whipped across her cheeks. The SUV was in the left-hand lane, tailgating the car in front of it. They were easing up on the right-hand side.

"Closer!" Elaine shouted, over the wind. *I hope to God this works*, she thought. As they neared the SUV, she aimed the gun at its spinning back tire.

"Closer!" she said. She wasn't taking any chances.

Dmitry pressed a little harder on the gas. Now the jeep's rear wheel was almost within reach of her arm.

Elaine pulled the trigger.

The tire exploded, then made a *flop-flop-flop* sound as the rubber began to shred.

Dmitry hit the brakes and let the SUV swerve in front of them.

"Now!" she said.

"*Bozhe moi*," Dmitry muttered, then let up on the brake. Two seconds later the front end of the Lada slammed into the rear of the SUV. It was enough to throw Elaine forward but not enough to do any serious damage to either vehicle.

Both cars came to a stop on the shoulder of the road. Elaine ducked down to the floorboard. Dmitry reluctantly opened his door. He looked terrified when he saw the big, pockmark-faced man open the door of the SUV and lumber towards him, scowling.

"*Durak!*" the man shouted. "What the fuck is wrong with you?"

"You stopped too fast," Dmitry said in Russian, walking cautiously towards him. "I—I was not prepared..."

The man stepped behind the SUV and peered down at the flat tire, cursing.

"I'll help you change it," Dmitry said, with no enthusiasm at all.

The man opened the SUV's rear door. "Get the hell out of here."

Dmitry did not need any more persuasion. He quickly walked back towards the Lada.

While they were talking, Elaine had slipped out of the car. She was squatting behind the Lada's bumper. Traffic was passing by, some of the cars honking.

As soon as the man bent down and tried to fit the jack under the car, she dashed forward.

The next thing the man knew, the barrel of the Sig Sauer was pressing into the back of his head.

"Lie face down on the ground," Elaine barked, adrenaline pumping through her veins. Pushing him down into the gravel, she grabbed both his arms and pulled them behind his back. She felt around and felt inside his jacket. There was a pistol in one pocket. She pulled it out and flung the weapon down the embankment, into the snow. In the other pocket, she found the data key.

"You're dead," he said, as she pocketed it.

She leapt off him and backed up towards the Lada. "Stay on the ground!" she said, but he climbed to his feet. There was a noxious sheen in his eyes.

Dmitry had the Lada's passenger door open for her. Just as she reached it, the man suddenly bent and plucked something from his ankle. An instant later the object was flipping end over end through the air towards Elaine, end over end, metal glinting in car headlights.

The stiletto tore through Elaine's wool coat and pierced her side.

Elaine gasped and stumbled into the Lada's back seat. Dmitry stared through the rearview, frozen with fear, his eyes wide.

"Go!" Elaine yelled.

Dmitry pressed on the accelerator, burning rubber.

The man ran at the car, smashing his fist into the passenger window, but the Lada grazed him and knocked him to the pavement.

"*Bozhe moi!*" Dmitry yelled.

"You are hurt!" Dmitry said.

Elaine braced herself, then yanked the stiletto out of her side. Blood spurted. For a second she was terrified, afraid she might have been seriously wounded. But the pick-like instrument had only pierced an inch or so of flesh. No internal damage had been done.

"I have medic kit," Dmitry said, fumbling to open the glove compartment.

"Just drive, Dmitry!"

With one hand pressing against her side to stop the bleeding, she opened the first aid kit, pulled up her red-stained blouse, and applied a stick-on bandage to her side.

Dmitry was looking nervously between the road ahead and the rearview.

"Where go now, Janyet? Where go now?"

Elaine looked out at the heavy traffic. She changed her mind about trying to go back to the airport. "Do you know where the American Embassy is?"

"*Da.*" He drove faster, tailgating the car in front.

If they could make it to the embassy, she could call the Treasurer, or the Secretary Treasurer, and explain everything over the phone. She would turn the data key over to the embassy staff. They would have to believe her.

She could hardly believe she'd gotten the data key back. But she'd done it!

Dmitry was looking distractedly into the rearview.

"What's the matter?" Elaine said anxiously. She was afraid to turn around and look. No way could it be the SUV—it would be impossible to drive with that shredded tire.

"Hummer," Dmitry said.

Elaine gathered the courage to look. The wide, menacing black vehicle was creeping up behind them. The glass in the Hummer's windshield was tinted so heavily that it was impossible to see inside.

"It is Mafia," Dmitry said, his voice wavering with fear.

"How do you know?"

"Mafia like Hummer."

Elaine fought panic—she wasn't about to let them catch her now, not after all this!

The traffic was thickening as they neared the center of the city. Ahead, she could see a river of red brake lights that looked like it went on for miles. The embassy was on the other side of town...they would never make it.

She glanced across the median to the other side of the road. The traffic back towards the Sheremetyevo Airport was moving along freely.

"Turn around," she said.

Dmitry hesitated. "But—"

"Turn around!" she said. "We're going back to the airport."

MIKE WELLS

The sky was growing lighter, a fine snow falling from gunmetal gray clouds. Elaine and Dmitry were only a few miles from the Sheremetyevo Airport, but the Hummer was riding their rear bumper.

If she could lose them, somehow, and make it inside the airport, she thought there was a good chance she could flee the country before they could catch her. She had the fake Irish passport, which nobody knew about, at least not yet. Sheremetyevo was a very busy airport, with flights leaving every couple of minutes to destinations all over the world. She had plenty of money—she could buy some clothes in one of the shops and disguise herself, then purchase a ticket on the first flight out.

Dmitry looked petrified, both his hands clutching the steering wheel as if he were holding onto it for dear life.

She looked back at the trailing Hummer again. "What about losing them on some small roads?" Elaine said.

Dmitry motioned to the rearview. "How? They have Hummer, we have Lada."

Elaine pointed the gun at the dashboard. "Open your road atlas and show me where we are."

Dmitry pulled out the frayed book and turned to the middle. They were just approaching a town called Burtsevo. Elaine leaned forward, studying the map.

"What about taking this route?" she said, indicating a small highway that branched off into a forest. It looked like it continued almost all the way to the airport. "Can you think of a way to lose them along here?"

"I know this *rejone* well, Janyet—I often fishing in river." She saw a thick blue line that snaked through the middle of the green area. "But there is no way lose them. I already say you—they have *Hummer* and we have Lada."

"A Hummer is very wide," Elaine said, "and your car is very narrow. Is there some place this car can go that a Hummer *can't* go?"

She saw the flicker of an idea cross his face.

"What?" Elaine said.

When he didn't answer, she pushed the gun against his neck again. "Speak up, Dmitry."

He swallowed. "In forest, trees very close together. Too close together for Hummer."

124

"Get off at the next exit."

Dmitry sailed down the exit ramp for Burtsevo as fast as the little Lada would go.

Elaine looked out the back window—the Hummer was following, but lagging behind. The driver had not anticipated the sudden turn Dmitry had made.

"Faster," she said, as they swung around the ramp.

Dmitry picked up more speed, the tires screeching. Fortunately, the snow had long been cleared off the pavement and the surface was clean and dry.

They came out onto a deserted road that ran parallel to the highway. Elaine held the atlas, tracking their route. They reached a crossroads— there was a sign pointing to the left, to the town of Burtsevo, but Dmitry kept driving straight ahead.

The pavement soon became rough, packed with several inches of snow, with only a few tire tracks.

Elaine looked out the back window again—the sudden exit had been unexpected, but the Hummer was gaining on them fast.

Just ahead was the beginning of the forest.

"Faster!" Elaine said.

Dmitry pressed harder on the accelerator, the little Lada now rattling and bucking as they hit ruts and ice-covered potholes. Elaine gasped as the car flew over a depression and slammed back down—the icon of Mary on the dash tumbled to the floorboard.

Dmitry swerved the car hard to the left. They were heading down a very narrow lane, the snow fresh and unblemished, the densely packed rows of birch trees coming up quickly. The Hummer was on their rear bumper now—Elaine could hear the thundering of its big engine over the weak whine of the Lada's.

Dmitry slammed on the brakes. An instant later, the Hummer banged into them, then lagged back as the Lada skidded ahead, thrown forward by the heavy vehicle. Dmitry took a hard left, straight into the forest, the white bark of the birch trees whizzing past their windows, coming within inches of the car on both sides. Elaine had dropped the road atlas and hugged the back of the passenger seat. The tree trunks were coming at them fast, Dmitry frantically twisting the wheel this way and that to avoid them. He was a very good driver.

"Are they still behind us?" Elaine asked.

"Yes, but not very..." Dmitry didn't complete the sentence, yanking the wheel hard to the left. There was a loud bang—the door mirror on Elaine's side snapped off. "...close," he finished.

Elaine looked out the back window. The Hummer was at least 50 yards behind, slowly picking its way through the trees, having veered off Dmitry's path to find clearance. She saw it simply run over a young, thin birch, the tree snapping partially up again as the heavy vehicle moved relentlessly forward.

If the Hummer caught up with them out here in the forest, they were both dead.

Elaine studied the road atlas, trying to determine where they were. The deeper they went into the woods, the longer it would take the Hummer to pick its way back out...

Dmitry slowed the car. Elaine looked up—directly ahead of them, a huge, fallen birch was blocking their path. It looked like there might be enough space to go under it, at least on the left-hand side.

Dmitry slowed the car, then pressed on the accelerator again, but he kept going straight.

Elaine said, "No! There's not enough roo—"

She was thrown forward and there was a loud crunch from the roof above.

Now the car was perfectly still.

Dmitry pressed on the gas pedal, the engine racing, but the vehicle was immobilized. Elaine looked out the back window. The wheels were only kicking up arcs of snow.

"We're stuck!" she gasped.

The Hummer was still approaching. It was moving faster now, threading its way through the trees, the driver become more adjusted to the terrain.

Dmitry slammed the transmission into reverse and tried to back out, but the car wouldn't budge. Elaine felt the rear of the Lada sink an inch or two farther into the snow.

"Stop!" she yelled at Dmitry. "You're just digging us in deeper."

He let up on the accelerator and the wheels stopped spinning. They sat there in abrupt silence, the Lada's little engine idling softly. Dmitry stared helplessly through the rearview as the approaching vehicle slowly threaded its way through the trees—it would reach them in a matter of a minute or two. By the look on his face, Elaine could tell he thought he was already as good as dead.

She threw the passenger seat forward and jumped out of the car. The tree branch was caught on the roof, snagged on the cracked TAXI sign. She held her pistol by the barrel and took several swipes at it, but the gun, made of plastics, was too light to have any effect.

Now Elaine could hear the rumble of the Hummer's engine. Dmitry dashed around to the trunk, and pulled out a tire iron, then came back and struck several heavy blows to the TAXI sign.

The sound of the Hummer's engine faded. Elaine turned back and looked. The vehicle had come to a stop perhaps 50 yards behind them. Doors opened. Several men got out, pulling pistols from their jackets.

"Get down!" Elaine said, just as the first shot rang out. The Lada's back window shattered.

Dmitry dove inside the car.

Elaine dropped into the snow. There were several metallic pings and thuds as bullets impacted the car. She crawled around to the far side of the open passenger door for protection. The window shattered above her head. She screamed, bits of glass spraying her in the face.

Using the top of the door to support her pistol, Elaine drew a steady bead on one of the men, the farthest to the left. He was crouched down, preparing to fire again.

She pulled the trigger.

The bullet went wide, not going anywhere near him. But all the men dropped to the ground. She fired again and again, mentally counting the ammunition remaining in the clip, as she had been trained to do.

Dmitry started the car. The wheels spun again, but it didn't move forward.

Elaine fired off another round. *Five left.* The men were staying down, but scurrying forward in little spurts, like soldiers trying to take out any enemy position.

"Keep beating the hell out of that sign," Elaine told Dmitry. "I'll cover you."

Dmitry looked at her like she was crazy.

Elaine fired off two more rounds.

He gave the TAXI sign several more blows, swinging at the sign as if his life depended on it. Which it did. Elaine fired off one more shot. *Two bullets left.* Dmitry was cursing to himself in Russian—the sign was beaten into a tangled mess of metal and plastic, but the debris was jammed underneath the tree branch.

Something warm was running into Elaine's eyes, blurring her vision. When she wiped it away, she saw that her fingers were wet with bright red blood. The glass had put a few tiny cuts in her forehead.

I'm going to die here, she thought. *I'm going to be gunned down in the middle of a goddam Russian forest.*

Taking another wide swing, Dmitry gave the car one more terrific blow, this time bringing the heavy steel bar down onto the roof just behind the sign. It caved in. He hit it twice more and the windshield shattered, the roof dented so deeply that Elaine could now see at least a half inch of clear space under the tree trunk.

She fired off one more round at the approaching men, then jumped into the car.

Dmitry stomped on the gas. The little Lada finally lurched forward, fishtailing a bit, and then cleared the tree.

Now Dmitry was madly twisting the wheel back and forth, trying to avoid more of the birches—it seemed they had gotten even closer together.

Elaine turned and looked through the gaping back window, vapor streaming from her mouth. The Hummer was far behind for the moment.

"Where's the bridge?" she shouted at Dmitry.

"Very near, I think."

"You *think*?"

He swerved around another tree. Suddenly they were in a small clearing. They sped across the open snow and entered another section of the woods, this one much less thick with trees. The Lada picked up speed. Dmitry tried to see through the shattered windshield, then stuck his head out the window. "There!"

Through the cracked glass Elaine could see a narrow bridge, made of wood. It was definitely not for vehicles, but for pedestrians.

"Are you sure this car will fit?" she said anxiously.

"I think so."

"Dammit," Elaine said, looking back out the rear window. The

Hummer was gaining on them again—the trees were spread far enough out that it was able to follow their path now. Elaine could see the river to the right—it was completely frozen over.

Dmitry swerved in the other direction, away from the bridge.

"What are you doing?" Elaine said.

"We need much speed."

To the left, the Hummer was barreling towards them. Someone was leaning out the passenger window, aiming at them.

Before the man could fire, Dmitry had swerved again. He fishtailed around a few more trees, and then they were headed straight at the bridge.

The Hummer swerved around, following their path.

Elaine dropped the pistol and grabbed hold of the dash, bracing herself for the impact. As the bridge rushed up at them, she could tell that the wooden side railings were not wide enough for the car to fit between.

The Lada hit the structure dead on, the nose of the car perfectly centered between the railings. The little automobile bounced violently as they flew across the narrow walkway, a hair-raising snapping of metal as the sides of the vehicle scraped through. Dmitry's remaining mirror and both door handles were ripped away. Then they were airborne for a half second...they sailed over a small depression on the other side of the bridge. The little car finally slammed back down to the ground, sliding sideways, out of control, Dmitry bellowing like a madman. As if moving in slow motion, it lost speed until the back end swung around, and finally, was stopped by another tree with a small, anticlimactic thump.

Now the car had completely spun around and they were facing the bridge. They both watched, open mouthed, as the Hummer roared towards it. The huge vehicle slammed into the two handrails, wood splintering, flying in all directions. It came to an abrupt halt halfway across, the wood bowed out on both sides. There was an eerie stillness for a second. One of the doors opened. The back end of the Hummer lurched downward a couple of feet. The other door swung open—she could hear shouting— and then the bridge collapsed. The back end of the vehicle dropped down to the ice, which was only a few feet below, with an ear-splitting crunch. Elaine could see one of the men trying to untangle himself from an airbag as he lowered himself down to the thick, cracked ice, peering at them, shouting something.

"Let's get out of here!" Elaine said.

Dmitry was so stunned it took him a second to snap out of it and get the car moving again.

It took them less than 10 minutes to reach the Sheremetyevo II terminal.

As they pulled into the long-term parking entrance, Dmitry rolled down his window. It was the only piece of glass left intact in the car—even the rearview mirror had been shattered. He plucked the time card from the machine, then drove to the far side of the lot, where there were only a few cars parked. After triumphing over the pursuers, Dmitry had experienced a few brief moments of glee. Now his expression was somber.

"That will take you to Arrival section," he said, pointing to a covered walkway.

Elaine got out, threw the seat forward, and climbed in the back next to her suitcase.

She started counting out money...but with the cash she would need for the ticket, and to buy clothes to disguise herself, she had almost nothing to spare.

She ended up handing him $500. "Dmitry, this is an insult, I know. I promise you, when I get back to the States, I will make sure that you're paid —"

"Money not so important now, Janyet," he said, gazing dejectedly out the window.

Elaine knew what he meant, and she felt sick. He was terrified for his life, and for the safety of his family. She was leaving him to face the wrath of the Russian Mafia all alone.

He reached over and picked up the tire iron. He handed it to her.

She stared at the heavy metal bar in her hand. "I can't..."

"You must, Janyet."

Elaine took the tire iron and slowly raised it above the back of his head. Her hand trembled. She couldn't hurt this poor man! He had risked his life to help her.

"You *must.*" He looked at her through the mirror with his sad, basset hound eyes. "If they think I want help you, they kill me."

She lowered the tire iron. "It would be better if I shot you."

His eyes widened.

She grabbed his shoulder through his overcoat, pinching the meat together and pushing the gun barrel up against the fabric. "You'll bleed like a stuck pig, but it won't cause any serious damage."

He grimaced. "*Da!* Do it, Janyet."

Gritting her teeth, Elaine forced herself to pull the trigger.

The gun went off, splattering blood all over the dashboard.

Dmitry lurched forward, groaning, cursing under his breath.

Elaine took hold of the suitcase and put one leg out the door. "Tell them I shot you because you wouldn't drive over the bridge. Tell them I threatened your family. Tell them—"

"I know what say them," Dmitry gasped, still doubled over in pain. Grimacing, he pulled a green checked wool scarf from the side pocket of his door and gave it to her. "You will be cold," he said.

She took it—it was old and frayed. "Thank you, Dmitry." She was touched.

She dragged her suitcase onto the icy pavement and shut the car door. She prayed that he would be all right.

Dmitry looked up at her.

"Janyet?" he grunted.

"Yes?"

"Good luck."

As Elaine rode the escalator up to the Departure level, she glanced around to see if anyone was watching. The space was so huge, and so crowded, it was impossible to tell.

She looked up at a gigantic display that showed the arriving and departing flights. There were five with the flashing BOARDING message—one to Lisbon, one to Bangkok, one to Paris...

She glanced at her watch. The Paris flight would be ideal—it took off in 30 minutes, which would give her just enough time.

Pulling her suitcase along behind her, she headed towards a cluster of shops. She quickly bought a jade, down-filled parka that came down to her knees, and a matching green cap with an extra long bill, almost the same shade as the jacket. She also bought a natural leather satchel, completely different from her black one.

Elaine found a disabled restroom and changed out of her soiled, bloody clothes. She washed the remaining blood from her face—there were a few small cuts just where her hairline met her scalp. When she finished, she pinned her hair up and applied a bronzer to her entire face, made an impossible-to-miss mole high on her right cheek, and made heavy use of eyeliner. She put on her reading glasses, donned the green hat, and then put on the long green checked scarf that Dmitry had given her.

When she peered at herself in the mirror, she thought she looked kind of arty and brainy. Like a graduate student in philosophy.

If she could make it to Passport Control, she could take off the glasses and wipe away the mole easily enough.

She slipped the data key into the secret compartment in the suitcase where the passport had been hidden. She ditched everything she didn't need, including her old satchel and the disassembled pistol, hiding it in the very bottom of the restroom trash bin. Hopefully she would be long gone before any of it was discovered.

She used her remaining cash to buy an economy class ticket on the Air France flight to Paris.

When Elaine reached Customs, she elbowed her way to the front of one of the shortest NOTHING TO DECLARE lines. Every now and then she glanced over her shoulder, but still did not see anyone following her.

As she approached the x-ray machine, she began to worry that the data key would show up in her suitcase and cause suspicion.

The customs officer watched as she placed her suitcase and handbag on the conveyor.

"You have with you Russian rubles?" he said.

"No," she said, handing him the Irish passport with a sweaty hand. When he saw the black diplomatic cover, his attitude softened a little. He gave as much of a smile as Russians ever give strangers, which was a kind of strained grimace.

There was a female guard watching a screen that monitored the x-ray machine. Elaine could see the screen. The image of the suitcase appeared. She could see the black cylinder, but it was only one of many shadows in the picture—her phone charger and other items masked it.

"Enjoy your flight," the officer said, handing her the passport.

Relieved, Elaine headed towards the check-in counters. *I just might make it out of here*, she thought.

There were a few people still queued up at the check-in counter for the Paris flight. An elderly couple, a pair of businessmen, and three nuns.

Elaine joined the line and nonchalantly glanced around. She still didn't see anyone watching—there wasn't even a security guard in sight.

Something caught her eye down the corridor. A female airport security guard was slowly walking along the check-in counters, scrutinizing the passengers. Beside her was the man with the pockmarked face.

Elaine looked straight ahead, moving a little closer to the nuns that were in front of her. She stole another glance to the right. Now the female security guard was hassling a blonde about Elaine's age, asking for her passport.

Elaine was so scared she couldn't move. She looked down at her suitcase. She had to do something with the data key or they would search her and find it.

She tapped one of the nuns on the shoulder. "*Pardonnez-moi. J'ai un problème.*"

The nun turned around. She was short and pudgy, perhaps sixty years old, and gazed up at Elaine through wire-framed glasses. "*Oui?*"

Elaine tried to appear as distraught as she could, bringing tears to her eyes. "*La—la ligne aérienne, ils—ils que mes bagages—*"

"You may speak English, dear."

"Oh, thank you! The airline told me I have too many bags. They want a hundred extra dollars. I don't have enough money to check this, I don't know what I'm going to do."

The nun looked sympathetic. "I am very sorry for you, *madame*, but I have very little mon—"

"I don't want money. Could you just check this one bag for me? Please? Just this one?" Elaine motioned at the suitcase. "You don't have much luggage, it wouldn't cost you a thing..."

Elaine stole a glance at the security guard and the other man—they were still questioning the blonde.

The nun looked down at the suitcase, hesitated, then glanced at the scant luggage she and her friends were carrying.

She asked Elaine, "There are no *narcotiques* in this bag...?"

"Of course not," Elaine gasped, as if shocked by the suggestion.

"Very well." The nun took the handle of the suitcase and drew it forward—her two companions had just approached the check-in desk. She whispered something to them.

Elaine moved a little closer to the nun and rested her hand on the check-in desk, as if she were simply impatient. She kept looking straight ahead. She held her breath when the ticket agent asked the nuns if anyone had given them any packages to carry with them.

"No," two of the nuns said in unison. The nun who had taken the suitcase remained silent. All four bags were placed on the conveyor. The one who had checked Elaine's suitcase nonchalantly pressed the claim check into her hand.

"Thank you so much," Elaine whispered.

Her turn finally came to check in. She handed over her ticket and passport to the clerk.

"No luggage to check?"

"No," Elaine said.

"You have seat Twenty-five E," the clerk said, handing her the boarding pass.

"Excuse me," a female voice said from behind her, and she felt a heavy hand on her shoulder.

She slowly turned around.

The female guard and the pockmark-faced man were both standing there.

"Passport?" the guard said, with a thick Russian accent. The woman looked as tough as nails.

Elaine gave it to her, avoiding eye contact with either of them.

The guard opened it. "O'Neill, Shannon..." she read, pronouncing the name "Shah-none."

"Havin' some kinda problem, are ya?" Elaine said, in her Irish brogue.

The two exchanged a glance.

"Your handbag, please," the guard said.

Elaine reluctantly slipped it off her shoulder. The woman searched it, the pockmarked man looking on uncertainly.

"*Nichevo*," she said to him.

"I trust yas have a bloody good reason for harrassin' me," Elaine said. "I werk for the Irish Department of Agriculture and I —"

"Did you check any baggage?" the guard interrupted.

Elaine peered down her nose directly at both their faces, which were nothing more than blurs through her reading glasses. "I did not."

The guard turned to the clerk at the check-in desk. In Russian, she said, "*Eta devushka registrirovala bagazh?*"

"*Nyet*," the clerk said, shaking her head.

Turning back to Elaine, the guard said, "Spread you arms, please."

"Ha! I suppose you'll be strip searchin' me next, then?"

"Spread you arms, please."

Elaine did so, an indignant look on her face. The guard carefully frisked her up and down, checking inside the coat. Elaine repressed a wince as the woman's hand brushed against her knife wounds.

When she finished, she and the pockmark-faced man glanced at each other. He uncertainly looked down at her right side, but there was no visible evidence of any injury there. Elaine saw him peering at the "mole" on her cheek, and then down at the natural leather satchel.

Elaine said, very loudly, "Are ya proud of yerselves, makin' a bleedin' spectacle out of an innocent pearson? I'll have yas both reported fer this."

Now all the people in the other queues were watching, and both of them were aware of it.

"You may go to gate," the guard said sheepishly. "Please excuse the intrusion."

At that moment, in Washington, D.C., Gene Lassiter was sitting in the back of a taxi that was heading towards Dulles Airport. He had a reservation under a false name on a red eye to Kennedy, where he would catch a flight to Berlin.

He was pleased with himself. By tomorrow afternoon, the Russians would wire the balance of his payment—eight million Euros—into his numbered Swiss bank account. Elaine Brogan was dead by now. It was a pity that she had to be sacrificed, but in the overall scheme of things, she was insignificant. By this evening, he and his beloved Gypsy would be together.

Gypsy.

The mere thought of that name sent sexual shivers through Lassiter's aging body. The thick mane of black curly hair, the dark, bewitching eyes.

And that figure!

Lassiter constantly fantasized about Gypsy. Their relationship had been flourishing for two years now, ever since they had met in Berlin. Those two years were the most glorious of Lassiter's life. For him, Gypsy was human Viagra. The relationship had liberated Lassiter, taken him to sexual heights that he never dreamed existed. The last time they were together he had shaved Gypsy's pubic hair, leaving the skin smooth and pink and childlike. The 30-year age difference only increased the sexual thrill, at least for Lassiter.

Yet for him, it wasn't merely a physical relationship. He was madly in love with Gypsy. He only truly felt at peace when they were together. The last time they met at a secluded little seaside hotel in southern Portugal. It had been like a dream, a magnificent, sensual experience that he wished had lasted forever. They had spent hours walking along the beach, hand in hand, watching the sea, the soaring gulls, the breathtaking sunrises and sunsets. Lassiter knew they were an odd couple. People stared. He didn't care.

Unfortunately, Gypsy had an insatiable appetite for the material things in life. Things that he could never afford on his lousy government salary. But Lassiter aimed to supply those things, no matter what it required. He only had a few more years to live, and he was determined to spend them with the one he loved.

Was that so wrong?

His cellphone started ringing.

When he pulled it out of his pocket, he recognized the number—the call was from Russia.

"Pull over," he told the taxi driver, the phone still ringing in his hand.

"What you say?" the man said. He was wearing a turban and didn't seem to understand English well.

"I said pull the car over for a second. I have to take this call."

Lassiter got out and shut the door, shivering on the side of the road as traffic whizzed by.

"Yeah?" he said into the phone.

"We have *problema*," a Russian-accented voice said.

"What problem is that?" Lassiter said.

"Your 'mule' has taken back the package."

"What do you mean, taken it back?"

"She was armed. Why you send us armed mule?"

Lassiter frowned. He couldn't believe that Elaine had taken a gun aboard a commercial flight. And where had she gotten it? He knew for certain that she had turned her Secret Service issued weapon back in before she left Bulgaria.

"I don't believe it," Lassiter finally said.

"No package, no money."

"Look, I delivered your goddam package! If your people are so incompetent they couldn't handle a woman—"

"No package, no money."

"Goddammit," Lassiter said. "Where is she now?"

"We do not know. We think she leave Russia from Sheremetyevo. Maybe."

Lassiter felt panicky, but managed to keep it under control—he had taken precautions in case something like this happened. "Look, I'll get the package to you, as promised. Give me a little time."

The line went dead.

"Shit," Lassiter muttered, getting back into the taxi. As the driver pulled out into the traffic, Lassiter opened his notebook computer and pulled up a GPS tracking program. When he had hidden the data key in Elaine's suitcase, he had hidden a small GPS tracking device there as well.

After a few seconds, a map of the world appeared on the screen. The little green blip looked like it was sitting right on top of Moscow. But when he expanded the map, he could see that it was actually about 100 miles to the west, slowly heading towards Europe.

She was definitely on a plane.

Lassiter quickly estimated the time it would have taken off from the Sheremetyevo Airport, and then went to the airport's website and checked the timetable for departing flights.

An Air France flight had left for Paris at almost the exact time he'd guessed. It would land at the Charles De Gaulle Airport, in about two hours.

"Pull over again," Lassiter said to the driver.

"What?" the driver said.

CHAPTER 2.6

When the Air France flight began its final approach into Paris, Elaine's heart was hammering so hard she thought the old man sitting next to her might actually hear it.

She knew there was a very good chance that someone would be waiting for her at the gate when the plane landed at CDG. The people who had almost caught her in Moscow could have checked to see if there was actually a Shannon O'Neill who worked for the Irish Department of Agriculture, and of course there was no such person.

"Excuse me," Elaine said, unbuckling her seat belt. "I need to use the restroom."

With a sigh, the man sitting next to her got up and let her out.

"Pardon," one of the flight attendants said, in a French accent, "You must take your seat. Ze plane is about to land."

"I'm sick," Elaine said, stepping around the woman.

She made her way up the aisle to the very rear of the plane. No one was in the galley—both of the flight attendants were busy up front, telling passengers to put up their tray tables, preparing to land.

Elaine opened the restroom door, and, hiding behind it, quickly glanced around the galley.

She spotted what she needed. In a flash, she grabbed it and hid it under her coat.

The Russian man waiting at the gate for the Air France flight to arrive from Moscow had an Interpol badge in his wallet, but he was not an Interpol agent. He stood back, casually pretending to read a copy of *Le Monde*, watching each and every passenger walk down the jetway.

The woman he was after was a slim blonde, mid-20s, 178 cm tall, wearing a long green parka, a green hat, and glasses. She might or might not have a mole on her left cheek.

The passengers walked steadily out of the jetway, but he did not see his target. When the flow began to thin out, the man began to shift uneasily from one foot to another. He couldn't have missed her...

With the exception of three nuns, who he had carefully scrutinized— all too short to be her—the plane seemed to be mostly filled with businessmen.

After another moment, the passenger flow trickled down and stopped completely. He couldn't actually see the door of the plane, as the jetway took a dogleg turn.

He went over to the gate desk. Flashing his badge at the attendant, he said, "Have all the passengers gotten off the plane?"

"One moment." The woman picked up the phone.

He looked impatiently back at the jetway, then turned and muttered *"Tvoyu mat,"* and headed towards it. His ass was on the line—if he didn't find this girl, he was in serious trouble.

The gate agent yelled something as he disappeared into the jetway.

When he went around the dogleg, he ran smack into an Air France stewardess, nearly knocking her down.

"You cannot board ze flight!" she said, straightening her hat. She pointed. "Return to ze gate at once!"

"Shut up," he said, brushing past her.

He reached the aircraft's door and stepped inside the cabin.

"Sir?" another stewardess said. "Were you aboard zis flight?"

He gazed past her, down the aisle.

The entire aircraft was empty.

CHAPTER 2.7

Three hours later, Elaine Brogan was sitting in a dark corner of a restaurant just around the corner from the CDG Lost Luggage Office, the baggage claim check clutched in her sweaty hand. She was afraid to move.

Her wounds were seeping blood and she was afraid that it would show on the light blue Air France overcoat she was wearing.

Elaine was sure that the man she had bumped into in the jetway had figured out what happened by now. He would have checked with the flight attendants to see if there had been a crew change. Fortunately, the man must not have known about her Irish passport or he could have had her stopped when she went through Passport Control.

At the moment, Elaine was mired down with indecision about whether to try and retrieve the suitcase she had given the nun to check for her. It was probably still going around and around on the conveyor in Baggage Claim, or had already been picked up and taken to the office for lost and unclaimed luggage. She thought she could probably make it back to Washington on the Irish passport, if she moved quickly. But Lassiter had framed her so thoroughly that without the data key, she would look guilty. It would appear that something had gone wrong, that she had perhaps not been paid for the product, and that she was trying to come back and blame Lassiter for it.

At the end of the day, it would be his word against hers. Who would they believe? A 26-year-old from the worst section of Pittsburgh with a criminal father, who had worked at Treasury for six months? Or a gray-haired man who had devoted his whole life to the department?

The answer was obvious.

Elaine gritted her teeth—it took all her willpower not to slam her fist down on the table, to overturn chairs, to scream her head off...the sneaky old bastard! He had used her in the coldest, most heartless way imaginable. All those months she had slaved away on his "secret project" for him, only so he could sell the resulting information to criminals and then frame her for it!

Had he lied to her about Nick, too?

He must have.

If she ever came face to face against Gene Lassiter, even if inside a courtroom, she didn't think she would be able to control herself.

Her back rigid with tension, Elaine walked down the corridor and passed by the door of the Lost Baggage Office, being careful not to look at it. Out of the corner of her eye she tried to see if there was anyone watching, but so many people were scuttling up and down the corridor, and sitting at a coffee shop directly across from the entrance, it was impossible to be sure.

She had ditched the green parka and hat, buying a cheap mustard-colored jacket and a black wool cap, stuffing her hair up under it.

After one more casual stroll past the Baggage Office, she finally decided to take the risk.

She opened the door to the Lost Baggage Office and went inside.

There were a dozen people standing in line. They all looked annoyed and frustrated—only one person was working behind the counter, a middle-aged Frenchman who looked like he moved at the same plodding pace regardless of how many people were waiting.

Elaine joined the queue, her shoulders two rigid blocks of anxiety. Every time she heard the door open, her heart skipped a beat. Her vision was fuzzy. She hadn't slept at all during the flight over to Moscow, and she had now been up for 30 hours straight. She took a few deep breaths, trying to clear her head, telling herself it was almost over. If the suitcase was there, all she had to do was claim it and then get to Washington.

After a few more excruciatingly long minutes, a second clerk appeared behind the counter. Elaine rushed over before anyone else could get there.

"*Oui?*" the man said.

"I forgot to pick up my suitcase when my flight came in," she said, making an effort to sound calm. She handed over the claim check the nun had given her in Moscow.

The clerk glanced at the paper. "One moment, please, it may still be out on the carousel."

He disappeared through a swinging door. Beyond it, Elaine glimpsed shelves stacked with rows and rows of suitcases, backpacks, sports bags, and various other unclaimed pieces of luggage.

She heard the door open behind her. She fought the urge to glance over her shoulder.

After a tortuous long minute or two, the clerk returned with a suitcase.

Elaine's pulse quickened—it was definitely hers.

He set the bag down in the gap between the counters, but not quite within her reach. "This suitcase belongs to you, *oui?*"

"Yes."

"Please make certain, *mademoiselle*. Many bags look alike."

"I'm sure it's mine."

"Anything to declare?"

Elaine tried not to think about the data key hidden inside it. "No, nothing."

The clerk stapled her claim check to a form and asked her to sign it. With a sweat-slick hand, she scribbled something illegible in the blank. He slid the suitcase through the gap in the counter.

"*Après, s'il vous plaît?*" he said, looking past her at the next person in line.

Elaine picked up the suitcase and quickly stuffed the receipt into her pocket. She turned around, half expecting to be arrested on the spot.

No one was there.

She prayed the data key was still inside the suitcase.

Feeling a little more confident, she went out the Lost Baggage Office door and into the corridor.

After taking only a few steps, a male voice said, "*Mademoiselle!*"

Elaine kept moving.

"*Mademoiselle!*"

She turned a corner.

There were footsteps behind her—the man was running after her. "*Mademoiselle!*"

A hand grabbed her arm.

She turned around.

A portly, red-faced man held out a piece of paper.

It was the receipt for her suitcase—it must have fallen out of her pocket.

"*Merci,*" she said, her legs nearly buckling underneath her.

She turned and shakily walked out of the airport.

As soon as she was outside, she looked up and down the sidewalk.

She needed to get away from here, and out of France, as quickly as possible. Her plan was to take a train from Paris to London and then fly from Heathrow to Washington. She knew that the Eurostar train left from the Gare du Nord station. She could take a taxi there.

She spotted the taxi queue, and headed in that direction, rolling her suitcase behind her.

Ahead of her, the red-faced man had stepped out of one of the doors, then looked up and down the sidewalk. There was a cellphone to his ear.

"*Merde*," he said, putting the phone back in his pocket. He looked at Elaine as she approached. "Can you tell me where the taxis are? My wife was supposed to pick me up, but it seems she has forgotten."

"That way," Elaine said, pointing past him.

He walked along beside her.

"You are going to the center of Paris?"

She glanced at him. "Yes."

"Perhaps we can share a taxi? They are very expensive."

She looked at him again—he seemed safe enough. *Why not?* she thought. It would be less likely for her to be spotted if she was with someone else.

His cellphone started ringing.

"Ah, *cheri*!" he said, "*J'ai pensé que vous aviez oublié votre mari* !" He stopped and looked out at the drive, then started waving. "*Ici, ici, ici*!"

A black BMW pulled over to the sidewalk.

He turned back to Elaine. "*Mademoiselle*, I would be happy to give you a ride to the center. Where are you going, exactly?"

"Gare du Nord."

"Ah, this is very close to our house! Please..." he said, opening the back door for her. "My wife will not mind."

Elaine hesitated. They had almost reached the taxi queue, and there was a long line.

"That's very kind of you," she said. "But—"

Before she could protest, he took her suitcase and slid it into the back seat, then held the back door open for her.

She leaned down to get in, but first glanced at the man's wife.

Behind the wheel was a man—the same man who had been waiting for her at the gate.

His hand shot out and a chemical sprayed into her face.

Elaine gasped, stars whirling before her eyes. As the other man shoved her into the back seat, she passed out.

CHAPTER 2.8

The sleek Gulfstream jet was cruising along at 38,000 feet above the Swiss Alps, glittering in the morning sun.

Elaine Brogan lay in a reclined seat inside the luxurious cabin, sleeping under a blanket. She was just beginning to stir.

The first thing she became aware of was a medicinal taste in her mouth.

I've been drugged, she thought hazily, as she fought her way to consciousness. She looked around, her vision going in and out of focus. There were some empty leather seats...a teak coffee table... a colorful bouquet of wildflowers...a row of oval windows.

She was aboard an airplane. A private jet, it seemed. Something was pinching at her waist. There was a seatbelt pulled around her, over the blanket. She struggled to release it.

"Oh, you are awake!" an accented female voice said from behind her.

A tall, rail-thin blonde stepped around to the front of her seat. She wore a tight-fitting skirt, blouse and jacket. Her face was stunning. "May I get you some coffee? Espresso, cappuccino...?"

It was all so strange Elaine thought she might be dreaming. "Where am I?" she said hoarsely.

"You are aboard Mr. Cattoretti's aircraft," the woman said. She gave a practiced smile. "Would you like a croissant? Some toast and caviar, perhaps?"

Mr. Cattoretti's aircraft. Elaine strained to look out the window—she could see snowy mountain peaks in the distance, and a flawless azure sky. It was early morning, she thought, or very late afternoon. When she looked back inside the cabin, she saw her suitcase sitting beside one of the coffee tables. What had happened to her? The last thing she remembered was that portly man who had offered her a ride to the center of Paris, and then being shoved into the car and having something sprayed into her face.

Memory came flooding back. Outrunning the Russian Mafia, fleeing to Paris, the data key...

Elaine felt sick.

"*Signora?*" the flight attendant said. She was still standing there, waiting for an answer.

"Coffee, I guess," Elaine finally said.

" *Caffè Americano?*"

"Yes. Fine."

The woman smiled, then turned and strutted up to a kitchen nook near a door that Elaine presumed led to the cockpit.

Elaine took the opportunity to unfasten her seatbelt, wincing as it brushed against her knife wounds. She had forgotten about those, too. When she pulled the blanket away, she was afraid of what she would see, but there was no blood on her clothes. She felt the bandage. It was fresh, thicker than the one before. Someone had changed it.

She looked back at her suitcase. Was the data key still there?

Her mind felt fuzzy again. She didn't have the strength to get up.

The cockpit door opened. A short, heavyset young man in a leather jacket emerged, saw her, and smiled. "How you feel?" he said, as he made his way down the aisle. He was dressed in expensive Italian clothes. "My father, he say he apologize how we take you from Paris."

"Your father...?"

"Giorgio Cattoretti." He smiled and offered Elaine his hand. "I am Luigi."

She numbly shook it. *Cattoretti*...the name meant nothing to her.

She glanced at her suitcase, and the man noticed. "Can I get you anything, *signora?*"

Who were these people? The buyers of the data key?

The stewardess brought the coffee and set it on the coffee table. "Sugar, cream," she said, pointing to a couple of elegant white vessels.

"Where exactly are we going?" Elaine said. "What am I doing here?"

Luigi and the woman exchanged a glance.

"We go to Milano," Luigi said. He glanced at his Rolex. "We will be arriving there very soon."

"And then...?"

"Do not worry, please. My father, he very good man." Luigi smiled. "He no hurt you."

Luigi's face went in and out of focus. "Where is Nick?" she said dully. "I want to go with h..."

She passed out again.

CHAPTER 2.9

Milan, Italy

If you drive east from Milan on the A4 motorway towards Verona, you will encounter an industrial area that stretches on for almost 100 kilometers. Both sides of the highway are littered with inelegant, sprawling industrial facilities—food processing plants, auto parts factories, and truck depots. Not the usual images foreigners conjure up when thinking of beautiful, romantic Italy. Yet, every country must have its industrial infrastructure, and Italy is no different.

One such establishment along this particular stretch of highway, virtually indistinguishable from all the rest, is a company called DayPrinto S.p.A. Housed in an expansive two-story turquoise building, the firm has been in business 30 years. It handles the printing of dozens of Northern Italian newspapers and magazines. The company employs 250 people and is owned, indirectly, through a complex tangle of offshore holding companies.

The sole stockholder is a very private man by the name of Giorgio Cattoretti.

This morning, Giorgio Cattoretti was standing in his elegant private bathroom that adjoined his DayPrinto office, admiring himself in the mirror. He had a bronze complexion, coal-black hair and brooding dark eyes. His face bore the imperious, hawkish look of a predator. A thick scar snaked its way down the left side of his jaw, from his ear to his sharply-defined chin. Though he was 53 years old, he still boasted the lean, aggressive figure of a boxer.

He straightened his Valentino tie, shot his cuffs out from under the sleeves of his Armani sport coat, and smiled at himself, his bleached teeth flashing pearly white.

The Cat was looking good.

His intercom buzzed.

"*Sì?*" Cattoretti said.

"Signore, Luigi is about to arrive with woman from the U.S. Treasury."

"*Bene*," Cattoretti said. "Have her brought directly to my office." He was looking forward to meeting Elaine Brogan.

CHAPTER 2.10

Elaine looked anxiously out the window of the Rolls Royce as it purred down the highway. She was sitting alone in the back seat, with Luigi in the front beside the uniformed chauffeur. The posh automobile had been waiting on the tarmac when the aircraft arrived at the private airport in Milan.

They had been driving for about an hour, and were now cruising through the Italian countryside. The after-effects of the drugs had mostly worn off. She displayed a calm-appearing veneer. On the inside, she was scared to death.

Luigi had said, *My father, he very good man. He no hurt you.*

Elaine hoped he was telling the truth.

The Rolls slowed down and pulled into the entrance of an industrial complex. DayPrinto, S.p.A., a blue sign said.

A printing company, Elaine thought. That was hardly a surprise.

They rolled up to the guard house, the gate sliding open as they approached. Luigi gave a friendly wave to the man in the booth as the car passed through.

The Rolls pulled around the back of the building to a loading dock area. The chauffeur hopped out and opened the door for Elaine.

"*Signora,*" he said, giving her a little bow.

As frightened as she felt, she could not help enjoying the celebrity treatment. It was a welcome change after all she'd been through. She doubted it would last long.

Luigi led her inside the building. The corridors were dark. As they walked through the facility, their footsteps echoed on the tiled floor. All the offices were empty. Elaine only now realized that it was a Sunday, and no one was working.

Luigi stopped at an elevator, entered a code into a keypad, and they rode to the second floor. They exited and Luigi stopped in front of an unmarked door and knocked on it.

"*Prego,*" a deep voice said, from inside.

As they entered, an elegantly dressed man stepped around from behind an enormous desk. He had dark hair and a bronzed complexion. He was in his 50s, his chiseled face dignified, almost aristocratic. Had there not been a thick scar running from his ear down to his jaw, he might have been a descendant of the Italian royal family.

He looked astonished when he saw Elaine. He gazed her up and down, as if overwhelmed. "Ms. Brogan! Why...this is an unexpected pleasure."

He gently took her hand and kissed it, then stepped back and peered at her again, as if admiring a work of art. "You could be a fashion model..."

Elaine pulled her hand away.

"Please excuse my bad manners," he said, smiling apologetically. "My name is Giorgio Cattoretti." He made a broad sweep of his arm. "I welcome you to DayPrinto S.p.A."

Elaine glanced uneasily around the office. The imposing desk was made of a single slab of polished stone. Behind it sat a leather-throne chair. A sensual Ruben painting dominated one wall—an original, Elaine guessed. The floor was a cool black granite.

Luigi opened his jacket and handed his father the data key that had been planted in her suitcase.

"Ah, *grazie*," Cattoretti said, with obvious satisfaction. He gave it back to his son. *"Prenda questo di sotto."*

Luigi left, pulling the door closed behind him.

"I must apologize for the way you were so rudely treated in Paris," Cattoretti said to Elaine, placing his hand over his heart. With a helpless shrug, he said, "My Russian business partners can be...well, uncivilized is the word."

"I'd like to know why you brought me here," Elaine said.

He smiled. "Americans are always so direct." He glanced down at her soiled, wrinkled clothes, and she saw a flicker of distaste cross his face. "Would you not prefer to freshen up before we talk?"

Elaine suddenly felt self-conscious. The man was immaculately dressed, in a tailored designer suit, decked out with gold jewelry—he looked like he could have stepped off the cover of *GQ*.

He motioned to the door beyond his desk. "Please take advantage of my private bath. It is fully equipped." He stepped back and appraised her. "What size are you, about a...seven?"

"Thirty-six," she said.

"*Bellissima*! I will find you some clothes that are more..." he glanced at her outfit again "...appropriate. I will also have breakfast brought in from our kitchen. You will find the food quite delicious. Our chef is from

Toscana."

A few minutes later, Elaine was sitting on an ornate brass loveseat next to the sink in Cattoretti's stylish private bathroom, staring into space. Opera music softly emanated from speakers hidden somewhere in the molded ceiling.

Giorgio Cattoretti had made quite an impression on her. He was so charming and confident. The man radiated a personal magnetism that was almost palpable. His English was perfect. He spoke with an American accent, so Elaine assumed he must have lived in the USA for at least a few years.

She wondered who he was, exactly, and what he wanted from her.

Rising slowly from the loveseat, she wearily took off her clothes. She was too tired to fight any more, too tired to think.

As she slowly folded her blouse and skirt and set them on the loveseat, she wondered if she might be on a hidden camera somewhere. *To hell with it*, she thought. If the man was a voyeur, let him get his jollies.

Elaine gazed at her naked body in the mirror, her eyes drawn to the bandage above her hip. Grimacing, she gingerly peeled it back. There were three neatly-made black stitches in the front and back knife punctures. Someone had sewn her up while she was unconscious. She wondered who had done it. She hoped it hadn't been Luigi.

She stepped inside the shower. The spacious stall was made of pink marble, the gold fixtures all of sensual Italian design. The stone floor felt warm against her feet—it must have been heated from underneath. She turned on the water and stood under the hot, steamy flow, careful not to get the bandage wet.

The bathroom door opened.

Elaine jumped, instinctively covering her breasts.

There was movement on the outside of the stall.

She backed against the marble, afraid to breathe. She expected the swarthy Italian to throw the stall door open any second, perhaps stark naked, with a grin on his face and an eagerly bobbing erection.

There was more movement. The fine hair on the back of her neck stood on end.

Then she heard the bathroom door quietly snap shut, and she peeked out into the room.

Her clothes were gone from the loveseat. In their place was a stack of new garments.

She finished her shower and picked up the dress, fingering the material. Cashmere and silk. It was black and short-sleeved, with a crew-neck top. She looked at the label. *Prada.* Her boots had been replaced with a pair of stilettos in 1970s green. *Fendi.* Underneath the outfit she found a new package of sheer tan hose, in her size. *Levante.* There was also a pair of panties and bra. *Valentino.*

Surely there hadn't been time for anyone to go out and buy all these expensive things for her.

Elaine held the posh dress in her hands. This garment alone was worth more than a few months of her government salary.

My government salary, she thought wryly. The only government salary she would ever receive now would be whatever they paid convicts to work in the prison laundry.

She tore open the package and put on the thigh-high stockings, smoothing the nylon up her legs. They made her feel better. She slipped on the rest of the underwear, telling herself not to think about the future, only the present. She strapped on the high heels, and then she began styling her hair.

The cabinet under the sink was loaded with fine cosmetics—*Kanebo, Estee Lauder, Shiseido.* She spent a few minutes applying makeup, laying it on thicker than usual.

She did not look at herself in the full-length mirror until she was fully dressed.

Her mouth dropped open. The reflection bowled her over.

Elaine Brogan was no longer there—someone else was standing behind the mirror, gazing back at her.

An elegant, ravishing someone else.

Elaine had always dreamed of owning clothes like these, ever since her days at the Rising Star Modeling Agency. She turned from one side to the other, taking herself in. She not only looked completely different, she *felt* completely different. More confident, and much more alive.

I could be on the cover of Vogue, she thought.

She felt ready to deal with whatever Giorgio Cattoretti wanted to throw at her.

When Elaine stepped back out into Cattoretti's office, there was a brass food cart parked in the middle of the marble floor. On it was an artful presentation of delicious-looking fruit and cheeses, freshly baked croissants, and a tall glass of fresh-squeezed orange juice. A slim vase held a long-stemmed yellow rose, glistening dewdrops clinging to its petals.

As the aroma of the warm pastries hit Elaine's nostrils, she realized she was ravenous. She picked up a warm croissant and bit into it, then strolled around the office in the slinky dress and outrageous stilettos. The heels made her legs feel ten feet long.

One wall was filled with bookshelves that were lined with leather-bound volumes. Some of them looked very old. She turned her head sideways and read some of the titles— *Machiavelli*, *Dante*, *Homer*...

She wondered if Giorgio Cattoretti had actually read all these books, or if they were just for show.

She noticed that behind his credenza, there were plaques and photographs of him with different well-dressed people. Local politicians and prominent businessmen, perhaps. The inscriptions were all in Italian, but it was clear that Cattoretti had donated a lot of money to charities.

Elaine felt a combination of dislike and intrigue towards the man. He was obviously a criminal, and yet he was so warm and charming and sophisticated, or at least appeared to be. She looked over at the door that led out to the hallway. She wondered if it was locked.

At exactly the same moment, the door opened. Giorgio Cattoretti entered the room. He looked Elaine up and down, taking in the dress, her long legs, and the high heels. *"Magnifico!* I knew that outfit would look splendid on you. Now you are a real *bella donna*."

Elaine felt a pang of pleasure at these words, but did not show it. She noticed that he had changed his outfit—now he was wearing a honey-colored suit with a chocolate tie. She wondered if he had changed on her account.

He offered his arm to her. "I would like to show you around my company. I think you will find what we do here very interesting."

Elaine hesitated. "If you don't mind I would like to know why I was brought here."

He raised his hands apologetically. "I honestly did not know what else to do, Ms. Brogan. My Russian partners called from Paris and told me that you had delivered the data key and told me all they could about you, which was scant—only that you were a U.S. Treasury Department employee. I told them to bring you here." He paused and studied her face. "Did I do the wrong thing?"

Elaine didn't know what to make of him.

"First, I didn't 'deliver' anything to anybody," she said. "The data key was planted in my luggage without my knowledge."

"I am aware of that, but it has nothing to do with me. I negotiated a contract with the Russians to buy the software updates that the U.S. Treasury was developing and that is exactly what they delivered to me. I paid a handsome price for those updates, and I intend to hold onto them." He offered her his arm. "Now, may I have the pleasure of showing you around?"

CHAPTER 2.11

Cattoretti led Elaine down the hallway and to a keypad-protected elevator, his warm hand holding hers. She still did not know what to make of his attitude and behavior. Was this all an act? She couldn't tell.

As the elevator doors closed and the lift began descending, she tried to hide her fear. She anxiously watched the display change from 2 to 1 to G and then -1, -2...

They were going to the basement.

Cattoretti glanced at her and gave her a relaxed smile.

When the display showed -3, the elevator came smoothly to a stop. The doors opened. Cattoretti led her down a long, wide, tiled hallway with keypad-protected doors on either side. There was a lot of activity on the other side of the walls—Elaine could hear the hum of machinery and a cacophony of voices speaking Italian and other languages, perhaps Chinese or Japanese, Elaine couldn't quite tell.

He stopped at one of the doors and tapped in another code. When they entered the room, the chattering dropped to a hush. Elaine expected to see the usual counterfeiting equipment—a printing press, a paper cutter, drying racks. Instead, the huge space was lined with rows and rows of middle-aged women sitting behind sewing machines.

"This is our designer clothing department," Cattoretti said proudly. Several of the women glanced curiously at Elaine as she passed by. Cattoretti seemed to be searching the workstations for something specific. He stopped and picked up a green dress. Elaine saw that it was identical to the Prada she was wearing. There was a pile of similar dresses on the table. She noticed a stack of Prada labels beside the sewing machine.

She glanced down at her own dress, wondering if it was a copy.

Cattoretti smiled. "You are wearing the original. All the copies you see here were made from a pattern created from it. When the labels are attached, they will be distributed for sale worldwide."

He paused, examining stitching in the garment. "*Lavoro magnifico,*" he said to the woman at the workstation.

"*Grazie,*" she said, beaming at his compliment. She looked like she worshipped the ground he walked on.

Far on the other side of the cavernous space, several Asian women were standing at tables with scraps of papers and various materials in front of them. They were chattering into headphones in Chinese, measuring various pieces of fabric, writing down information on yellow pads.

"It is far too expensive for us to manufacture most of our lines here," Cattoretti explained. "Eighty-five percent of our copies are made in Taiwan."

So he was a manufacturer of designer knockoffs, Elaine thought. She wondered why he was showing her all this.

They entered another similar room that smelled strongly of glue and leather. At least 50 people, both men and women, were at work at long wooden tables.

"This is our footwear center," Cattoretti said. There were boots, high heels, and sandals in various stages of assembly, all copies of famous designer products. The room was huge. Tables extended as far as she could see.

They entered another vast room. "This is where we make our handbags and purses." There were hundreds of items in all stages of production, everything from copies of Gucci wallets to Valentino satchels and cosmetic cases.

"And this," he said, leading her through yet another door, "is our jewelry department."

They walked down several rows of benches with workers peering through magnifiers, tapping with small hammers and filing stones with grinders. They were making necklaces, bracelets, rings...

"Let us choose something nice for you to wear with that dress." He led her all the way back out into the hallway, and they turned another corner. At the end of that corridor was a massive iron door that looked like a bank vault.

Cattoretti entered a code into a computer touch screen that was mounted on the wall. There was a heavy thump. The massive door slowly swung open—it must have been two-feet thick.

"We simply call this, '*la volta*,'" Cattoretti said. "The vault."

The inside of the room looked like a high end jewelry store, with floor-to-ceiling display cases.

Cattoretti led Elaine over to one cabinet, pulled out a key, and opened a glass door. Behind it were dozens of Chopard necklaces. The diamonds glittered and made little prisms of red, blue and yellow on the glass.

"Those look real," Elaine said, her mouth a little dry.

He chuckled. "Ms. Brogan, everything in *la volta* is genuine, purchased legitimately, at retail prices." He paused. "May I call you Elaine? Please call me Giorgio." He smiled warmly at her. "I think we will become very good friends, Elaine."

She had her doubts about this.

He motioned to the shelves. "This is where we keep all the expensive originals...not only our jewelry, but our clothes and accessories as well. The moment a new design is available, we acquire it and begin the copying process. Once the design is captured, the originals are kept here."

He inspected several of the necklaces, finally settling on a brilliant blue sapphire and diamond necklace in white gold. Taking it from the box, he stepped behind Elaine and drew it around her neck.

"How do you like it?" he said, both their faces visible in the mirror behind the glass.

Elaine swallowed, gazing at the stones against her neck. It must have cost a fortune. *He's trying to buy me*, she thought. *And it just might work.*

"It's beautiful," was all she could mutter.

Cattoretti placed it inside a plush Chopard box, and handed it to her. "You can wear it to the opera tonight."

"The opera?" she said, taken aback.

"*Madame Butterfly* is playing at La Scala in Milan. It is opening night. Andrea Bocelli is performing. Would you do me the honor of accompanying me?"

"Well, I..."

"Unless you have other plans..."

Other plans? She almost smiled. That was a good one.

"Please, come this way—I want you to pick out some more things."

They went farther into the space. Elaine could see it was the beginning of a long tunnel. It was illuminated by soft, recessed ceiling lamps. The passageway stretched as far as she could see, narrowing to a vanishing point hundreds of feet away. There were rows and rows of gowns, dresses, skirts, tops, lingerie, shoes, handbags...

Cattoretti pushed a button and the shelves rotated, a new shelf appearing above, and the one at the bottom disappearing. He plucked a pale blue evening gown from the nearest shelf and held it up to her shoulders, cocking his head to the side. "This Versace would look splendid on you." He draped it over her arm and moved on. From another hanger, he removed a chinchilla fur coat. "These will go together well."

Elaine looked numbly at the luxurious garments— together they must have cost twenty or thirty thousand dollars.

Leading her deeper into the tunnel, they reached the shoes. "Choose a nice pair of flats to complete the outfit." He glanced at his watch. "If you will excuse me a moment, I have some pressing business I must attend to. Please feel free to look around all you want, try things on—take whatever suits your fancy." He gave her a winning smile. "Put together a few nice ensembles, won't you? It would give me great pleasure to present such a lovely woman with a few of these pieces—they just sit here in this vault, collecting dust."

He left her alone in the tunnel, the door cracked open.

Elaine wandered down the rows and rows of lavish designer attire. *Gucci, Loretti, Casadei, Bergamo...* It was mesmerizing. She had never seen so much beautiful clothing in one place. *The tunnel of love*, she thought.

A pair of grey satin flats by Miu Miu caught her eye.

She unstrapped her green stilettos and tried on the slippers. Her feet melted into them.

Wandering down the tunnel, she became lost in all its apparel. She tried on anything that struck her fancy. She lost all track of time.

This almost makes up for all the bad things that have happened to me, she thought. *If there's a special heaven for women, this is it.*

As she tried on garment after garment, she decided that she didn't care if Cattoretti locked her in and left her here forever. Her emaciated body would be found clad head to toe in Prada, with a goofy smile on her face.

When Cattoretti finally returned, she was trying on a pair of Bergamo sandals.

"*Sì!*" Cattoretti said, cocking his head to admire them. "An excellent choice."

Elaine slipped them off and stepped back into the stilettos.

The sight of the man in the flesh, the brooding eyes and the scar running down his jaw, yanked Elaine back to reality.

"I can't accept these things," she said, reaching behind her neck to unfasten the necklace.

Cattoretti looked honestly surprised. "Why not?"

"I think you know why not."

He gazed at her with a mixture of puzzlement and curiosity. He did not look offended.

"Come," he said, taking her hand again. "I want to show you something else."

CHAPTER 2.12

When they emerged from the vault, Cattoretti led Elaine back to the elevator and up one level. They passed through a maze of endlessly crisscrossing hallways. She was growing afraid again. Maybe she should have accepted the clothes.

They finally reached another heavily guarded door. She could feel a familiar vibration beneath her feet. "I think you will appreciate what you are about to see," he said, as they passed through the door.

Elaine took only two steps inside before she stopped in her tracks, gaping.

There it was, the centerpiece of the room—a KBA Giori intaglio printing press, exactly like the model used at the Bureau of Exchange and Printing. The roaring contraption was blasting out page after page of wet green banknotes, the sheets flying through with such velocity they were only a blur. Beyond it, men in blue DayPrinto coveralls were feeding stacks of the freshly printed bills into a large paper cutter. On the far side of the room, a half dozen more men were crawling over two gigantic copies of $100 bills that were spread out on the floor, examining them on their hands and knees.

"Impressed?" Cattoretti shouted over the din.

Dumbfounded was the word. Elaine stepped closer to the printing press, peering at the manufacturer's plate attached to the side. It was genuine, the words KBA GIORI—WURZBURG, GERMANY stamped into the metal.

"If you don't mind me asking," Elaine said, "how did you—"

"There was a bit of a mix up in a shipment to South America," he said, with a smile.

Elaine remembered what Nick had told her about the Giori press that had mysteriously disappeared en route to Chile.

Elaine stared at this strange man, trying to figure him out. An expert manufacturer of designer knockoffs, and a master currency counterfeiter? To somehow intercept a KBA Giori printing press on its way to the government of Chile?

She found herself strangely attracted to him. She was tired of fighting, and his power offered much-needed security.

The huge press slowed, then came to a halt. Cattoretti plucked a freshly printed sheet of $100 bills out of the hopper and handed it to her. The uncut banknotes were printed in the same format used by the U.S. Bureau of Engraving and Printing, 32 to a sheet.

With a feeling of unreality, Elaine stared at the paper in her hand, the smell of the damp ink flooding her nostrils.

She suddenly felt sick. Teetering, Cattoretti grabbed her arm and settled her down into a metal folding chair.

"It is shocking for you?" Cattoretti said uncertainly.

"That's an understatement."

"Let me get you some water," he said, and he trotted over to a cooler and returned with a full paper cup.

Elaine drank. The room kept spinning—the men, the machines, uncut stacks of fake $100 bills...

This is what I swore to stop, she thought queasily. *And this is what killed my poor father, and landed Nick in jail.*

She wondered where Nick was, wracked with guilt again, feeling like she was somehow responsible. She pushed the thoughts from her mind— Nick was out of her life, and she would never see him again. All of that was in the past.

Cattoretti was squatting beside her, holding her hand. "Are you all right?"

Elaine didn't answer. She had been fairly certain that some criminal had been using a real KBA Giori press to make the counterfeits, but it was still a shock. She had never seen or heard of a counterfeiting operation of this magnitude. The typical bogus moneymaking setup consisted of one or two technical types working out of a small basement or an abandoned warehouse, usually with cobbled together equipment that could be broken down and moved at the first sign of trouble. In contrast, this operation not only had a real KBA Giori printing press, it looked as sophisticated and permanent as the one at the BEP itself. Even the paper cutting machine was just like the ones used at the BEP.

"Drink some more water," Cattoretti said.

Elaine took another sip. She began to feel a little better. As she gazed across the room at the men studying the blowups of the $100 bill, her curiosity grew. She shakily rose from the chair and approached the huge, taped-together enlargements.

She noticed everyone had stopped working and were all watching her.

"If you're feeling up to it," Cattoretti said, "will you do me the honor?" He handed her a magnifying glass, then motioned down to the page of freshly printed banknotes—she had forgotten she was still holding them. "To pass muster with someone from the U.S. Treasury would be a real coup for us."

The men were all standing there, watching curiously, mostly with their arms crossed.

Elaine raised the magnifier and methodically began checking the freshly printed sheet of banknotes the way she had checked thousands of others. First, she rubbed the paper between her thumb and forefinger, testing the texture. Of course it was printed with an intaglio press—the machine was sitting right in front of her. But she was testing for something else. Most laymen did not know that the paper itself was a major stumbling block for many counterfeiters, even the pros. This paper had the distinct feel of the genuine U.S. mix, 75% cotton, 25% linen. She peered at the edges through the magnifying glass. It also contained the different lengths of red and blue fibers. They weren't merely printed onto the paper, the way amateur counterfeiters did it, but woven right into the material, just like genuine U.S. currency.

She held the page up to the light. The required graduated watermarks were there, too. All of them looked right.

These were the same bills she had been checking the last year, only they were of even better quality now. They had continued to improve.

Elaine glanced at Cattoretti—he was watching her with a knowing smile. He was well aware of everything she was checking. But did he know that she was the one who had been in charge of developing the software updates? He didn't seem to.

Next came the security threads. The super-thin polyester strips were properly woven into the paper. With the magnifier, she checked the tiny *USA 100* that was micro printed on the strip. The characters were clear and sharply defined. The magnifier wasn't strong enough for her to check the mistake in the zero on the set of numerals.

She switched on the magnifier's built-in ultraviolet light. The security thread glowed red, just like it was supposed to.

"The threads are right," she muttered.

Cattoretti glanced at the other men, pleased.

Next she turned her attention to the color-shifting ink in the *100* denomination in the corner. She slowly tilted the page and watched the numbers shift from copper to green all down the page. The hues looked spot-on, but a technician would have to check them with a spectrometer to be sure.

These were the bills she had been checking the last year, there was no doubt in her mind now.

Cattoretti smiled. "So have we passed with flying colors?"

"Not just yet," Elaine said. She had a feeling that if she wanted to remain alive, she better find some additional faults than the ones the new software updates would search for. He hadn't had a chance to check the "salt shaker" yet, but he would soon. He wouldn't need her anymore unless she could spot some new defects in his counterfeits that no one had found before.

She moved closer to the huge enlargements of the $100 bill spread out over the floor.

"The blowup on the left is genuine," Cattoretti advised.

"I know," Elaine said.

Cattoretti raised an eyebrow, but did not ask how.

Elaine started to step out onto the paper, then remembered the high heels. She slipped off the bright green stilettos. All the men were watching, a few obviously enjoying it. She also noticed that most of them had skeptical expressions on their faces.

Elaine padded onto the paper in her bare feet and began moving from one area of the enlargement to another, searching for defects that were not included on the data key.

"For starters," she said, "the face on this clock isn't right." She pointed down at the image of Independence Hall on the back side of the $100 bill.

"It shows ten past four," Cattoretti said defensively. This feature could only be seen under magnification.

"That's not the problem. The roman numerals aren't shaped correctly."

The other men glanced at each other, unable to grasp her English.

"*Numeri romani,*" Cattoretti said, translating.

One of them, a short man with teardrop glasses, said, "*Stronzate!*" and began babbling angrily in Italian, speaking with his hands. It sounded like he was saying "How can you listen to this stupid bimbo," or something to that effect.

"*Comparero!*" Cattoretti barked.

The men reluctantly gathered around the blown-up clock and began to compare it to the clock in the original.

Elaine moved on, slowly making her way across the paper, checking minute details, until she reached the front side of the bill. She stopped with her bare feet on the bridge of Benjamin Franklin's nose.

"What is wrong now?" Cattoretti said.

"Franklin's chin isn't drawn correctly."

"How so?" Cattoretti said, looking skeptical himself.

All at once, the men across the room began talking excitedly. The one in the teardrop glasses called to Cattoretti. "*Otto e dieci sono errati?*"

"On that clock, is it the eight and ten?" Cattoretti asked Elaine.

She nodded.

Now the men were looking at Elaine with respect.

When she finished her inspection, Cattoretti led her out of the basement and back up to his office. She had only revealed a fraction of the finer mistakes she had seen.

An off-putting grin appeared on his face, as if he had just discovered some kind of secret.

"What's wrong?" Elaine said uneasily.

"I know who you are," he said, pointing at her. "You are the woman who used to work at the Secret Service office in Bulgaria. The one who has 'an eye for a fake.'"

Elaine didn't react.

He smiled knowingly. "Do not deny it, Elaine. I know it is true. Everyone involved in counterfeiting across Europe heard about you. The rumor was that you could spot a counterfeit as fast as any automatic machine. Your own field offices were sending bills to you, instead of back to the States, to get quicker turnaround. Then, you disappeared—no one knew what happened to you." Cattoretti chuckled. "I should have known the U.S. Treasury Department would not let someone like you waste away in a godforsaken place like Bulgaria." He gave a big belly laugh. "I cannot believe it! And here you are, standing right here with me in my very own office!"

Cattoretti waited for her to say something, but she remained silent.

His mouth slowly opened, and then he pointed at her again. "You were the one in charge of creating the software updates, too. Am I right?" He slapped his forehead. "Of course I am! That is why you disappeared from Bulgaria—you were transferred to the Treasury Department to help create the software updates. It is true?"

Elaine still said nothing.

"It is true? Yes, it's true!"

"So what if it is?" Elaine finally said.

"Is it not obvious? You and I—we could make history together!"

She couldn't believe this. "You actually expect me to *help* you with your counterfeiting operation?"

Cattoretti looked genuinely surprised. "Is that such a far-fetched idea?"

"You destroyed my life!"

"Me?" Cattoretti said. "You are terribly mistaken, Elaine. I told you before, my Russian partners were responsible for obtaining the data key. I had nothing to do with it. I told them what I wanted, and they handled the rest. All I knew was that they bribed some high level Treasury official, a man—"

"Gene Lassiter."

"Is that his name?"

"Yes. He was my boss," Elaine added bitterly.

"In any case, I knew nothing more about it. There are very good reasons that I must maintain my distance from the United States. I had no knowledge of any other details, how the Russians were acquiring the data key." He paused. "You must understand— I really have no choice but to work with them. Only an organization of their size can launder the amount of money I can produce with that Giori machine. I cannot risk changing the money to Euros in Italy—I sell every last dollar to the Russians for laundering."

Elaine wanted to believe him, but it was difficult. She would have to think about all this later—if there was a later.

Cattoretti looked sympathetically at her. "I am truly sorry that someone as lovely as you became a victim in this project, Elaine. If I had known this is the way it was being handled, I would have put a stop to it."

He paused, studying her. "Of course, I cannot reverse what has happened...but I can make it up to you. If you join me in my efforts, I can certainly do that. I will be glad to do that! And why not? I can pay you very handsomely for your work."

Elaine looked at the door. "And if I refuse to help you?"

Cattoretti frowned, looking insulted. "You continue to misjudge me, Elaine. You are not a prisoner here." He motioned to the door. "You are free to leave whenever you wish."

She looked into his dark eyes. He knew damn well she had nowhere to go. Lassiter had probably called in the Secret Service by now, which meant Interpol was looking for her as well. She wouldn't stay on the streets long.

He watched her for a moment, then said, "There is no need for you to rush to any decision. All I ask is that you think about it. What have you got to lose? As long as you are in Italy, under my protection, you have nothing to fear—no one can touch you here." He gave a relaxed smile. "I would suggest that you go to my villa and have a good rest, reflect on the situation. My staff will cater to your every whim. We have an indoor swimming pool, a sauna, a private chef, and a masseur with absolutely magical fingers. Spend some time letting yourself be pampered, Elaine. You deserve it."

Without waiting for a response, Cattoretti picked up the phone on his desk. "Luigi? I want you to escort Ms. Brogan to Fontanella."

A few minutes later, Elaine was again sitting in the back of the silver Rolls Royce as it glided along Italian countryside, Luigi and the chauffeur in front.

As she gazed out the window, she considered what Cattoretti had said. Was it really such an outrageous thought, helping him? She had been blamed for the theft of the data key, but was reaping none of the rewards. On the other hand, the thought that she was helping a man like Giorgio Cattoretti was abhorrent to her. He may have been elegant and sophisticated, but he was still a criminal, just like the man who had destroyed her father.

How many lives had he destroyed? But, on the other hand, how many had he saved by creating hundreds of jobs in an economically repressed part of Italy? His employees did not seem to fear him—they seemed to admire him, to hold him in awe.

The Rolls slowed, approaching a four-way stop. There was a sign that said FONTANELLA – 3 KM and pointed to the right.

They turned in that direction. In a few minutes, the Rolls soon slowed again and turned off the highway, down a smaller paved road. They drove down an easy grade, through the woods, and then up a steeper rise. There were PROPRIETA' PRIVATA signs posted every now and then.

They finally came to a high stone wall with a massive wooden gate. The entrance was medieval style—it might have been the entrance to a castle.

After a few seconds the gate began to open inwards, revealing a gigantic set of stone buildings in the near distance.

It *was* a castle.

Elaine leaned forward as they rolled along the road that approached it. Two imposing stone towers formed the front of the structure. The wheels of the expensive car thumped softly as they crossed a little bridge...there was actually a moat. The water looked black and oily. They drove along the curved driveway and passed two men in dark blue suits that were walking Doberman Pinschers. Luigi waved, and the men waved back. They approached an arch in a section that stretched between the two towers—there was a heavy, closed inner door and an outer shield of sharp wooden spikes that was lowered halfway to the ground.

Elaine expected that door to open as well, but the chauffeur made a sharp left and parked next to the tower.

Luigi stepped around to the trunk and retrieved her suitcase and the Balenciaga handbag. As they approached the bottom of the tower, a door opened and a man appeared.

"*Signora!*" he blurted, grinning at her. There were deep dimples in his cheeks. "Ah, you are more-a lovely than the boss said." He was rail-thin and had a drooping black mustache. He was wearing a long white apron that covered a dark suit. "My name Antonio!" He took her hand and squeezed it. "But you canna call me Tony."

He led her inside the building. The circular foyer was filled with antiques, the stone floor covered with a worn oriental carpet. The room smelled ancient, a combination of old stone and wood.

"Let me take-a your coat," Tony said. He slapped his own cheek, staring at her again now that he could see the designer dress. *"Mama-mia!* That dress-a, it's-a perfect on you. Prada, *sì?"*

Elaine couldn't help smiling at his exaggerated, childlike admiration.

He grabbed the Balenciaga handbag and her suitcase from Luigi. He glanced down at the stone floor and frowned at the driver. "Get out-a here, your big feet-a messin' up my floor!"

Luigi snickered and walked past him, calling him a *finocchio*, which Elaine sensed was a slur about Tony's sexual orientation.

To Elaine, Tony said, "I'm-a the little boss around here. Signor Cattoretti, he the big boss. Tony the little boss." He grinned and grabbed Elaine's hand and led her up a winding staircase, his hips swinging prissily. "I'm-a gonna give you the best room in-a the house, signora, the Blue Suite. The view is *spettacolare!"* Elaine nearly slipped on the narrow, worn steps and Tony stopped. "You gotta be careful with those-a heels, *signora...*" He peered more closely at them, looking envious. "Fendi, *sì?"*

Before she could answer, he turned and led upwards again. "The Blue Suite, is-a much better than the Red-a Suite."

When they had climbed up the equivalent of about three flights of steps on the circular stone staircase, Tony stopped and opened a door for her. *"Signora, prego..."*

Elaine cautiously stepped inside the room. The first thing she noticed was the vaulted ceiling—it was covered with faded pastel blue murals showing armored knights on horseback that looked original to the castle. Along one curved wall, also painted in a pastel blue, was a canopied bed with an oak frame that must have weighed five hundred pounds. There was a marble washbowl, an old spinning loom, a painting of a curly-haired boy petting a dog...

The stone floor was worn to a polished sheen in places.

"How old is this place?" Elaine asked, fascinated.

"The oldest section was-a built in the Eighth Century," Tony said smoothly, as if he had answered this question many times.

Elaine started when she turned around—there was a full suit of armor beside the door, the face mask closed, a sword grasped in one metallic glove.

Tony patted the helmet and grinned. *"Signor* will-a protect you." He set the bags down and admired Elaine's looks again. He slapped his hands together. "The boss say you want-a rest. But maybe you like-a go for swim first? We have a swimmin' pool, it's-a heated."

"No, thank you, I—"

"Maybe you like-a massage? Or a sauna?"

"Maybe later. I'd like to take a little nap."

"*Sì, signora.*" Tony bit his lip, thinking. "But maybe you like-a something to eat. A little *focaccia* with some buffalo mozzarella—"

"No, I'm really—"

"Or some *proscuitto*? I just cut-a some fresh—"

"No, thanks, but I'm really not hungry. I had a big breakfast at..." Elaine didn't know what to call it. "...the office."

"Ah! No wonder you no-a hungry! You ate the cookin' of that-a Tuscan *dilettante*. The man calls himself a chef...could not make-a *focaccia* bread! He spend-a too much time up in France, those French people and their odd-a ways of cookin'!" Tony looked more closely at her, concerned. "Maybe I get you some-a Pepto-Bismol?"

Elaine laughed. "No, I'm fine, really."

Tony leaned forward and spoke conspiratorially. "Between you-a and me, I wouldn't let that so-called chef make-a food for my dog..." He gave a helpless shrug. "But if the boss wants to hire a fry cook to feed his workers, whatta can I do?"

Tony looked her over again, nodding approvingly. "You a real classy lady, just like-a the boss said."

Tony turned and pointed to a rope that hung from a hole in the ceiling. "You need anything, you just-a pull on this string, it make-a ding-a-linga down in the kitchen. *Bene?*"

After Tony left, Elaine looked at the two bags, hesitating, then decided to hang everything up in the wardrobe. She went over to the window and opened the heavy wooden shutters.

She found herself overlooking a courtyard, the inner area of the castle. Only the "courtyard" was huge, more like an Italian *piazza*, paved with cobblestones and lined with streetlamps and statues. There was a stone well in the middle, with a wooden bucket hanging from a rope. Along one side was a row of automobiles, all under canvas covers—antiques, she supposed. There was a long row of beautiful fountains on the other end, flanked by two cannons. At the farthest point, there was also something else under a tarp, an object that looked much larger than a car. Perhaps a boat on a trailer.

It was so tranquil—she could hear birds chirping in the woods beyond the castle's wall. There was a sense of unreality to it all.

Princess Alana, Elaine thought. *Maybe I've arrived at my true home after all...*

She looked back into the room, and the suit of armor, at the steel face mask. It made her think of Lassiter—cold, hollow, and untouchable. She wanted to kill him. He had caused all this. He had caused her to be kidnapped and taken to Italy, blamed for stealing top secret information from the U.S. Treasury Department, pressured into helping an international counterfeiter perfect his currency.

And she wondered: had Nick really been under investigation, or had Lassiter merely made all that up to separate her from him?

She knew the answer to that. Lassiter was the criminal, and not Nick. She hated herself for believing the wicked old bastard, and not listening to Nick.

She looked longingly at the bed. She was too tired to think anymore. She debated whether or not to take off the Prada dress before she slept.

She spotted pajamas on a shelf under the nightstand. Pure silk.

She changed into them, then finally lay down on the huge bed and curled up in a blanket.

CHAPTER 2.13

When Elaine awoke from her nap she felt surprisingly fresh and energized. She started to reach for the bell to call Tony, then decided to explore the castle on her own, if she could get away with it. She was in a much better mood, and ravenous.

She changed into a comfy cotton lounge suit she found in the wardrobe, it did wonders for her figure. It was by Gucci. Of course. The heather-gray hue enhanced her clear complexion.

Castle life suits me, she thought happily, as she opened the bedroom door. She descended the stairs, barefoot, the smooth stones cold against her soles. When she reached the bottom spiral staircase, she went through a dark, arched hallway. It opened into what appeared to be the drawing room, or at least one of the drawing rooms. A monstrous stone fireplace dominated the space, the hearth ablaze. The mantle was composed of solid marble, carved into the form of a seashell and supported by two buxom nymphs on either side. The beam-vaulted ceiling was alive with frescoes in orange and blue pastels.

She wandered through the ancient structure, passing a two-level library with another spiral staircase, then a billiards room. Luigi was leaning over the table, lining up a shot, while another dark, burly man looked on. They both glanced at Elaine and she continued on. She expected Luigi to come after her, but she heard the soft click of billiard balls, the men talking casually to each other in Italian.

She turned down another corridor and entered the kitchen so big it would have held her entire apartment.

Tony was at a counter, kneading dough. He looked up. "Ah, *signora*! You slept well?"

"Yes, thank you."

"That Gucci look-a real good on you." He wiped his hands on his apron. "You want somethin' to eat now? Maybe something light, like a *mozzarella* and tomato salad?" Before she could answer, he quickly prepared the salad for her. The cheese was delicious, the tomatoes so fresh they exploded in her mouth. She wolfed it down right at the counter, too hungry to move to a table. Tony smiled with pleasure, watching her.

When she finished, he said, "Maybe I show you around the castle?" He grabbed her hand and led her out of the kitchen and into another huge room.

"This room they call-a the Great Hall," he said.

Elaine tilted her head back, looking up at the vaulted ceiling. It must have been three stories high. The stone walls were covered with tapestries and paintings, a few statues near the doorways.

"It's incredible," Elaine said, her voice echoing in the vast space.

Tony looked pleased. He gave her a formal tour of the castle, pointing out various paintings and other works of art. There was a Picasso, a Rembrandt, a Goya, and three Rubens. She wondered if Giorgio Cattoretti liked Rubenesque women, or if he simply liked Ruben's style. There were statues by Boccioni, Rodin, and Houdon. It was like a museum.

Tony stopped in front of a spiral staircase that only led downward. "You wanna see the dungeon, *signora*?"

"There's a dungeon?"

"*Si*. It is a very dark and wicked place. Many horrible things happened down there."

Nothing was more repulsive to Elaine than physical torture. No form of human behavior was more loathsome.

"Of course I want to see it!"

The dungeon gave Elaine the shivers. There were no electric lights—Tony had to use a candle to show her around. The area was composed of several rooms, some with heavy wooden medieval doors that had only tiny, barred windows in the middle. Another cave-like space had a large fireplace in it, which Tony explained was used to heat up "*strumenti*" used to extract information from victims. Another room housed an ancient, cobweb-covered rack. There were heavy, rusted shackles attached to the walls.

When Elaine saw a shadowy blob scurry across one corner of the stone floor—a blob that looked like it had a long tail— she jumped. Standing there in her bare feet, it felt like the creatures were nibbling at her ankles.

"I've seen enough," she said, clutching Tony's arm. "Let's get out of here."

When they were back upstairs, Tony led her into a modern wing that had been added on to the castle, complete with tile floors and fluorescent lights. The clean, brightly lit space was a welcome change from the dungeon.

"As you can-a see, this part of the castle has-a been renovated," Tony said, in his tour guide voice. They walked down a wide, modern-looking hallway with skylights. "That's-a the swimmin' pool, and there's a sauna across the hall."

They passed a long, narrow room with a massage table where soft, soothing music was playing. There was a bronzed young man in white chinos, working out with two dumbbells, the muscles rippling under his white polo shirt. He gave Elaine a dimpled smile as they went by. He could have been a Chippendale's model.

"That's-a Mario," Tony said. "He's our personal trainer and masseuse."

Tony stopped in the hallway. "Maybe you like-a massage now?"

That's tempting, Elaine thought. Then another doorway caught her eye—it opened to an exercise room with mats scattered all over the floor.

In the center, suspended from the ceiling, was a punching bag. It hung there perfectly still, begging to take a beating. And Elaine was just the person to do it.

"Do you have any exercise clothes I can wear?" she said.

Tony raised his hands as if it was a ridiculous question. "Do we have clothes? *Signora*, this is Giorgio Cattoretti's house!"

Tony showed her to a comfortable changing room that was packed with workout clothing, everything from tennis outfits by Givenchy and Dolce & Gabbana to high-end Nike and Rossignol pants and athletic bras, much of it still with tags attached. It was almost all women's attire. It seemed that Cattoretti had a lot of female friends. She had noticed that all the bathrooms in the castle were stuffed with expensive women's cosmetics, as Cattoretti's private bath at DayPrinto had been.

Elaine chose a simple pair of yoga pants that fitted loosely, and a top.

When she came out of the changing room, she slowly approached the punching bag. She gazed at it for a moment, breathing hard. In her mind, Gene Lassiter's sneering face appeared on it. And then Giorgio Cattoretti's.

Elaine suddenly whirled around and gave the bag a powerful roundhouse kick. Her arms and legs became windmills as she peppered the leather with a combination of kicks and punches—jabs, backfists, crescents, axes, hooks. She felt a sting in the side as her stitches tore, but she didn't give a damn—all her pent-up frustration was pouring out of her body, and it felt wonderful. At times the bag became Ronald Eskew and Bill Saunders. She pounded the bag mercilessly, until sweat poured into her eyes.

She finally began to tire, the punches and kicks slowing, then coming to a stop. Elaine stood for a moment in front of the bag, panting.

She whirled around and gave the bag one last, mighty roundhouse kick. It flew up so high that it nearly knocked her down on its backswing.

A voice behind her said, "I hope it is not *me* you imagine there!"

Elaine turned around.

Giorgio Cattoretti was standing at the doorway in his Armani suit, watching her.

"I've made a decision," she said.

He looked surprised. "You have?"

"I've decided to help you with your project."

Cattoretti clapped his hands together. "*Magnifico!*" He opened his mouth, hesitated, and then said to himself, "Oh, why not? I was about to offer you a sweetener to help you make up your mind, and it still stands."

"What 'sweetener'?"

He motioned to her. "You are the one who carried the data key out of the United States, not Gene Lassiter. You should receive the balance of the payment, not him. Is that not fair? I think it is."

"How much is the payment?"

"Eight million Euros," Cattoretti said smoothly.

She swallowed. Eight *million* Euros. It was hard for her to think in such large amounts of money.

"Of course, there is a chance he will come after it," Cattoretti said.

Let him come, Elaine thought darkly.

"With eight million Euros," Cattoretti went on "you can live anywhere in the world—you can simply put the money in a bank account and live off the interest. I can have a completely new identity made for you— a passport, birth certificate, driver's license—everything. You want a university degree? I can earn you a PhD from Yale, or a masters from

Oxford."

Elaine smiled. "What exactly would I have to do for this eight million Euros?"

"You must help me make my currency as perfect as possible. My god—with your help, we do not even need the data key! We can make my counterfeits so perfect that the Treasury Department will have to develop a whole new set of software updates, which will take them another six months, at least."

True, Elaine thought.

"All I ask is for you to help me make my counterfeits good enough to pass through the bank verifying machines again, with the updated software. Do that, and the money is yours."

Eight million Euros, she thought headily.

The notion that she could usurp Lassiter's money had a delicious sense of poetic justice.

"I'll do it," she said.

CHAPTER 2.14

Less than an hour later, in Paris, Gene Lassiter hobbled up to a pay phone on the Rue de Rivoli. He glanced up and down the street, then tore the plastic off a new international telephone card. He used it to call a number in Switzerland.

As he waited for an answer, he glanced at his watch. It was now 5:40 pm. The second payment should have arrived.

"Banque Cantonale du Valais," a woman said, in a French accent.

"Yes, good afternoon. I have an account at your bank and I would like to check the balance, please."

"One moment." Lassiter glanced up and down the street again to make sure he wasn't being observed.

A clerk came on the line and he gave her his account number.

"Your balance is exactly five hundred thousand U.S. dollars." The clerk paused. "Will there be anything else?"

"Only five hundred thousand? Are you sure? I was expecting a wire this afternoon."

"Just a moment." There was a long pause, with clicking sounds in the background. "I'm afraid there were no wires received at all today for this account."

Lassiter slammed the phone down. *Goddam Russians!* After he had corrected their screw up in Moscow and helped them recover the data key, they thought they still weren't going to pay him!

There was no way he could support Gypsy on a measly five hundred thousand Euros. He wiped the sweat from his brow and forced himself to calm down.

He glanced up and down the street again, then used the phone card to make another call. This one was to Moscow.

These people had no idea who they were dealing with. They didn't know that he had planted a GPS device in Elaine Brogan's suitcase. He'd just checked and now his computer showed the device was at a location east of Milan, Italy. Where he had damn good reason to believe the buyer—and the Giori printing press—were located.

He waited impatiently as the phone rang on the other end.

"*Da*," a voice said, sounding bored.

"It's me. I want to know why you haven't wired the rest of the money. I just called my bank and it's not there." Lassiter fought to control his temper. *Be diplomatic,* he thought. *Don't assume they're going to screw you.* "Perhaps there's been some mistake..."

"Mistake?" the voice said calmly. "There has been no mistake."

"You listen to me, you prick. I know for a fact your buyer has the product—I put it into his goddam hands myself, after you guys screwed it up. I want to know why I haven't received the second—"

"Your services are no longer necessary."

Lassiter frowned, not sure he had heard correctly. "Excuse me?"

"Your services are no longer necessary."

"What the hell is that supposed to mean?"

"It means *Do sdvidanya,* sucker."

The line went dead.

"Hello?" he said, clicking the hook a few times. "Hello?"

Lassiter flagged down a taxi, went back to his hotel, and made plans to catch the first flight out from Paris to Milan.

He was going to get his money, even if he had to pry it free from the buyer's cold, dead fingers.

CHAPTER 2.15

Elaine was in Cattoretti's bedroom, dressed in the Versace gown, just about to clip the Chopard necklace around her neck.

Luigi appeared at the door. "Excuse me, Ms. Brogan, but Gene Lassiter was caught trying to climb over the fortification wall."

"*Grazie*, Luigi," she said elegantly.

She slowly turned from the mirror and then was floating down the wide, marble staircase. Gene Lassiter was at the bottom of the steps in the Great Hall, standing between two of Cattoretti's men, his arms firmly in their grip. As she descended, he stared up at Elaine, his mouth agape.

She floated to a stop three steps from the bottom, peering down her nose at him.

"On your knees," she said coldly.

"Elaine, I'm sorry, I never meant to—"

The two men forced Lassiter down, his cane dropping from his shaking hand and rattling against the stone floor.

"Your gun," she said to Giorgio Cattoretti, who had materialized by her side. She took the cool weapon into her hand and pointed it at Lassiter's forehead.

"Please have mercy on a stupid old man!" Lassiter cried. "I am a fool, an imbecile! I should never have—"

"Did you really believe that you could take advantage of *me*?" Elaine said. She cocked the gun. "Nobody messes with a Brogan."

Cattoretti clapped his hands together, watching her with delight.

"Please," Lassiter begged, a filament of spittle dangling from his lower lip. "You can have the money! Take it! Take it all! I am nothing, a powerless nonentity, unfit to be in your presence." Lassiter was trembling so badly that his kneecaps beat out a tattoo on the floor. "The reason I used you was because I was so madly in love with you. I was excruciatingly jealous of Nick! I know that a shriveled up, pathetic excuse for a human being like me could never hope to so much as kiss the ground you walk on. Please show mercy on a disgusting, selfish old man!"

Elaine enjoyed his groveling for a long, luscious moment. She finally let her finger off the trigger. Handing the pistol back to Cattoretti, she said, "He's not worth wasting a bullet on. Shall we have dinner, darling?"

Elaine rolled over onto her stomach, so that Mario could work her upper back. It was a delicious fantasy, almost as delicious as the handsome young Italian's fingers felt kneading her aching muscles.

As Mario began massaging her shoulders, she pressed the REWIND button in her mind and watched her fantasy again, this time with even more satisfying dialogue.

Elaine showered and dressed, then came downstairs for dinner at 5:30. The opera started at 8:00, so they were dining early. The long mahogany table in the Great Hall was arranged only for two, one place setting on the near end, and the other immediately to its right.

Giorgio Cattoretti was decked out in an Armani tux, his hair slicked back, his bleached teeth gleaming. If it wasn't for the scar that ran along his jaw, Elaine thought that he would have been too good looking.

"You look ravishing," he told Elaine, pulling the latter chair out for her. She was wearing the Versace gown and Chopard necklace, and she had pinned up her hair with a diamond-studded barrette Cattoretti had given her from the vault. As she sat down at the table, she felt the warmth of his breath on her shoulder.

Tony sashayed into the dining room, wearing a formal black suit. He grinned at Elaine, his dimples showing. "*Signora*! You look stunning in-a that Versace! *Belissima*!"

"Thank you."

He draped a white napkin over one arm and began pouring wine. "I hope-a your appetite come back now."

Cattoretti gave Elaine a concerned glance. "You have not been well?"

"Of course she has not been well!" Tony said. "She ate-a breakfast at DayPrinto." He nodded to her. "Don't-a worry, *signora*. My cookin' will get-a your system back to normal. I made some *gnocchi* with truffle that gonna melt inna your mouth, *porchetta*, some *vincisgrassi*, and *spiedini*...not that heavy Northern saucy slop that *dilettante* serves...

"Tony," Cattoretti warned, as he poured the second glass of wine.

Tony indignantly left the room. Cattoretti looked a bit embarrassed. "Those types make the best cooks, but they are very difficult to manage."

"I think he's wonderful," Elaine said.

Cattoretti merely grunted.

Elaine looked around the spectacular room. Covering nearly one entire wall was a faded tapestry depicting several robed figures sitting in a garden. Hanging on the adjacent wall, in a heavy, gilded frame, was a large portrait of a hooknose man with long black hair parted down the middle, painted in a Renaissance style. There was something vain in the man's expression. He had a cruel-looking mouth.

"That is Galeazzo Sforza," Cattoretti said, "the man who built this castle. Back in the Fourteenth Century, he was also Duke of Milan once. He constructed this as a summer retreat."

"Quaint little place," Elaine said.

Cattoretti smiled. "Sforza had a reputation for extravagance, and also for being wicked and tyrannical. He took hundreds of lovers. When he tired of them, he passed them on to his court. He made many enemies as well. It is said that he nailed one of his betrayers to his own coffin, still alive. There is another story of a poacher—on this very property, in fact—who he forced to swallow an entire hare, fur and all."

Elaine sensed a trace of admiration in Cattoretti's tone.

"In his day, the dungeon was always filled to capacity," Cattoretti went on. "Did Tony show it to you?"

"Yes, he did," Elaine said, giving a little shiver.

"Sadly," Cattoretti said, "Sforza was eventually assassinated. His body was dragged through the streets of Milan by an enraged mob." Cattoretti added, with a sigh, "It's a pity. The man was a great contributor to the Italian culture, a noble patron of art, the theater, music..."

Elaine had the distinct feeling Cattoretti was talking about himself.

Tony entered with his arms full of small plates. He spread them precisely around the table, making sure each one was positioned so that the presentation of the food was oriented their way. He pointed to one and said, "This we call-a *fontina tartlet*, it has-a fontina cheese and—"

"Please leave us, Tony. We do not need an explanation of every ingredient you used."

"*Si*, boss." Looking a little hurt, Tony gave a little bow and disappeared out the door.

Cattoretti dipped a piece of bread in olive oil, and he gazed again at the portrait of Sforza. "You know, sometimes it amazes me the lengths that some men will go to for love." Raising an eyebrow at Elaine, he said, "Did you know everything Gene Lassiter has done is for the sake of a lover?"

Elaine was shocked. "No, I didn't."

"It is true. The Russians told me."

"Who is she?"

Cattoretti gave an odd smile. "German. Goes by the name of Gypsy. The Russians know very little—the two lovebirds are very careful about communicating with each other. They do know that Gypsy is much younger than Lassiter is. *Much* younger. And lives in Berlin. Nothing more."

Very interesting, Elaine thought. It explained a lot—no wonder Lassiter was always going to Berlin to visit "family." The man had always seemed sexually neuter to Elaine—he had never looked at her the way many men did, or shown any interest in any other women. She'd heard he was married once, long ago, and had been through a terrible divorce.

Elaine wondered what this Gypsy looked like. She imagined some fresh, Heidi-like 16 year old that Lassiter bounced on his knee. Probably with long blonde pigtails with a frilly white frock. Probably called him "Papa."

"Apparently, his darling 'Gypsy' is very beautiful," Cattoretti said, as if reading Elaine's thoughts. "Or at least Lassiter thinks so. Dark eyes...thick curly black hair, tall, with long legs..."

So much for Elaine's idea of her appearance. "How do you know what she looks like?"

"Lassiter's messages to her. Apparently he is quite the Casanova. The Russians have enjoyed reading his correspondence to her."

Elaine felt disgusted by the thought of Lassiter with a girl young enough to be his granddaughter, and the thought that he would ruin Elaine's life on account of her.

All the more reason Elaine would enjoy taking his money away from him.

She wished she could see the look on his face when he found out.

CHAPTER 2.16

The opening of *Madame Butterfly* at La Scala, with Andrea Bocelli, was a gala event. It brought out the media in droves.

When Cattoretti's silver Rolls Royce pulled up to the theatre entrance, there was a rope line set up that led from the sidewalk to the front doors, with reporters and TV crews swelling up against it.

Elaine watched as camera flashes popped—a celebrity couple was climbing out of a limo in front of them. When Elaine and Cattoretti emerged from the Rolls, no one paid much attention, though a few photographers snapped off pictures just in case they turned out to be famous. It seemed to Elaine that Giorgio Cattoretti was virtually anonymous.

That changed when they went to the private reception for the theater sponsors. It was held in a large, elegant room with inlaid teak floors framed with beautiful cream pillars. There were shouts of "Giorgio!" and "The Cat!" as people caught sight of him entering the room. He blossomed into full form, hugging his friends, kissing them on both cheeks Italian style, shaking hands, squeezing shoulders—he seemed to know everyone in the room.

He could not introduce Elaine under her real name, of course. On the way to the theater, they had come up with the alias "Marie De La Fontaine," and decided that she would be French, but educated in the USA, at Stanford. Elaine wasn't sure she liked the name—Marie De La Fontaine either sounded like a countess or a stripper, she couldn't decide which.

In any case, Marie De La Fontaine was introduced to government ministers, pop stars, ambassadors, business magnates, artists, writers, and politicians. Elaine could tell by the way that people looked at her that Giorgio Cattoretti went about town with a different lady on his arm every night. Even the older women who looked like inveterate gossips regarded Elaine with little more than mild curiosity and soon moved on to scrutinize more interesting specimens.

One thing puzzled her—Cattoretti introduced her to two world-famous fashion designers, and both of them seemed to be good buddies with Cattoretti. Didn't they know what he was doing in the basement of DayPrinto?

By the time curtain call was announced, she had downed three glasses of Dom Perignon and her head was spinning. They stepped inside Cattoretti's private box, and Elaine went to the railing, taking in the La Scala theater. It was breathtaking. The seats were covered in plush red velvet, the stage framed by ornate gold-gilded carvings. There were no walls, but multi-storied rows of boxes that formed a semicircle up to the stage. A majestic three-tiered crystal chandelier descended from the ceiling.

Elaine felt overjoyed, like a little girl living out a fantasy. Only this wasn't a daydream—this was real.

"Did you notice the fireplace?" Cattoretti said, touching her on the shoulder. There was a bricked rectangle cut into the back of the box.

"This was the personal box of Giuseppe Piermarini," Cattoretti said, "the architect of this magnificent theater. There was no central heat back then, of course, so fireplaces were necessary in winter. Also, at that time, operas were full day events—food was often cooked in between acts to keep the audience happy." Cattoretti looked down at the stage and chuckled. "There is nothing actors fear more than a cold, hungry audience."

Elaine sat down on one of the velvet seats and peered down over the railing at the handsomely-dressed crowd beneath them. The air was rich with the smell of expensive perfumes and colognes. She could see directly into the orchestra pit—the musicians were all warming up, the mishmash of violin and flute notes charging the atmosphere with excitement.

Directly across from them in a box on the second tier sat yet another one of Milan's top fashion designers. The man gave Cattoretti a nod and a knowing smile. Cattoretti smiled back.

"I don't understand," Elaine whispered.

"What do you not understand?"

"Why are all these designers so friendly with you?"

Cattoretti smiled. "Are you not familiar with the old adage, 'Imitation is the sincerest form of flattery'?"

"Yes, but still, your knockoffs cost them money. Don't they?"

"*Cost* them money?" Cattoretti laughed. "My dear, my knockoffs *make* them money."

"How—do you give them a cut or something?"

"Elaine, you do not understand marketing and consumer psychology. Every time someone buys one of my knockoffs, it is a free advertisement for the genuine article. My customers cannot afford the real thing...yet."

He raised his hands. "I do not sell knockoffs, Elaine—I sell *dreams*."

He looked over the audience and smiled at another famous designer, who smiled back. "My business is not only good for the designers, but good for society as a whole. My clients feel a profound longing to own the real product, not a mere 'knockoff.' Nobody in their right mind believes they are buying a genuine five-hundred-dollar Gucci handbag for fifty dollars. The very idea is absurd. Their heartfelt desire to own the authentic product motivates them to work harder and to make more money, which is good for everybody." He motioned to her. "Surely you can appreciate that. Is it not the American way?"

"Yes, of course it is," Elaine admitted. She was beginning to admire Giorgio Cattoretti. She could learn a lot from him.

Taking her hand, he said, "The curtain is about to go up."

BOOK 3

MURDER

CHAPTER 3.1

About the time the opera started, Gene Lassiter's flight was just touching down at the Milan Airport. He was flying under false ID, which he used to rent a car.

Using the many secure resources he had at his disposal, he had already traced the location of the GPS to a castle east of Milan, and he already knew a good deal about the owner, a Mr. Giorgio Cattoretti. One of the things he had learned was that Mr. Cattoretti was one of the benefactors at La Scala, and he also learned there was a premiere at the theater tonight.

As soon as he was on the outskirts of Milan, he pulled over and called Gypsy. He was supposed to be in Berlin yesterday, and Gypsy was probably mad.

When the cellphone rang, Gypsy was luxuriously reclined on a canopied bed in an expensive apartment in Berlin, reading a German copy of *Cosmopolitan*.

"Where have you been?" Gypsy said. "I've been waiting for your message for twenty-four hours."

"I had a snag," Lassiter said. "But I'm almost finished with my little project. Please be patient, my love."

"I think I've been patient enough," Gypsy said, gazing out the window at the depressing weather. The city was engulfed by low-hanging gray clouds, the streets wet with a tedious drizzle that had been going on for a week. "You aren't the only fish in the sea, you know."

"Please don't be like that, my darling. You know that no one cares for you as much as I do. If all goes well, we can meet tomorrow."

"Where?" Gypsy said skeptically.

"How does Milan sound?"

"Italy?"

"Yes, my darling."

"Well..." This was sounding better. "Why don't I just come now? I can do some shopping and—"

"No!" Lassiter said. "I'll let you know exactly when and where in a few hours." He made some disgusting kissing noises in the phone. "I can't wait to see you."

"Yeah," Gypsy said. "Don't call me anymore—only send text messages. Dieter is getting suspicious."

"Of course. I just had to hear your voice, my precious."

"I understand," Gypsy said.

Dieter entered the bedroom. Gypsy quickly cut the connection.

"Who was that?"

"None of your business," Gypsy snapped.

Dieter just stood there in his stupid PROST! apron, gazing like a hurt puppy.

"When will dinner be ready?" Gypsy said.

"Soon, *schatz.*"

"I hope we are not having Koenigsberger Klopse again. I'm tired of that."

"No, *schatz*! I am making Schweinshaxe tonight." He smiled. "Your favorite."

Gypsy grimaced. German food was such a bore, and so were German men. It was high time for a change. Dieter's coffers had been drained dry. He had spent every last Euro he had on expensive clothes and jewelry. It was time for Gypsy to find a new benefactor. Gene Lassiter promised to deliver a long and fruitful run. The aging American had agreed to buy a beautiful house in Switzerland, no strings attached, where Gypsy could live in a fitting lifestyle. Gene Lassiter planned to keep his job at the U.S. Treasury for a few more years, which meant he wouldn't be around much. That would leave plenty of time for Gypsy to find more appealing—and financially generous—lovers.

Dieter was just standing there in his apron, pouting.

Gypsy rose from the bed and sat down at the Louis XV vanity, a birthday present from Dieter. The robe split, revealing Gypsy's smooth, freshly waxed legs.

Dieter stared.

"Call me when dinner is ready," Gypsy ordered. "I think I'll do my nails."

Half an hour later, a nondescript sedan pulled up at the guard house at Castello Fontanella.

The driver's window rolled down as the guard on duty came out to the car.

"I have an appointment with Mr. Cattoretti," the man said in English.

The guard peered into the car—no one else was inside. The man looked fairly old, in his sixties. A cane lay across the front seat, the handle in the shape of a horse's head. It looked expensive.

"*Signore* Cattoretti not here, sir."

"I know that. He's at the opera right now, but he told me to come here and wait for him."

"What is your name, *signore?*"

"Malcolm Price. I am one of DayPrinto's best customers, a personal friend of Giorgio's."

"*Un momento.*"

The guard went back into the building and looked at his list. There was no Malcolm Price on it. Glancing back at the car, he called Luigi.

"There's a man here at Fontanella who says he has an appointment with your father."

"Who is he?"

"Malcolm Price."

"Never heard of him."

"Says he's a DayPrinto customer."

"I said I've never heard of him."

"What do you want me to do?"

"Get rid of him," Luigi said, and hung up.

The guard hesitated, looking back down at the list. Giorgio Cattoretti would be very upset if this man was a close friend. Cattoretti was exacting about how guests were treated.

Better to call Tony.

"Send him in," Tony said, after the guard explained. "I will entertain him until the boss gets back."

Tony seated Mr. Price in the Great Hall. The man was very well dressed and seemed distinguished and sophisticated.

"Would you like something to eat or drink?" Tony said. "You like-a Chianti? We have some new from a winery down in Tuscan, it's-a very nice."

"Chianti will be fine," the guest said, with a warm smile. With a trembling hand on his cane, he glanced around the room's vast interior. "This is incredible. I've been to DayPrinto many times, but I have never been to this castle before. Giorgio said I would be impressed, and I certainly am."

"*Si*," Tony said, pleased. "Maybe you want some *gnocchi* with truffle? I made it this afternoon."

"No, no, I don't want to trouble you."

"Oh, it's-a no trouble, believe me! I bring you *pronto*."

As Tony returned to the kitchen, he thought, *Such a nice, well-mannered gentleman. It's a pity he's ill.*

Tony brought the *gnocchi* out on a silver serving tray, along with a selection of their best cheese.

The aging man took one bite of the gnocchi, and his eyes closed.

"*Signore*—are you all right?"

The eyes slowly opened and he started chewing again, an ecstatic look on his face. "My god...this is the best *gnocchi* I've ever tasted!" He stared at Tony in awe. "And *you're* the one who made it?"

Twenty minutes later, Tony was proudly showing Mr. Price around the inside of the castle. When they went upstairs, he stopped in front of Cattoretti's bedroom.

"Is that...no! It can't be! An *original* Monet?"

"*Si*, it is original. But *Signore* Cattoretti, he don't like..."

It was too late. The guest had already entered the bedroom. He hobbled over to the Monet painting. Leaning on his cane, he started inspecting it closely.

"Incredible." He glanced at Tony. "Did you know, Claude Monet is one of my favorite artists?"

"*Si*," Tony said uneasily, glancing back at the door. He didn't want to be rude, but the bedroom was off limits to everyone—he wasn't even allowed in here himself. Signore Cattoretti would blow his top if he knew.

"Oh, no!" Mr. Price said. "It looks like something splashed on the corner here." He pointed.

Tony leaned closer. "Where?"

Suddenly there was a gun barrel thrust into his side. "Move and I'll blow a hole in you, you prissy faggot."

CHAPTER 3.2

It was after midnight when Elaine and Cattoretti left the theater.

The whole evening had been like a dream. After the opera had ended, Cattoretti took Elaine backstage. She met Andrea Bocelli and other members of the cast in person. It was thrilling to meet him—he had a larger than life presence, even more so than when he was on the stage.

Elaine had been to the opera before, in Washington, and the performances were moving, but nothing compared to what she had witnessed this evening. Seeing *Madame Butterfly* at La Scala, the very theater where Puccini's masterpiece had premiered over a hundred years ago, and cast with some of the best performers in the world, was an experience she would never forget.

When the Rolls Royce turned down the road that led to Castello Fontanella, Cattoretti was holding her hand, stroking it, still talking about the opera. She knew that he wanted to sleep with her tonight—it was obvious. She wondered if he considered that "part of the deal." And she wondered what would happen if she resisted.

"Did you live in America once?" Elaine asked curiously.

Cattoretti raised an eyebrow. "Yes I did. Why?"

"Your English," she said. "It's perfect."

"Thank you, *cara*. But I would rather not discuss my time in the United States." He absently touched the scar on his cheek. "It was a very long time ago, and I am a different person now."

As they turned down the driveway, he squeezed her hand and said, "Before we move ahead with our plan, there is an understanding we must have between each other."

"What's that?" she said uneasily.

Cattoretti turned and looked into her eyes. "You must reveal to me every defect you see in my money, Elaine. Every mistake."

"Of course I will," she said.

"No holding back, like you did today."

"No," she said, shaking her head.

"Good." Cattoretti smiled, and he stroked her hand. "I would consider anything less a betrayal."

When the Rolls Royce passed the guard house, Cattoretti turned sharply and peered at it. No one was inside. The front gate was wide open.

Cattoretti said something to the driver, concerned. There was a brief exchange. Cattoretti looked angry.

As the car pulled into the courtyard, Tony came running out the kitchen door, his face white as chalk. Cattoretti got out of the car. Tony was talking rapidly in Italian, waving his hands, apologizing for something. He looked terrified. Elaine couldn't understand a word.

Cattoretti brushed past him and went inside the Castle.

"What happened?" Elaine asked Tony.

"Oh, Tony in big trouble! Tony in *molto* trouble!" He skittered back into the kitchen, wringing his hands.

Elaine found Cattoretti standing in the Great Hall, yelling at his son. Luigi was looking at the floor, ashamed.

"*Sciocco!*" Cattoretti shouted, and slapped him. "*Perchè non mi avete telefonato?*"

Luigi said something to defend himself. Cattoretti pulled his cellphone from his pocket. Elaine remembered that he had switched it off when the opera started, but he hadn't pulled it from his pocket since.

So angry he didn't even see Elaine, he turned and trotted up the marble staircase, leaving his son standing there with stinging red cheeks.

Elaine started to ask Luigi what happened, but when she saw the look on his face, she changed her mind.

She slowly went upstairs and cautiously entered Cattoretti's bedroom. She had not seen it before, as the door had been closed when Tony had shown her around the castle. All the furniture in the room was turned over, drawers scattered everywhere.

Cattoretti was standing in front of the open door of a wall safe. There were bundles of money inside—he was counting through it.

"*Merda!*" he hissed. He slammed the heavy iron door shut.

"What happened?" Elaine said.

Cattoretti whirled around, his eyes seething with rage. "He took your money, that is what happened! Eight million goddam Euros!"

"Who took it?" Elaine said, dumbfounded.

"Gene Lassiter!"

Elaine was shocked, and she looked around the room. Lassiter had gotten into the castle?

"But...how?"

"That idiot Tony let him in here," Cattoretti said, running his hand through his hair. "I...I cannot believe it—he just walked right into my house and walked away with millions!"

Elaine looked back at the safe. "But how did he open—"

"I keep the damn combination on a piece of paper under a desk drawer. I am a bigger fool than my son." He ran his hand through his hair again. "I never thought anyone could get past all the..." His mouth still open, he looked suspiciously at Elaine. "How did Lassiter find me?"

She backed away slightly. She didn't like the cast in his eye.

"I have no idea how he found you."

"To find me, he must have found *you*."

Cattoretti's arm shot out and grabbed her wrist. "How did he know where you were?"

"You're hurting me," Elaine said, yanking her arm free.

Cattoretti kept looking at her, but suddenly his expression changed. "Your suitcase!"

He briskly walked out of the room and down the stairs. Elaine followed along, but lagged far enough behind to stay out of his reach. He went through the ground floor and up into the East Tower, to the bedroom.

Glancing around the room, he spotted her suitcase. He picked it up and threw it on the bed, then began rifling through it, unzipping pockets, roughly pulling items out, tossing them this way and that. The little wind-up turkey Nick had given her hit the stone floor.

"What are you looking for?" Elaine said, picking it up.

Cattoretti found something in the lining. Pulling out a pocket knife, he made a small slit in the fabric. The object was a little black box the size of a small makeup compact.

"What is it?" Elaine said.

"A GPS tracker," he said, peering closely at it. He dropped it on the stone floor, then stomped on it with his heel. It shattered to pieces, electronics spilling out on the stones.

He looked at her accusingly.

"I had no idea it was there," Elaine said. "Lassiter must have hidden it there when he put the data key in my suitcase."

Cattoretti just stared at her, breathing hard, the air whistling though his nostrils.

"Do you think—do you think I would actually be in *cahoots* with Gene Lassiter?"

Cattoretti stared at her another moment, then his anger suddenly faded. "No, of course not." He reached for her, and she flinched.

"I'm not going to hurt you," he said, gently touching her upper arm.

Elaine swallowed. She hadn't realized how afraid she had been.

He ran his hand through his hair again. "It is just that I have never had anyone come into my own house before and do something like this..." He looked at the window. "It makes me feel like all my security here is a joke! Jesus Christ—what do I pay those people for? And that goddam Tony—"

"I'm sure it wasn't Tony's fault."

Cattoretti looked at her again, and sighed. "No, of course you are right. It is not Tony's fault, he is like a child." Cattoretti looked down at her hand—she was still clutching the little wind-up turkey. One of the plastic feet had broken off.

He reached for it, but she moved it away.

"Sentimental value?" he asked, when she looked back at him.

"Yes." For some reason, she didn't want him to touch it.

After he left the room, she glanced at the Chopard necklace on the dresser, and then at the little gadget in her hand. It was ironic, she thought, that a broken toy an orphan would likely toss aside meant more than all the expensive gifts in the world.

When Cattoretti went back downstairs, he poured himself a cognac to calm his nerves. He pulled a Cuban cigar from the humidor in the Great Hall and then went outside and took a slow stroll around the courtyard, as he often did before he went to bed. The cool air relaxed him and cleared his mind.

He paused by the drinking well, looking up at the window in the East Tower, where Elaine Brogan was sleeping.

Did you live in America once? she had asked.

Giorgio Cattoretti absently touched the scar on his face, and he remembered when he had decided to move to the United States.

CHAPTER 3.3

Cattoretti grew up in the Cinecittà or "Cinema City" section of Rome, where the Italian film industry was located. While Frederico Fellini and his peers may have made their masterpieces in Cinecittà, there was nothing else glamorous about the suburb. Giorgio grew up in a microscopic two room flat that housed his parents and his four brothers and sisters. His father was a bricklayer and his mother worked in a shoe factory.

Giorgio was the eldest. By age 13, he was roaming the streets, desperately trying to find a way out, any way out.

One hot summer afternoon he slipped into the side door of an air-conditioned cinema, merely to escape the heat. What he saw on the big silver screen by chance on that sultry afternoon changed his life forever. The film was *The Godfather*. It had just taken Italy by storm. Giorgio had of course seen plenty of gangster movies before, but the splendor in which the fictitious Corleone family thrived in America left Giorgio utterly awed. To the young and impressionable Italian, the characters in the story were all real people—Michael and Sonny and Fredo and Don Vito—living thrilling, dangerous, fascinating lives in New York City...the complete antithesis of the hopeless future Cattoretti saw stretched out in front of him.

Giorgio saw the movie a total of 16 times, until the manager caught him and threatened to turn him in to the police. He became obsessed with Americans and all things American. He began reading everything he could get his hands on about the United States, and he soon fully grasped the concept of the ubiquitous American Dream. It seemed that anyone could go to "the land of the free"—anyone of any race, creed, or culture—and become anything he or she wanted to be. There were no limits.

This prompted him to apply himself at school, particularly to his English language classes, with the fuzzy idea of somehow moving to the USA when he finished and making the big time.

He began to imitate Americans, to dress like Americans, to mimic their various regional accents—Texas, New York, Midwest. He watched American movies and TV shows, even the soap operas, paying fine attention to every detail. He soaked it up like a sponge—he told himself that everything he learned might be useful in the future, when he went to the USA.

Giorgio took any part-time job he could get and began to save his money in order to achieve his ambition. He mainly washed dishes, delivered groceries, swept floors. Every now and then he was lucky enough to get a job as an extra in a movie that was shooting an exterior scene in Cinecittà. One was a Fellini film, and he actually met Frederico Fellini himself, for a fleeting instant. A stack of movie posters was nearby, and Giorgio grabbed one and got the director to sign it for him. It became Cattoretti's most prized possession.

The only thing he spent any money on was clothes. He saw himself as a younger version of Michael Corleone—he actually favored Al Pacino, his friends said, with his trim build and swarthy good looks.

"You dress like a gangster," his mother often said.

"I dress like an American, mama."

"American, American, American," she muttered, her hands on her broad hips. "Would you explain to me what's wrong with being Italian?"

Giorgio would look at her helplessly. She simply didn't understand.

Whenever he could afford it, he would take the bus over to the ultra-chic Via Veneto area to watch all the beautiful, well-dressed women. He would find a prime seat at the Gran Caffe Doney or the Caffe Busse and order a single Negroni, sipping it as slowly as possible, taking in the action until one of the waiters would finally shoo him off.

The women he saw there were incredible. Dressed in the latest fashions out of Milan, they would sashay up and down the street, chatting with each other in reserved tones, window shopping, or sitting at the outdoor tables for cappuccinos, their long, well-pampered legs crossed demurely—women from all over the world, the most beautiful and richest and well-educated dames one could imagine. He loved to inhale their combined fragrance.

The heady, sweet aroma of *class*...

Giorgio knew he was nothing to these exquisite female specimens, just a scruffy teenage boy with a square jaw, dark eyes, and a pleasant face. He would often catch their gaze, and sometimes there would be a fleeting instant of provocative eye contact, but the next second they would notice the rest of him, his cheap double-breasted jacket and pointed, two-tone shoes, and they would look away as if he were lower than dirt itself.

He assured himself that one day, after he moved to America and built his empire, he would have scores of such women. He would marry one and have children with her, and then keep three or four more as mistresses, like Michael Corleone. He would be so rich and so handsome and so worldly that such women would be almost disposable to him, like cigarettes. Smoke it and toss the butt aside.

When Giorgio was 17, his dream finally began to materialize.

An uncle who had immigrated to the USA returned to Cinecittà for a short visit. Silvio Lombardi was a ferret-faced, pot-bellied man who had grown up in a village near Pescara. Giorgio only knew him as Uncle Silvio. He had entered the USA illegally and owned some sort of import business in Manhattan. Giorgio was sure that the business was a cover, and that Uncle Silvio was a Mafioso as big as Don Corleone. He wore pinstripe suits with gold cufflinks and smoked thick cigars. He had to be Mafia.

Silvio immediately took a liking to Giorgio, who would only address him in English.

"So, you like-a America, Giorgio?" he said one day, puffing on a cigar.

"Of course I do. I'd give anything to go there!"

"You speak-a English almost good as me. How you speak-a English so fine?"

Giorgio shrugged. "Cinema."

Silvio sized him up. "You find your way to America yourself, I help-a you when you-a get there. I give you a job." He produced a slim silver box from his sport coat and handed Giorgio a business card.

Silvio never expected to see his restless young nephew again.

He had grossly underestimated Giorgio Cattoretti.

Three months later, Giorgio was standing at the door of his family's squalid little Cinecittà apartment, a scuffed up suitcase in his hand. His mother and father were both slumped on the couch, watching TV.

Imitating Michael Corleone, he said in English, "Uncle Silvio made me an offer I can't refuse."

His mother and father looked blankly at each other.

Neither one understood a word of English.

The cargo ship, called *Bianca*, was docked in Trieste. Cattoretti not only had to pay the captain the equivalent of $1,000 in lire for the privilege of being a stowaway, but was expected to work alongside the other deck crew aboard the aging vessel while it was out on the open seas.

The ship cast off early in the morning. With dry eyes, Giorgio watched the Italian shoreline slide by as the huge container vessel chugged its way south through the Adriatic Sea, around the tip of the "boot" of Southern Italy.

"Good riddance," he muttered to himself, as the last glimpse of his motherland sank into the sparkling blue-green waters of the Mediterranean.

The *Bianca* carried an international crew of merchant marines, and to Cattoretti's delight, everyone communicated in English. The captain assigned a young, brawny blonde-haired Swede named Anders to show Cattoretti the ropes. Which Anders did, literally.

The first day he taught his young apprentice how to make several of the most common seaman's knots—the reef, timber hitch, bowline, the sheet bend. Cattoretti found the deck work was exhausting—painting, splicing broken lines, mopping—but he loved every minute of it.

Cattoretti found the container ship and all the equipment fascinating. He asked Anders endless questions about it. The Swede was enthusiastic about his vocation and only too happy to oblige—he was an Ordinary Seaman diligently working towards his Able Seaman certificate and hoped to be a ship captain someday.

"How big is this ship compared to other container ships?" Giorgio asked.

"Relatively small. The *Bianca* has a length of one hundred sixty-two meters, a breadth of twenty-three meters, and a TEU of eleven hundred—"

"What is TEU?"

"Ton equivalent unit. A standard forty-foot container equals two TEUs. Which means this ship can hold about five hundred fifty containers."

By the end of the week-long trip, Cattoretti's brain was overflowing with detailed information about the ship and its operation. He filed it all away in his head—it might be useful later.

One night, while they were gazing out across the dark water, Anders said, "So, Giorgio, someday are you planning to work aboard a container ship?"

"No," Cattoretti said. "I'm planning on owning a whole fleet of them."

As they neared the Eastern coast of the USA, they encountered a terrible squall. The *Bianca* was tossed about like a cork all night long. Cattoretti was deathly sick, and threw up over and over again into a steel pail.

The storm finally broke at dawn, and the waters were mercifully calm at last.

Giorgio took the pail up to deck to empty overboard. When he wandered around to the stern of the ship, he noticed that a couple of steel cables were running from the top of the rearmost container stack out into the water. The cables were taut, vibrating every now and then.

Cattoretti looked up and saw that there was a gap in the stack of containers—one of them was missing.

He scrambled back up to the bow and told Anders.

"Container overboard!" Anders shouted, "Container overboard!"

The captain brought the great ship to a halt. Using the crane, it took the crew over an hour to get the rectangular iron box back onboard and strapped into place.

"It's a good thing you noticed," Anders said, when they were underway again. "We might have hauled that damn thing through the water all the way to New York."

"Nobody would have felt the drag on the ship?" Cattoretti said.

"Are you kidding? The engine on this vessel is so powerful the drag would be negligible."

As the *Bianca* entered the New York Harbor, Giorgio climbed into his cramped hiding place, behind a false wall in an anchor storage compartment.

When they passed Governor's Island, Giorgio managed to peek out a porthole and glimpse the Statue of Liberty.

The sight of the monument he'd seen so many times in pictures gave him goose bumps. *Give me your tired, your poor, your huddled masses...*

Giorgio may have been poor, but he wasn't tired, nor was he part of any "huddled masses." He was destined for great things. The United States of America—the land of opportunity—was going to give them to him.

Soon, he would step off the ship and set foot in America.

Soon, he would be an American.

CHAPTER 3.4

Uncle Silvio was shocked when Cattoretti showed up on his doorstop, but kept his promise and took his nephew in. He let Giorgio sleep on the sofa in the living room of his cluttered apartment. He arranged for a fake birth certificate and driver's license for his surprisingly resourceful young relative.

Cattoretti soon learned that his pot-bellied uncle was hardly Don Corleone, just a two-bit criminal among thousands in the sprawling metropolis of New York City. Silvio was into "a little of this, a little of that." He sold fake Rolex watches, operated a small escort service out of the apartment, supplied "actresses and actors" for a small-time porno movie producer, dealt a little cocaine, and, of late, had "diversified" into making fake documents, such as college diplomas and Social Security cards.

There was always a girl staying in the apartment. When Cattoretti arrived, it was a bleach-bottle blonde who called herself "Fantasia." She was in one of the films Silvio was producing. She had a large tattoo on her lower back, needle tracks on her arms, and silicon breasts the size of basketballs.

One night Cattoretti woke up with her kneeling beside the couch, groping under the blanket for his cock. When she touched it he gasped, and despite his best efforts, he found himself erect. The next thing he knew the girl was squatting in front of him, giving him a blowjob.

In the middle of all this, Silvio opened the bedroom door and walked by in his ratty bathrobe and slippers. He merely glanced at them and continued to the kitchen.

A moment later, he returned, eating a pastrami sandwich. He paused, watching as if distracted by something mildly interesting on television. After a moment he went back into the bedroom and shut the door.

Cattoretti tossed and turned on the sofa all night, wondering what his uncle would do to him the next morning.

To his surprise, when he went into the kitchen for breakfast, Silvio set a cup of coffee in front of him and chuckled. "You're hung like a horse, Giorgio. You wanna be in one of my porno movies?"

Giorgio Cattoretti was not interested in being a porno star. He wanted to become a rich and powerful Mafioso, like the characters in *The Godfather*.

He started by selling fake watches for his uncle. Silvio had carved out a humble slice of the counterfeit Rolex business in lower Manhattan, but the Mafia was getting into the same market. Things were beginning to heat up. Silvio had spent several years developing his own source for the product, two nervous Taiwanese importers who received the fake watches directly from the Far East.

Giorgio was very good at recruiting new salesmen and training them to sell the watches on the street.

Their problem was that they could not bring in large enough quantities to compete with the Mafia. The Mafia controlled all the docks in the New York area. At the moment, Silvio and his Taiwanese partners were paying people to smuggle the watches into the country on commercial flights, inside suitcases.

One night when they were all having dinner at an Italian restaurant, Cattoretti said, "Why don't you just bring a whole damn container of them over?"

"How we get past custom?" one of the Taiwanese said. "You such a boy-genius."

"Easy." Giorgio remembered the experience he'd had on the voyage over. "You can drag a container behind the ship."

The men all laughed. "What the fuck you talk about? Drag container behind ship. You drink too much whiskey, boy!"

They all laughed again.

Pulling a pen from his pocket, Giorgio picked up a napkin and started making a sketch. "If you build a container like this, with tapered sides, you can haul it behind the ship. Then, when the ship comes into the New York harbor, you can pick up the container with a motorboat and take it somewhere else to unload it."

The three men looked at each other.

They were no longer laughing.

The importers had the special submersible container made in Taiwan. Completely waterproof and welded together with iron plates, it was tapered on both ends to keep drag to a minimum. There was a single, sealed hatch used for loading and unloading. It looked like a huge gray cigar.

The first run from Taiwan went flawlessly. The container ship dragged the "cigar" into the harbor, and Silvio and Cattoretti easily snagged it by passing behind the ship in a large, rented motorboat.

They hauled the container to a remote spot on the Jersey shore, and then transferred all the merchandise to a waiting truck. The container was filled with water and sunk, the location marked with a small fishing float. It was later dragged back to Taiwan behind the same boat and used again.

Within a few months, Silvio's fake Rolex business was thriving. He was making more money from that than all his other businesses combined.

"You're doin' good, Giorgio," he said. "I'm gonna make you a partner."

Several more months went by, and Giorgio soon understood that Silvio had no intention of making him a partner.

And Cattoretti had no intention of wasting any more brilliant ideas on his greedy, ungrateful uncle.

Two nights before a new shipment was due to arrive in New York, Cattoretti deliberately carried a small box of watches into Times Square, which he knew was controlled by the Mafia. It wasn't long before he felt a hand grab him by the back of the collar. He was dragged into an alley and slammed up against a brick wall, the hand holding him by the throat. The box fell on the ground, some of the watches spilling out onto the pavement.

"What the fuck do you think you're doing?" the man said. He had a face like a bulldog.

"I want to make a deal with your boss," Cattoretti grunted. "I have something to sell."

The bulldog laughed, sending his garlic breath into Cattoretti's face.

"I know where you can get a whole container of fake Rolexes."

The thug let Cattoretti slide down the wall until his feet touched the pavement. He picked up one of the watches. It was a new model, one that had not been sold in New York before—a copy of a Rolex Sea Dweller.

He raised an eyebrow and looked at Cattoretti.

Half an hour later, Cattoretti entered an abandoned warehouse in the garment district.

"Siddown," the bulldog-faced man said, shoving Cattoretti into a chair that was bolted to the floor.

There was nothing in the musty room but a rickety wooden table and a few folding chairs. Beer bottles and cigarette butts were scattered across the concrete. There were dark, sticky spots that could have been dried blood. Cattoretti tried not to look at them.

A tall, olive-skinned man entered the room, an expensive-looking wool coat draped around his shoulders. He wore black leather gloves and smoked a long, slim cigar.

He puffed on the smoke, appraising the young Italian.

This guy is the real thing, Cattoretti thought. He had a feeling it was Joey Russo, a powerful Mafia kingpin who had a big stake in the fake Rolex trade.

"Vito tells me you know somethin' about a container of watches, and you want to make some kinda deal."

"That's right," Cattoretti said.

He snickered. "You got balls kid, I give you that. Punk like you, wantin' to make a deal with Joey Russo. Don't he got balls, Vito?" He made a gesture with his hand. "Balls like a fuckin' stallion."

Vito chuckled.

Russo picked up one of the fake Rolexes and inspected it, turning it back and forth under the bare light bulb. "Not bad. Where are the rest?"

"I'll sell you that information."

Russo started laughing, revealing fine teeth, like a barracuda's. "You talk shit, kid. You know how I know you talk shit? Because I got my finger on every import channel in New York. There ain't no fuckin' way a whole container of watches comes in without me knowin' about it."

"It's coming," Cattoretti said.

"Yeah?" Russo looked back at the watch.

Cattoretti remained silent.

Vito grabbed him by the collar, but Russo stopped him.

"How much you want for this info, kid?"

"Five thousand. Half in advance, and half after you get the watches."

Russo glanced at Vito, then studied Cattoretti's young, determined face for a moment, smoking his cigar. He pulled out his wallet.

"Boss, I don't think we—"

"I don't pay you to think, Vito."

Russo counted out 25 crisp one-hundred-dollar bills and handed them over.

Cattoretti pocketed the money, looking nervously at the two men. "Take me to a public place. I'll tell you where you can pick up the watches."

They drove Cattoretti to an Italian restaurant on the Lower East Side, and he told them the route that the truck would take after it was loaded on the Jersey shore. He did not tell them how the watches were brought in from Taiwan. When Russo asked, he claimed he didn't know. He was saving that for later.

Cattoretti used the cash to check into a decent hotel in midtown, where he was continuously watched. The next morning, he went shopping and bought himself a tailored suit, much like the one Joey Russo wore.

He was followed everywhere he went.

At about 11 pm the next evening, Russo's men stopped Silvio's truck and hijacked it, leaving Silvio and two of his helpers dumbfounded in the street.

That night, Joey Russo waited for the other shoe to drop. He didn't know which of the other New York families he had hit, but he knew they would retaliate.

Nothing happened.

"Who the fuck does this kid work for?" Russo said, looking from one face to another. Vito and several of his other men were sitting in his office.

"He don't work for Conti, I checked," Vito said.

"Not for Morella, either. I know every one of his guys."

"Then who?" Russo said. "Maybe one of the Vegas families is runnin' this?"

"Nah," Vito said. "They don't deal in Chink watches."

Joey Russo and his men were baffled. The truckload of watches they had stolen seemed to have dropped out of the sky.

The next day he and Vito came to Cattoretti's hotel room. They didn't knock.

"Nice threads, kid," Russo said, handing him the remaining $2,500 and admiring the new suit. "With my help, you could go places. Now, you gonna tell me who you work for? It ain't one of the gangs here in Manhattan, I know it for a fuckin' fact."

Cattoretti said nothing. He and his uncle were so small, and so unknown, that in the overall scheme of things, they were anonymous. In this case, his insignificance was working in his favor.

Russo motioned to him. "Okay, what about the watches? You gonna tell me how they come in here?"

"I told you, I don't know," Cattoretti said. The submersible container smuggling idea was far too valuable to hand over free of charge. He planned to sell it to them, too, just like the information about the truck. But for a much higher price. "I might be able to find out if you guys back off, give me some breathing room. I think they're using a new smuggling method."

Russo and Vito glanced at each other.

"'New method'? Whaddya mean?"

Cattoretti shrugged. "Something clever that's never been done before. Something to do with container ships."

Russo looked at Vito. "Do you believe this kid?" He motioned to Cattoretti. "A cockroach don't so much as fart over on those docks without me knowin' about it. In fact, they ask permission. Am I right, Vito?"

"They ask permission," Vito said.

"So when you talk about some 'new method', you're talkin' shit, kid."

"I was right about the truck, wasn't I?"

Joey Russo sighed, glancing at his sidekick. "Okay, kid, you win. Come on Vito, let's give him some breathing room."

Giorgio Cattoretti spent a stressful few days trying to figure out what to do. He knew he was in over his head. He didn't have a plan. The fact was, he had no idea what he was doing. The money he'd been paid wouldn't last much longer. His uncle was after him for selling him out to

Russo. And it was only a matter of time before Russo found out who Silvio was—a nobody. Then Cattoretti knew he would be in deep trouble. They would beat the information about the submersible container out of him, and probably kill him. And Silvio, too.

He decided to go talk to Russo again.

"I've changed my mind," he said, after he was frisked and ushered into Russo's office.

The gangster rose slowly from his desk. "What are you talkin' about? We had a deal."

"We still have a deal. But I don't want to be paid with money."

"What do you want to be paid with?" Russo said suspiciously.

"I want a job in your organization. A good job."

Russo and Vito looked at each other.

"Not a bagman, either. Something important."

Russo studied him a moment, then walked around from behind his desk. Cattoretti's pulse quickened.

Russo warmly put an arm around his shoulder.

"I'm flattered, kid, you want to come work for me." He looked at Vito. "Makes me feel like a fuckin' role model." He patted Cattoretti on the back. "You get me the info I'm waitin' on, I'd be glad to find you a place within my organization. We got plenty of spots. Right Vito?"

"Well, yeah, sure boss."

When Cattoretti left, Vito said, "What'd you tell him that for?"

Russo shrugged. "Keep him motivated."

An hour after Cattoretti left, one of Russo's men came into the office.

"I found out who the kid is."

"Who?"

"Name's Giorgio Cattoretti. Traced him through a guy makes fake driver's licenses. He works for his uncle, guy named Silvio Lombardi."

"Silvio Lombardi? Never heard of him."

"That ain't a surprise. The guy's a nobody. Makes porno movies, has a two-bit escort service on the Lower East Side. He's nothin', boss."

Russo puffed on his cigar, thinking.

The next day, when Cattoretti returned to his hotel after dinner, he noticed two well-groomed men in suits sitting in the lobby.

When he stepped onto the elevator, both of them rose from their chairs and headed towards him.

As the elevator went up to the third floor, his heart beat furiously. With a little luck, he could get away by climbing down the fire escape from his room.

When he stepped off the elevator and unlocked the door, he found two more men waiting for him.

There was a satchel on the bed he'd never seen before, sitting wide open. Five fake Rolex Sea Dwellers were in it, still in their boxes.

Silvio. His goddam uncle had framed him. Who else would have put them there? He had no other enemies in New York.

"FBI," one of the men said, flashing a badge.

The other patted him down.

"You're under arrest, you stupid Dago."

Giorgio Cattoretti was taken to Midtown North Precinct Station. He found himself surrounded by the lowest flanks of humanity— prostitutes, pimps, drug dealers, muggers and their victims.

He was photographed, fingerprinted, and booked for two separate crimes: trafficking illegal merchandise and violating U.S. immigration law. Both were felonies. A desk sergeant kindly informed him that he faced a sentence of up to five years in prison.

He did not take advantage of his right to one telephone call. There was nobody to phone.

He was led into the courtroom before a stern-looking female judge. The Hispanic woman peered down at him from the bench as if he were an insect. Cattoretti heard the words float past him as she talked to the arresting agents. "The State is requesting—" "—recommend that bail be set—" "trafficking counterfeit Rolexes—"

The judge was asking him a question.

"What?" he said dully.

"I said, are you represented by counsel?"

Cattoretti stared blankly up at the woman. The words meant nothing to him. His life was over.

"Do you have a lawyer?" she said.

"Lawyer? Um, no."

"Then the court will appoint one for you. You are ordered held in jail, in lieu of one hundred thousand dollars bail." She banged the gavel down. "Next case."

Cattoretti had no recollection of being led to the cell.

Cattoretti plunged into a state of utter despair. Only eight months in America, and already arrested! And with nowhere to turn for help.

His life was down the sewer.

Sometime early the next morning, the cell door clanged open. Cattoretti was curled into a ball on his bunk.

A clean-cut young man in a blue pinstripe suit entered. A briefcase was in one hand, a small metal folding chair in the other.

"Hello, Mr. Cattoretti," he said, sitting down. "I'm Stephen Petit, your court-appointed attorney. You want to tell me what happened?"

Cattoretti looked into the man's eyes. Suddenly, some survival instinct took over.

"He forced me to do it," Cattoretti blurted, on the verge of tears.

"Who forced you?"

"My uncle. He—he said if I could find a way to get to America, he would give me a job. I had no idea he was a criminal." Cattoretti started to blubber, but checked himself, pretending to be ashamed. "He t-told me I had to sell the watches, or he would throw me ou-out on the street."

"Who is your uncle? What's his name?"

Cattoretti wiped his eyes. He hesitated, remembering *omertà*, the Mafia's code of silence. But Silvio wasn't in the Mafia, he was just a small-time crook, a nobody. "His name is Silvio Lombardi."

Stephen Petit came back the next day.

"Your uncle was clean," he said. "The police searched his apartment and came up empty."

I should have known he would have been prepared, Cattoretti thought. "My uncle is a snake. I never should have come to America." He started crying again.

Petit sympathetically put his hand on Cattoretti's shoulder. "Look, you're just a young guy who's been taken advantage of. I've already spoken to the DA. He isn't interested in ruining your life—what he's interested in is stopping all these fake Rolexes from pouring into the city. He's under a lot of pressure from the mayor. It's bad for tourism—people buy those watches around Times Square, get ripped off, complain to the police." He paused. "If you could give them something to go on, something that would lead them to the *source* of these watches..."

Cattoretti hesitated. It was his only bargaining chip. "I...I'm not sure."

Petit leaned forward confidentially. "Look, I know how it is with Italians, Giorgio, with Silvio being family and all. But you've got to look out for yourself. America is dog-eat-dog, especially in New York City. If you know who's sourcing your uncle's watches, I can cut you a deal with the judge. You can plead guilty and get off with six months, and the sentence will be suspended. You won't serve a day behind bars."

Cattoretti didn't understand the American legal system. To plead guilty sounded dangerous.

"Are you sure about this?"

"Of course I'm sure about it, I'm your attorney. It's called a plea bargain, it's done every day. You change your plea to guilty and spill where the watches come from, and you're off the hook. Nobody is interested in punishing small fry like you—our prisons are overcrowded as it is." Petit motioned to him. "You look the judge in the eye and say you made a mistake, you're sorry, that you learned your lesson. It's your first time—that's all he needs to justify letting you off with a slap on the wrist."

Cattoretti swallowed.

There was a distinguished-looking man seated on the bench in the courtroom. He had a craggy face and thick, styled hair. He looked down at Cattoretti.

"The court has been informed that the defendant wishes to change his plea from not guilty to guilty," he said. "Is that correct?"

"Yes, Your Honor."

The judge looked at the others. "All parties in agreement?"

Stephen Petit nodded. "Yes, Your Honor."

"The State agrees, Your Honor," the district attorney said.

A wave of relief passed over Cattoretti.

The judge looked down at him, silent for a long moment. "One reason this city is such a cesspool of crime is due to people like you, vermin who enter the country illegally and then prey on our good citizenry, selling them counterfeit goods, drugs, and God knows what else. People who thumb their nose at the laws of this great country. People who have no respect for honest, decent Americans." The judge's voice trembled with righteousness. "There are some judicial systems which coddle such people. In Manhattan, we punish them to the fullest extent of the law."

Cattoretti had a panicky feeling. He glanced at Stephen Petit, but the man just stood there, his hands folded, his eyes fixed on the judge.

"Giorgio Cattoretti, you were caught red handed in a hotel room with counterfeit merchandise, with a clear intent to sell said merchandise. To make an example of you, I sentence you to serve five years at the state prison in Attica, New York. After you pay your debt to society, you will be deported from the United States."

The room began to spin. Stephen Petit was calmly closing his briefcase.

"There's been a mistake!" Cattoretti shouted, as the bailiff grabbed his arm. "My lawyer lied to me...I'm innocent! I was framed by my uncle! I was framed!"

He was dragged away screaming.

For an instant, he glimpsed the face of Joey Russo, who was standing in the back of the courtroom.

There was a smile on Russo's face.

CHAPTER 3.5

The men at the Attica State Prison fought over the young, handsome Italian like horny dogs.

Life became a living hell for Cattoretti. The first few weeks he was auctioned off nightly, like a prime piece of beef. He fought the rapists tooth and nail, had his nose broken repeatedly, along with his jaw, several ribs, both wrists...but of course in the end he always lost. When things settled down, three trustees ended up sharing him, passing him from one cell to another. The only way he kept his sanity was to tell himself that he was lucky they didn't kill him.

He vowed that somehow, someday, he would get even with the three of them.

As the days turned into weeks and the weeks into months, Cattoretti developed a deep loathing for the American government and legal system. The thought that this was a country where someone could be subjected to years of nonstop torture for selling a few fake watches was unthinkable to him.

"The Land of the Free." "Liberty and justice for all." *What a joke,* he thought. The United States was just as corrupt as Italy, the judges and lawyers and criminals all paying each other off. Stephen Petit had been bought off by Joey Russo, and for all he knew, the DA had been bought off by Russo, too.

A year after Cattoretti was sentenced to prison, Joey Russo was bringing massive amounts of heroin into New York using submersible containers exactly like the one Cattoretti had designed.

Giorgio Cattoretti was released from Attica after serving two years, three months, and eight days.

Only 22 years old, he was already a broken man. He went through the deportation proceedings in a stupor.

This time, when he saw the Statue of Liberty slide by the cargo ship on his return voyage—paid for by the U.S. Department of Immigration—she seemed to be laughing at him.

CHAPTER 3.6

When Giorgio Cattoretti arrived in Italy, he felt so utterly defeated he could not bear to face his family or friends. He did not return to Cinecittà. Instead, he settled in a seedy section of Milan. He took a manual laborer position in a shoe factory, like his pitiable mother.

But Giorgio Cattoretti was a survivor. *The Cat always lands on his feet*, he told himself.

In Milan, Cattoretti observed that Italy lagged far behind the USA in the sales of fake goods, particularly knockoffs of the Italian designer clothing labels. He began to think he could carve out a healthy niche in that business sector, living in the center of the world's fashion industry. He could gain access to new designs very fast and beat his competitors to the market.

Cattoretti knew that to get into the design and production of fake clothing, he would need a base of operation, a legitimate business of some kind that could serve as a front.

In Attica, he had kept his ears open. He had learned a lot of unusual approaches to entice people to do what you wanted them to do.

After several months of research, he narrowed his choice down to one particular company, a printing outfit. It was called DayPrinto, S.p.A. and was located one hour by car east of Milan. The facilities included printing presses and a large graphics design department, along with plenty of basement and warehouse space.

This firm was owned by a 52-year-old Milan businessman named Reggio Martino. He owned a score of other companies in the area, and was a pillar of the community.

He was perfect.

Every weekday from 4 to 5 pm, Reggio Martino went to the same tearoom off the Via Torino and had a cognac and a cigar and read *Il Giorno*.

One day, when he went out the door, he ran smack into a blonde carrying a bag of groceries. Or rather, she ran into him—she wasn't watching where she was going. She fell down on the wet sidewalk, tomatoes and apples rolling in all directions.

"*Signora*, are you all right?" Reggio said, taking her hand to help her up. "I'm terribly sorry..."

"My ankle," she said, wincing. She looked up at him with big blue eyes that nearly stopped his heart.

He squatted beside her. She couldn't have been more than 16 years old. More like 14, he thought, looking at her more closely.

"Let me help you to my automobile—I'll give you a ride to the hospital." Reggio put his arm around her to support her, and guided her over to his car.

"I'm fine, really," she said, but he opened the door and helped her inside.

"Let me get your groceries," he said.

As he bent over the sidewalk, picking up the fruit and vegetables, he wondered if anyone had seen what had happened, but as far as he could tell, nobody was paying any attention because of the rain.

When Reggio got in the car, the girl was inspecting her slender, delicate ankle. It was hard for him to pull his eyes away.

"It's not broken," she said. "If you could just take me home..."

"Certainly," he said, starting the engine.

She told him where she lived. As he drove, he glanced over at her often, making polite conversation. She was from a small village in Umbria, went to secretarial school and shared a flat with her sister, who was a seamstress.

"This is a beautiful car," she said, glancing around the interior.

"Thank you," Reggio said proudly. It was a 1967 Lancia. He kept it in perfect condition.

She was massaging her ankle again, her blonde hair hiding her young face. She was stunning. Reggio asked God to help him fight the thoughts he was having.

When they reached her neighborhood—a run-down section in the northeast quarter of Milan—she guided him down several side streets. "This is where I live," she said quietly. She looked ashamed.

Reggio parked in front of the shabby building. He walked around to her door, cradling the groceries as he helped her out. They went inside the dingy entrance.

"I live on the fifth floor," she said, turning towards the stairs.

"There's no elevator?"

"No, but I can make it."

Reggio helped her up two of the steps, but it was clear that the poor girl was in terrible pain. He bent and scooped her up in his arms, trying not to grunt.

"You're very strong," she said softly, slipping her hands around his neck.

Reggio smiled. He tried not to show the strain as he carried her up flight after flight of steps. Her sweet perfume tickled his nostrils, causing the troubling but exciting thoughts again. Whenever he glanced down at her face, it seemed that there was a dreamy look in her pale blue eyes.

He felt himself getting an erection. He hated himself for it—she was a mere child!

When he reached the fifth floor, he gently set her down at her apartment entrance, breathing hard, his forehead slick with sweat.

"Thank you so much," she said, and fumbled in her purse for her key, teetering on one high-heeled shoe. She opened the door and they entered, Reggio helping her over to a grimy-looking couch.

The one-room flat was depressing, dark, and smelled of stale tobacco. There were two single beds, a battered coffee table, and a wardrobe. A terrible place for two young women to live. At least one side of the room was relatively clean and orderly—there were a few feminine knickknacks scattered around.

"Where's your sister?" Reggio asked, as he wiped his balding head with his handkerchief.

"She works nights."

"Oh." He glanced at her lovely legs as she propped them up on the table, then quickly looked away.

"Would you mind making some coffee?" she said. "You're probably thirsty, too, after carrying me up all those steps."

Reggio glanced at his watch. He needed to get home...and he didn't trust himself with her. He had slipped a few times over the years, but unlike most of the men he knew, he managed to be a faithful husband. He didn't need this temptation.

Reggio went to the microscopic kitchen nook and prepared the coffee. He poured two cups and brought them back to the living room.

"Thank you," she said gratefully, taking a sip. "Would you mind getting me some aspirin from the bathroom?"

He set his cup down and stepped into the small room. He opened the medicine cabinet, which was all but empty—only a tube of toothpaste, safety razor, and a bottle of aspirin.

Strange.

"How long have you and your sister lived here?" he called, trying not to sound suspicious.

"Just a few days. We haven't had a chance to move our things from our old flat."

"I see." If Reggio hadn't known better, he would have thought a bachelor lived here, and not a very tidy one at that.

He brought her back the aspirin. As she took one of the tablets, he picked up his coffee and sipped it. The muck tasted terrible, but he was so thirsty from his exertion he downed it in two gulps.

"Well, I really must be going," he said.

"Would you mind doing just one more thing for me before you leave?"

He sighed. "What's that?"

"Get me some ice from the refrigerator? I'd like to put some on my ankle to keep it from swelling."

Reggio stepped into the kitchen nook, retrieved some ice, wrapped it in a dishtowel, and brought it back to her.

"You're too kind," she cooed. "I'm so sorry to put you to all this trouble..."

"It's nothing."

She leaned forward, awkwardly reaching for the ankle strap on her shoe. "Can you help me...?"

Reggio swallowed hard, then knelt in front of her. Why was he doing this? He knew better.

With a shaking hand, he unfastened the strap and slipped off the high-heeled shoe. He stared at the ankle, which was only inches from his face. It didn't look the least bit swollen. In fact, it was the most beautiful ankle he had ever seen.

Suddenly there were two ankles, then three ankles, then four...

Unable to control his limbs, he fell forward and spastically collapsed on the floor.

Giorgio Cattoretti emerged from the wardrobe.

"Is he out?"

"Cold," Polina said, raising one of Reggio's eyelids. She was a 15-year-old junkie-prostitute Giorgio had found peddling her wares along Viale Renato Serra.

"Hurry up, he won't stay that way long."

As Polina stripped out of her clothes, Giorgio quickly retrieved the studio light from under the bed, set up the tripod and umbrella, then pulled out the rest of the props—a couple of teddy bears, a heart-shaped pillow, and some school books—and scattered them around.

"Get him upright," Giorgio said. They struggled to pull the unconscious man off the floor, then forced him into a kneeling position, using the arm of the couch to support him.

Polina had put on the top of the schoolgirl uniform—a white blouse and black sweater with a red monogrammed insignia. From the waist down, she was stark naked.

She seated herself on the bed directly in front of Reggio, her legs spread apart, her freshly shaved vulva only inches from his face.

Giorgio peered through the camera lens. "That's good, but put his hand on your thigh...yes. Make sure the wedding ring shows..."

A week later, Reggio was sitting behind his desk in his office, pouring over financial statements. He had nearly forgotten the unsettling incident with the young blonde. He had woken up alone in her apartment, and wondered if he'd had a stroke—he couldn't remember anything that happened. The next morning he had gone to the doctor for a checkup, but was told that other than being a bit overweight, he was in excellent physical health.

His secretary buzzed the intercom.

"You have a visitor," she said. "It's your nephew."

"Nephew?" Reggio said. "What nephew?"

There was a pause. "Giorgio."

"I have no such nephew. Get rid of him."

A moment later, the intercom buzzed again. Sounding embarrassed, his secretary said, "He says he's the..." she lowered her voice to a whisper, "...illegitimate son of a relative of yours in Pescara."

Illegitimate son...Pescara. What was this nonsense?

"Send him in," Reggio barked. He would teach this numbskull a lesson—some salesmen would say anything to get a foot in the door.

A young, dark-haired man entered his office. He was dressed in a long, expensive-looking overcoat and scarf, woolen slacks, and finely-polished black shoes. A wavering, thick scar ran down his jawline.

"Hello, Reggio," the man said amiably. There was a peculiar gleam in his eyes that Reggio could not quite interpret.

He had an envelope in his hand. He slid it across the desk.

Puzzled, Reggio opened it. When he saw the glossy black and white photographs, he gasped and shoved them back inside.

He stared at the dark figure in his office. "W-who are you?"

The man smiled. "My name is Giorgio Cattoretti. I am your new business partner."

CHAPTER 3.7

Over the next ten years, Giorgio Cattoretti developed DayPrinto into the largest fake designer fashion goods operation in Europe. Reggio Martino was bought out. As it grew, the Cat used the profits to buy a dozen other businesses, all related to his counterfeiting operations. A textile factory, a trucking firm, a plant that made adhesives, a manufacturer of buttons and shoe-soles.

He loved working in the center of the world's fashion industry. Like many Southern Italian men, he had a penchant for tall, rail-thin natural blondes, the exact opposite of the type of women he grew up around in Rome. He dated some of the most striking young models in the industry— Finns, Russians, Swedes, Belgians, Polish—bedding them down one after another with his charm and his dark good looks. Life was grand. He thought of his younger days back in Rome with great satisfaction, when he loitered on Via Veneto in his scruffy clothes and all the chic, well-dressed women looked down their noses at him.

Let them look down their noses at me now, he often thought.

The Cattoretti conglomerate grew and the various divisions achieved an enviable synergy. Each supported Cattoretti's illegal activities, keeping costs of goods low and profits high. At the same time, each protected the other, the continued legitimate activities holding the Italian authorities at bay.

Cattoretti became an expert manager of people. He saw himself as a kind of artist—he viewed his businesses as his canvas, his employees as his palette. He reduced turnover to zero by paying his people 50% more than they could earn anywhere else.

He owned all the companies outright, through a spiderweb of offshore holding companies that became more and more complex.

The Cat took no partners.

One of the first things that Cattoretti did, when he started making good money, was take care of some "loose ends" back in the USA.

The first of the three Attica rapists, who had been released shortly after Cattoretti had been deported, was found floating in the Hudson River, his severed penis tightly sewn into his mouth with fishing line. Cattoretti was delighted to hear that the New York City coroner had determined that the grotesque "surgery" had been performed while the man was still alive.

The second rapist was found in his prison cell with one of the guards' billy clubs shoved so far up his rectum that he died of internal injuries.

The third was found in a Bronx playground one morning, beaten severely about the head and neck. His testicles were missing. They were later discovered in his stomach.

Joey Russo, Vito, and two of his men died in an explosion. It occurred in the Hudson Bay, at night.

On a motorboat.

Cattoretti was particularly thrilled when he got his hands on a shipping company that owned a dozen container vessels. While he never forgot his enemies, he also never forgot his friends—especially the people who helped him, and were kind to him.

The day he took control of the company, he began to track down Anders, his Swedish crewmate on the *Bianca* so many years ago.

It took him three months, but he finally reached Anders, at a hotel in Trieste.

"Anders, this is Giorgio Cattoretti. Do you remember me?"

There was a long silence. Then: "Giorgio! My god...you cocky bastard. How long has it been? Ten years?"

"Twelve."

"Are you still in America?"

"No. I live in Italy now. And you?"

"Still a crewmember on the *Bianca*. Believe it or not." He sounded a little embarrassed. "So, did you get your fleet of container ships?" His voice was laced with sarcasm.

"As a matter of fact, I did."

Now there was an even longer silence.

"Anders, I never forget my friends. I'm calling you because I want you to be captain of the largest vessel."

When Cattoretti reached his 35th birthday, he decided it was time to marry. He had already reestablished his relationship with his family and had bought his parents an elegant apartment in Rome. He asked his mother to help him find a suitable bride.

He was soon set up with Isabella Scarso, a plain, well-mannered young woman who worked as a bookkeeper in a large department store. There were no great sparks between them. On their third date, Cattoretti knew she was the perfect wife for him.

They were at an expensive restaurant and enjoyed a long, luxurious dinner. After dessert, he slid a small jewelry box across the table to her. "Isabella," he said sincerely, "I think you are a wonderful woman. I want you to be my wife. If you agree, you will live in security and comfort the rest of your days. Our children will attend the finest schools and will be raised like royalty. But..." he motioned to her. "...I will only spend a few days each month here in Rome. My business is in the north, in Milano. When I am in Rome, I am one hundred percent yours. When I am away, I belong to no one." He paused. "Do we understand each other?"

"Yes, Giorgio, of course."

By the time Cattoretti was 45, he became bored with the knockoff designer clothing business. He decided he wanted to take on the ultimate counterfeiting challenge—making fake paper money.

He started with the Euro, but then switched to the American dollar. Counterfeiting American money gave him greater satisfaction, knowing that, in his own small way, he was hurting the government of the country that had treated him so shabbily.

He acquired new printing presses and modified them, but he soon discovered that he would never make a high quality counterfeit U.S. $100 bill without actually using one of the intaglio sheet-fed presses made by KBA Giori, in Germany. But it was impossible for anyone but official government printing offices to buy them.

Cattoretti applied all his experience and know-how to the problem. He considered building one of the machines from spare parts, but the sale of spare parts for the Giori presses were reported to Interpol.

Cattoretti learned that the KBA Giori plant was located in Wurzburg, Germany, on the railroad line. The printing presses were carefully packed and loaded directly onto trains bound for northern Germany, where they were either air-freighted or sent by container ship to their final destinations.

Cattoretti finally concluded that the only way to get his hands on a KBA Giori press was to steal one of them. And the only way he could do that, and get away with it, was when the machine was in transit, when it was between the Giori factory and the purchaser.

He considered trying to have his shipping company certified as a KBA-approved vendor, but that would take far too long and might raise suspicion.

There were other ways, ways that were more certain and with which he had much more experience.

Cattoretti began to go to Germany often, traveling to Wurzburg under false documents and posing as a distributor of auto parts for Italian cars. KBA Giori was the largest employer in the little city of Wurzburg—it seemed virtually everyone worked at the factory. The place had tighter security than the Vatican.

Cattoretti spent many hours drinking in beer gardens and mixing with the locals, making friends, playing the role of friendly traveling salesman, slowly amassing information. It amazed him how much people would say when they were drunk. It did not take him long to track down a few different men who worked in the KBA Giori shipping and receiving department.

He checked them out one by one, looking for dirt. If he didn't find any, he would create some.

He finally lucked out when he casually struck up a conversation with a man named Niklas Kaiser. Kaiser was 40 years old and weighed 300 pounds, divorced, with a 15-year-old daughter he visited on weekends.

He also worked as an accountant in the KBA Giori shipping and receiving department.

Cattoretti soon observed that Niklas Kaiser exhibited odd behavior, behavior that held promise. Kaiser often went to the library and several bars that offered computers with free Internet access.

Yet Kaiser had his own notebook computer and subscribed to wireless Internet at home.

One morning when Niklas got out of bed, he was shocked to find a strange man in his kitchen. The intruder was sitting calmly at the table, peeling an apple with a long-bladed knife.

"*Guten tag*, Niklas," the man said. He had a dark complexion, salt and pepper hair, and wore black gloves. A long, frightening scar ran down his jawline.

Niklas backed away, terrified, his blubber shaking under his bathrobe. "Who are you?"

"Incest," Cattoretti said.

"What?"

"Incest," Cattoretti said again, motioning with the knife.

On the corner of the table sat three printouts. Niklas recognized them, and had a sinking feeling. The three titles, translated into English, were *Father Knows Best, Wicked Stepmother,* and *Taboo Easter.*

Niklas looked back at the man in his kitchen.

"You have quite an imagination," the intruder said, carving out a slice of the apple and popping it into his mouth. "I particularly enjoyed *Taboo Easter.* I never would have thought of doing something like that with a hard-boiled egg...especially to my own daughter."

Niklas blushed.

"Do you make much money writing this filth?"

Niklas was too stunned to answer.

"It does not matter, I was simply curious. In these trying times, a man has to do what he can to make a living." The intruder motioned to the picture on the coffee table. "I was also curious as to what your daughter would think if she read these stories and knew that her dear old *Vater* was the author." The bastard smiled. "And your ex-wife—I wonder how she would react if she knew her bastard ex-husband was actually Birget Schmidt, the German incest porno king?"

Niklas didn't wonder how she would react. He knew. The shrew would take him to court, have his visitation rights revoked, and he would never see his daughter again. Worse, it would create a terrible scandal—a juicy story like that would be all over the TV and newspapers. KBA Giori would fire him instantly—it was a 200-year-old firm, and extremely conservative.

"What is the matter, Niklas? The cat got your tongue?" The man laughed as if this was some private joke.

"What do you want?" Niklas whispered, his throat dry.

"Very simple, Niklas. I want information."

"W-what information?"

"I want to know each and every time a KBA Giori printing press is shipped to South America. I want to know the name of the vessel, the container number, and the final destination."

Niklas stared. What this man was asking him to do could put him in jail for 20 years. He looked back at the printouts, and at his daughter's picture.

"That's impossible," he said. "I don't have access—"

"But you can *gain* access, Niklas. I have already seen how good you are with computers."

That same evening, Cattoretti called Anders on the *Stella*, the largest of his container ships.

"Anders, this is Giorgio. How would you like to make a million Euros?"

There was only a brief pause. "I'm listening."

"You will need to take a leave of absence from the *Stella* and work as an Ordinary Seaman for a while..."

Over the next 18 months, Niklas Kaiser dutifully informed Giorgio Cattoretti of the KBA Giori container shipments to South America. One to Argentina, one to Brazil, one to Ecuador. It was only on the fifth shipment when Anders happened to be a crew member on the particular German ship carrying the KBA Giori printing press.

The machine was bound for Santiago, Chile on a ship called the *Emilie*.

Two weeks before the scheduled departure, Giorgio Cattoretti traveled to Bremerhaven, Germany, still using the false identity of the Italian auto parts distributor. There, he arranged for a container of his goods to be shipped to an auto parts distributor in Chile.

From the docks in Bremerhaven, he silently watched the *Emilie's* crane pick up the container and then set it down on top of a stack, with dozens of others.

All the rusty brown metal boxes looked exactly the same.

The only way you could tell them apart were by the numbers stenciled on the sides.

Fourteen days later, a truck arrived at the loading dock at the Ministry of Finance in Santiago. Three armed guards emerged and they began unloading the unmarked crates that contained the new KBA Giori printing press they had ordered.

Using a crowbar, one of the ministry workers carefully opened the crate, with the others looking on.

When they removed the packing, they all gaped at each other.

They found themselves looking at stacks and stacks of brand new Pirelli tires.

The Chilean intelligence department and Interpol were immediately called in. It seemed that somehow, the numbers on the containers had been mixed up on the German ship's cargo manifest. A simple mistake— the tires could be sent to the rightful owner, and the printing press recovered.

The rightful owner of the tires proved difficult to track down. It turned out there was no company in Chile by the name that was listed on the shipping documents. The address listed in Santiago proved to be that of a massage parlor. There were no records of the truck that had picked up the contents of the KBA Giori container at the docks, and no one could remember what it looked like.

On the other end, in Europe, it also turned out that the name of the Italian company that had shipped the tires was false. No such company was registered in Italy. The address given for it in Trieste turned out to be that of a school for the hard of hearing.

All payments had been in cash. There was no way to trace it.

The investigators then realized that it was not the cargo manifest that had been modified, but the numbers on the containers themselves. Someone aboard the vessel had managed to climb up onto the stacks, cover the numbers with rust-colored paint, and stencil on new ones in white.

By this time, the *Emilie* had already arrived back in Germany. One of the crewmembers, a blonde man from Norway, had disappeared, presumably in Chile. Further investigation of his records showed that he had been signed onto the crew using false documents.

After six months of investigation, the authorities exhausted all their leads and concluded that the stolen Giori press would probably never be recovered.

An insurance claim was filed.

Shipping procedures were changed at KBA Giori so that nothing like this could ever happen again.

One year later, Giorgio Cattoretti was using the complex machine to turn out his first crude but promising fake U.S. $100 bills. It took him another two years before he could manufacture them well enough so that they would pass through automatic verifying machines. Then the U.S. Treasury hatched the idea of programming the machines to recognize his fakes...

"Papà!" Luigi said, breaking his reverie.

Cattoretti was still standing in the castle courtyard, gazing at the East Tower. He had been so lost in his memories that his cigar had gone out.

"What?" he said, turning to his son.

Luigi was walking towards him across the cobblestones. There was something in his hand.

"I found this in your bedroom," he said, giving the cellphone to his father. "Gene Lassiter must have dropped it when he was looking for the combination to the safe."

Cattoretti turned it on, then scrolled through the names in the contact list one by one, reading them.

When he saw the name GYPSY, he stopped.

There were a half dozen text messages sent to that number, the last one only a few hours ago.

He read through them, then looked up at Luigi and chuckled. "We are going to get the eight million back, my son. Every last Euro."

CHAPTER 3.8

Elaine Brogan slept badly the night that Giorgio Cattoretti's castle was robbed.

She had tangled dreams of Gene Lassiter lurking around the castle, of Giori printing presses spewing out mountains of paper money, and of Giorgio Cattoretti and the opera.

She also dreamed of Nick. She slept with the broken wind-up turkey he'd given her as a present under her pillow. She and Nick were in the Ethiopian cafe across the street from the Secret Service office in Sofia, where they were "synchronizing their DOPS." They were talking and laughing and immensely enjoying each other's company. During the dream, she realized that those days were over, and they had been the happiest moments of her life. She wondered if Nick had enjoyed those times as much as she had.

Elaine was awakened by the soft beeping of a small alarm clock on the nightstand, one that she didn't remember being there when she had gone to bed. It was just getting light outside, but too dark to see the time. She flicked on the light and squinted at the display of the little alarm clock.

6:45.

When she glanced across the room, she noticed that there were flowers on the dresser, red roses in a lovely antique vase. Attached to the vase was a note.

She climbed out of bed and read it.

The note was written with a fountain pen, on cream monogrammed stationery, a fancy *G* and *C* embossed in gold at the top. There was a bold, showy flair to the handwriting.

Good Morning Elaine,

I am truly sorry about what happened last night, and how suspiciously I behaved towards you. Can you forgive me?

I selected this outfit from the vault and had it sent out to you. I hope it cheers you up.

Giorgio

Outfit? she thought, looking around the room. Then she saw the business suit—it was hanging on the handle of the wardrobe door. A Dolce & Gabbana—of course— a navy wool-twill blazer with light blue pinstripes and matching city shorts. Underneath was an Oscar de la Renta sheer silk ruffle blouse. The shoes were Lanvin, a pair of braided black satin sandals.

Then she noticed a P.S. at the bottom of the note:

You will find your work schedule for today on the dresser.

She picked up the computer printout and read it.

TODAY'S WORK SCHEDULE

6.45 Wake up

6.45 - 7.15 Quick swim in mineral water pool

7.15 - 8.00 Custom-prepared healthy breakfast. (Consultation with dietician for future preferences)

8.00 - 9.00 Makeup and hair stylist visits

9.00 - 9.30 Get ready for work (chauffer will wait in courtyard for you)

9.30 - 10.00 – Arrive at DayPrinto

10.00 – 13.00 Work

13.00 - 14.00 Free time —on site cosmetic salon open Monday, Wednesday, and Friday

14.00 - 15.00 Lunch (prepared by DayPrinto chef)

15.00 - 18.00 Work

18.00 - 18.30 Travel back to Fontanella

18.30 - 19.30 Exercise as desired

20.30 - ? Dinner, hopefully with me (?)

Elaine smiled to herself. What a "work" schedule!

She looked back at the business suit, touching the lush fabric. The man certainly did know how to cheer a woman up in the morning.

As she donned the luxurious silk robe and padded down the spiral staircase, she thought of her typical day working the last six months for Gene Lassiter and the U.S. Government.

7:00 Drag ass out of bed

7:00 – 7:30 Gulp down instant coffee and try to wake up

7:30 Shower & eat (yogurt & frozen juice)

7:30 – 7:45 Slog through rain and snow to Metro station

7:45 – 7:55 Stop and buy shampoo and hand lotion (don't forget coupons!)

7:55 – 8:30 Stand on packed train between a man who doesn't bathe and a woman who talks to herself incessantly

8:45 – 9:00 Slog through rain and snow to Treasury Building

9:00 – 12:00 Work

12:00 – 1:00 Grab a sandwich and drop off dry cleaning (don't forget coupons!)

1:00 – 5:00 Work

5:00 - 5:30 Slog back through rain and snow to Metro station

5:30 – 6:00 Stand on packed train between teenager with bad breath and creepy man who rubs up against young women

5:45 – 6:30   Dash through rain and snow to snag space in walk-in yoga class (don't forget coupon!)

7:30 – 8:00 Trudge home through rain and snow

8:00 – Eat microwave dinner and collapse in front of TV set

10:00 Drag ass into bed.

A few minutes later, she was swimming a relaxed backstroke in the heated mineral water pool, watching the early morning sunlight filter through the skylights.

Now this is living, she thought.

The water felt like velvet.

When she went to the Great Hall for breakfast, Tony made her a perfect omelet, along with some fresh-squeezed orange juice.

He still seemed upset about the robbery.

As she began to eat the omelet, he said, "Do you think Tony did wrong-a thing last night? I only try to make *Signore* happy. He want me treat all-a guests very well, and that is what Tony always do."

"I'm sure you didn't know the man was dangerous," Elaine said.

"No!" Tony said emphatically. "How could I know this? He old, he walk with a stick, he look ill—how I know he was *bandito*?"

"It wasn't your fault, Tony."

He looked greatly relieved by this. "Thank you, *signora*. I hope you tell *signore* this—he listen to you, he like you very much."

"I told him already."

"*Grazie!*" Tony gushed. "*Grazie, signora!*"

Just before ten, the chauffeur let her out at the entrance to the DayPrinto main building.

As Elaine got out of the Rolls, she checked herself in the reflection of one of the large lobby windows—she was stunning in the D&G suit.

She went inside the building with a heady feeling, wearing the fancy outfit, with the Gucci satchel over her shoulder. A powerful, international businesswoman. She also felt kind of silly, as there was nothing in the satchel but one piece of paper—her Agenda for the day.

Just as the receptionist greeted her, Luigi appeared.

"*Buon giorno*," he said, and gave a polite smile. "Follow me, please." He led her down a hallway. The facility seemed very different on a weekday—there was a lot of activity in the offices, workers walking up and down the corridors carrying papers. Several glanced curiously at Elaine.

"This is your office," he said, stopping in front of a door and opening it. Elaine stepped inside. "Before, our production manager work here. Now he work for our shipping company in Trieste."

The luxurious space was furnished much like Cattoretti's, with a marble floor and desk made of polished stone, only there were no original masterpieces on the wall, only a framed Monet print.

Elaine set the Gucci satchel down on the sleek desk. "Thank you."

"Greta come soon," he said, and left the room. A few seconds later, a woman appeared at the door, rapping formally on the frame. She was dressed in a smart grey business suit, with a heavily starched blouse.

"I am Greta," she said, with a strict-sounding German accent. "I am your personal assistant." She gave a formal smile and shook Elaine's hand, her grip strong and confident. "I trust you had a pleasant drive in this morning?"

"Yes," Elaine said, a little taken aback. The woman stood as if at attention, her sensible black pumps precisely together, her hands folded in front of her. "Is there anything you need? Coffee, perhaps?"

"Not just now," Elaine said. She wasn't used to this. She had never had an administrative assistant before, let alone a PA.

"Very well. Was the work schedule I prepared for you, with Signore Cattoretti's guidance, satisfactory?"

"Yes, it's fine, thank you."

"*Sehr gut.*" Greta gave a formal nod and motioned to the door. "Signore asked me to escort you down to the production area, if you are ready."

When Elaine entered the huge room that housed the Giori printing press, all the technicians were so busy that they barely noticed her. There was a new set of enlargements spread out on the floor, and the workers were poring over them.

Cattoretti walked up and kissed both her cheeks, Italian style. "*Buongiorno!*" He admired the D&G business suit and glanced down at her long legs. "*Bellissima!* You set a new standard of elegance for all businesswomen in Italy!"

Elaine blushed as a few of the workers looked up at her.

"You picked the suit," she said clumsily. "Anyone would look good in this outfit."

"What is it with you American women that you cannot take a compliment?"

Elaine felt like a debutante on a date with an older man.

Cattoretti beamed at her. The suspicion he'd shown the night before had completely disappeared. "Shall we get started?"

Elaine spent the entire morning going over new enlargements that had been made since the last version of the fake $100 bill. The technicians had been up all night correcting the mistakes she had found yesterday.

As the morning wore on, the headiness she felt about her new "career change" began to fade. Every now and then a rude voice would surface inside her and say *These people are criminals* and *This is exactly the kind of operation you were trained to hunt down and destroy.*

She tried to ignore the voice. But every now and then, she found herself looking at the scar that ran down Cattoretti's cheek.

At 2 pm, Cattoretti and Elaine went to his office for the scheduled private lunch. The meal was served by the DayPrinto *"dilettante"* himself, on Cattoretti's conference table, with glimmering Tiffany tableware.

Cattoretti's high spirits had been boosted even higher by the progress they were making today.

"Your nails look very nice," he said, as he unfolded his napkin.

"Thank you," she said. Before lunch, the manicurist had come in from the outside, apparently one that Cattoretti and some of the other DayPrinto executives used.

As they started eating, Cattoretti said, "This dish is called *Cotoletta all orecchio di elefante.* Do you know what that means?"

"No. I hope it doesn't actually come from an elephant."

Cattoretti laughed. "I am afraid there are not many elephants in Italy. The name literally means 'elephant ear cutlet,' but it is made from pork."

Whatever the ingredients were, the dish was one of the most delicious Elaine had ever tasted. This was not something she would share with Tony, however.

As they ate, Elaine became more and more uneasy about the agreement she had made with Giorgio Cattoretti. Would he really pay her the eight million Euros he promised, after Lassiter had stolen it?

When she thought it was just the right moment, she said, as casually as she could, "When do you think the passport will be ready?"

"Passport?" Cattoretti said.

"The one you promised yesterday," she said casually.

"Oh." He cut a piece of the meat. "Luigi is handling that. These things take time. He promised me he would have it by five o'clock this afternoon." Cattoretti paused, eying her. "You are not thinking of leaving so soon, are you, *cara?* After we finish these revisions, I hoped you would stay on with me, help me continue to improve my currency when the American government catches on and makes another round of software updates for the verifying machines."

"I intend to stay on," Elaine lied. "It's just that when we're done with this, I'd like to take a little vacation."

"A well-deserved one," Cattoretti said.

The truth was, she was afraid that if she stayed here even a few more days, she would become so addicted to all the luxury and power that she would be unable to make herself leave. The mineral water swims, the massages, the thousand dollar suits, chauffeured Rolls Royce, rubbing elbows with international celebrities...it was all incredibly seductive. She could easily see how honest people could cross over to the other side and stay there.

She also didn't trust Giorgio Cattoretti.

He cut another piece of the meat and chewed slowly, smiling at her. "At the rate we are progressing, it seems we might finish this revision today. Which means we will be ready to go into full production tomorrow. The Russians are very anxious to get their hands on these new counterfeits. Do you think that's possible?"

"It's possible," Elaine said. She would make certain of it.

They worked nonstop the rest of the afternoon. On the next set of plates, Elaine helped them correct all the errors that were stored and marked in the data key, the errors she had been finding the last 6 months when working for Lassiter.

Just after 6 pm, yet another set of plates was done and she found three more discrepancies, errors she thought Treasury could easily create new verifying machine software to look for. The technicians were exhausted. Many of them hadn't slept in more than 40 hours.

Elaine's eyes were bloodshot and her neck ached, but she kept working, determined to get the job finished today.

At 7:30 pm, the computer-controlled engraving machine finished carving out yet another set of plates. Hopefully, the final one.

Elaine checked the new sample bills when they came out of the intaglio press, and spent more than a half hour comparing them to a genuine $100 bill of the latest series. She could not spot a single mistake. Everything had been fixed.

It was eerily quiet in the room. Cattoretti had put on the soundtrack from *Madame Butterfly*, and the sorrowful music drifted through the space. All the worn-out technicians were standing there in their DayPrinto coveralls, watching her, their ink-stained hands in their pockets, waiting.

For what seemed like the 50th time today, she kicked off her new Lanvins and slowly walked across the latest set of enlargements, barefoot, reviewing every detail. The tension in the room was almost palpable.

At last, she turned to Cattoretti. "I've gone over this with a fine-toothed comb, and I can't find a single...mistake." Something caught Elaine's eye, something on the back side of the bill. She turned her head, peering at the words IN GOD WE TRUST. She silently traced the arc of the engraving line from the corner of the "D" in GOD to the dome at the top of the building.

It was off by one engraving line. On the blowups, it looked like a glaring error, but in reality, it was out of position by only one ten-thousandth of an inch. But it was plenty large enough to be caught by any currency verifying machine, even older models.

"Is something wrong?" Cattoretti said.

Elaine turned back to him and gave a winning smile. "Everything is perfect."

The men went wild, jumping up and down, slapping each other's backs. Champagne corks popped. Cattoretti started spraying them all with Dom Perignon. Somebody switched the music to a hard-driving Italian pop song and a few of the younger men started dancing around on the enlargements.

When the ruckus eased a little bit, Cattoretti clapped his hands together until everyone was quiet. In Italian, he said, "We will begin full production tomorrow. But first, let us take a few minutes to print out a million dollars, just to show we can do it!"

There were more cheers, and everyone scrambled to fire up the big Giori press.

Half an hour later, Elaine was sitting alone in Cattoretti's office, waiting for him to come up from the basement.

She didn't know why she had chosen to betray him at the 11th hour.

It was incredibly risky. No, it was suicidal. As soon as Cattoretti or one of his people tried to change even one of the new bills at a bank or a currency exchange, he would know what she had done.

But she had not been able to go through with it. Some part of herself had held her back, a part that did not want her to help a man like Giorgio Cattoretti.

She had to get away tonight. She didn't know where she could go, but she would just have to take it one step at a time. The banks and currency exchanges were all closed right now and wouldn't be open again until tomorrow morning.

But then they might find out.

The door opened. Giorgio Cattoretti entered the office, a small leather Gucci bag in one swarthy hand. He was smiling ear to ear, the scar along his jaw stretched into a white line.

"You do not know how happy I am," he chuckled, setting the bag down. "Do you know how long I have been working on this project, Elaine? Six years! Six long *years*. First I had to perfect the paper, then the ink, then the security thread, the microprinting, and finally, the minute details only a KBA Giori press can produce, which meant snatching one. It took a year just to understand how that blasted machine worked. If not for you, the U.S. Treasury Department would be knocking me out of business as we speak."

Elaine smiled. On the inside, she was terrified.

He opened the bag—she could smell the freshly printed bills from across the room. He pulled out one of the $100 notes and gazed at it, his eyes misty. "Behold! A veritable masterpiece!" He gazed up at the oil painting on his wall. "Our friend Rubens would be proud."

Elaine could see the back side of the bill in his hand. She tried not to look at it. To her, it seemed that the words IN GOD WE TRUST were so far out of place that even a layman would notice it at 20 yards. But of course that was ridiculous.

He glanced back at Elaine. "Are you not happy, *cara?*"

"Yes, of course. I'm just tired." She closed her eyes and rubbed them, mainly to avoid looking at him.

"Of course you must be exhausted," he said sympathetically. He moved closer and tenderly caressed her neck. "You worked very hard today."

It was well past five o'clock, and she had not seen any sign of Luigi. But she was afraid to ask about the passport—she didn't want to risk making him suspicious.

"We must celebrate our victory," Cattoretti said, taking her hand. "Tonight, we will dine at the best restaurant in Milan."

CHAPTER 3.9

The restaurant, Il Luogo de Aimo e Nadia, was located in the central part of the city. Instead of being chauffeured there in the Rolls Royce, Cattoretti drove himself, in a shiny metallic-blue Porsche cabriolet.

The interior of the restaurant was styled with modern simplicity—stark white walls that were only broken by a few splashy abstract oil paintings. It looked very Italian.

Cattoretti brought along the Gucci bag and set it in one of the empty chairs.

The food was delicious, but Elaine had trouble eating. All she could think about was the counterfeit money in the bag. He had told her that every last dollar he printed would be sent to Russia and laundered there. Yet, if that was true, then what was he planning to do with this money?

Elaine's worst fear was that he would use some of it to pay for the meal. She guessed that the bill would come to several hundred Euros—Cattoretti ordered a bottle of wine that cost over €300 alone.

As they had coffee and *tiramisù*, Cattoretti snapped his fingers at the waiter and asked for the check.

The man brought it in an elegant little tray and left them alone.

Cattoretti just sat there sipping his coffee, gazing pleasantly at Elaine. "You seem distracted, *cara*. Did you not enjoy your meal?"

"No, it was delicious." She smiled and touched her stomach. "I just ate a little too much, that's all."

"Nonsense," he said, glancing down at her figure, "you eat like a bird."

"I—I was just wondering. Have you heard from Luigi, about the passport?"

"Oh. Yes. I am afraid I have some bad news about that."

Elaine tensed. "Bad news?"

"Yes. Unfortunately, it will take a little longer than expected. Our contact at the ministry was taken ill today. Luigi says it will be at least two more days before it is delivered. Probably not until the end of the week."

"That's all right," Elaine said, her stomach churning. The end of the week! They would discover the flaw in the counterfeits long before then.

Cattoretti's cellphone started ringing. He pulled it out, glanced at the display. "Excuse me," he said, and he took the call out in the lobby.

Elaine shifted uneasily in her chair—she could still see him through the doorway, talking on the phone, nodding. He was still looking at her.

Please don't let anybody discover the error in the fakes, she thought. *Please?*

When Cattoretti came back to the table, he smiled and sat back down. He glanced at the bill sitting on the little silver tray, and he reached for the Gucci bag.

Elaine dug her fingernails into her palms.

Cattoretti pulled his wallet from the bag, opened it, and dropped his credit card on the tray.

She breathed a great sigh of relief.

The waiter came with a portable credit card machine and Cattoretti keyed in his PIN.

"And now," he said, rising from the table, "I have a little surprise for you."

They were back in the Porsche, heading across the center of Milan. Elaine's stomach was tied in knots, the coffee and dessert gurgling up every now and then.

Surprise? she thought. *What kind of surprise?*

They had been driving for several minutes. Cattoretti had not said a word.

"May I ask where we're going?" Elaine finally said.

"*Cara*," he said, admonishingly. "I told you—it is a surprise. You don't want me to spoil it, do you?"

"I've never really liked surprises," Elaine said weakly.

"Really? It is my experience that most women love surprises—surprise gifts, trips, and so on."

"Well, guess I'm not like most women."

He chuckled. "No, *cara*, but I am not like most men. You will always love my surprises."

At a traffic light, he turned sharply to the right and sped down a narrow street, the tires burning a little rubber. He seemed relaxed, steering with only one hand on the wheel, casually shifting gears.

Elaine could feel sweat running down her side. "You're not angry with me about anything, are you?"

"Angry?" Cattoretti reached over and squeezed her hand. "How could I be angry with you, after you so brilliantly exorcized every little error from my counterfeits?"

Elaine fought the panic that gripped her. Was there a slight sarcasm in his tone? She couldn't tell.

He suddenly slowed the car, peering past her, out her window. He seemed to be looking into the windows of a bar. With no warning, he made a U-turn that tossed Elaine into the door.

"Sorry," he said. "I saw a parking space down this way. They are hard to come by."

He brought the Porsche to a stop, then expertly parallel parked between two big motorcycles.

He turned off the ignition. Smiling at her again, he took her hand. "All right, I will stop keeping you in suspense. We are going to get your money tonight. All of it."

"My money?" she said, confused.

He motioned across the street to the bar, "In a few minutes, Gene Lassiter's beloved Gypsy will arrive there." He smiled with satisfaction. "We are going to trade Gypsy for the money."

Gene Lassiter was in the throes of his fifth or sixth anxiety attack since he had made off with the money from Cattoretti's castle.

He was sitting in front of his laptop computer in his Milan hotel room, hyperventilating, his palms sweaty, refreshing the computer screen every minute or two, hoping to find an email from Gypsy. He was terrified that he had lost his sweet love forever. If that had happened, he didn't know what he would do.

He had no way to contact Gypsy by phone. He had not dared write down the number anywhere—the only place he'd kept it was in his cellphone, which he had evidently lost somewhere last night, possibly at Cattoretti's. He knew that Gypsy was living in Berlin with some man named Dieter, but that was all.

He looked over at the bag full of cash he had taken from Cattoretti. What good was all that money without Gypsy? Everything he had done was for his cherished lover. Without Gypsy, all that money was nothing more than ink on paper.

The hotel room was a disgusting mess, dirty plates and cups and glasses from room service scattered everywhere. Lassiter was afraid to leave the building. He hadn't stepped outside the room since he had checked in last night, afraid that Cattoretti's men might somehow find him. He had a feeling Gypsy was coming to Milan that day, despite the fact that he had forbade it.

Gypsy was maddeningly impulsive. Which was part of the attraction.

Lassiter refreshed the screen again, his face twisted with anguish. The notion that Gypsy no longer was interested in him was too much to bear.

Then, a horrifying thought struck him, one that he realized had been lurking just beneath the surface of his awareness the entire day.

What if Gypsy really had found another lover?

Holding his head in his hands, Gene Lassiter began to cry like a baby.

The bar was sleek and stylish, with comfortable sofas scattered around, the walls decorated with moody impressionist paintings. It was filled with a hip, 30-something crowd, all locals, all well dressed, and was so packed it was hard to breathe.

Cattoretti greeted a few people as he led Elaine to a stand-up table in one corner. It was partially hidden by a pillar, but still afforded a good view of the front door.

A waitress came to the table. Cattoretti ordered Chianti for both of them.

On edge, Elaine glanced around the room, surveying all the people. The last thing she cared about right now was getting the money. She no longer wanted it. She only wanted to escape. Maybe she could excuse herself and go to the ladies' room, and get out the back door.

But with no passport, and Interpol and God only knew who else looking for her, she didn't think she would get far.

Cattoretti was watching all the people, searching for Gypsy.

Elaine looked around the room—just within her field of view, there were quite a few tall women with long, dark curly hair.

"How will you recognize her?" Elaine said.

"At nine o'clock, Greta will call the bar and ask for Gypsy." He smiled. "When she comes to the phone, we will know her."

As the minutes ticked by and Elaine watched all the people drinking and chattering to each other, her curiosity began to outweigh her desire to flee. She wanted to see what Gypsy looked like, what kind of girl Gene Lassiter would go to such great lengths for.

At precisely nine o'clock, there was a faint sound of a phone ringing. The bartender answered it.

"That is Greta's call," Cattoretti whispered, watching.

The bartender listened for a moment, then lowered the receiver and glanced around the crowd.

"Gipsy *è qui?*" he shouted. "Gypsy?"

Elaine leaned forward, watching all the people. Nobody seemed to react.

"Gypsy!" the bartender shouted louder.

"Maybe she—" Elaine began, but then noticed the crowd parting near the bar to allow someone through.

"There she is," Cattoretti whispered.

A tall, slim figure moved through the crowd. The young lady was only visible from behind, a thick mane of curly hair that came down to the small of her back. She was wearing a skintight pair of black leather jeans and a white sweater.

When she reached the bar and picked up the phone, Elaine glimpsed long fingernails that were painted with black or very dark blue polish. She listened for a moment, and then said a word or two and handed the phone back to the bartender.

The girl disappeared into the crowd again, now heading for the front door.

"Let's go," Cattoretti said, already on his feet.

They went outside and started following Gypsy down the street. She was walking purposefully along, her hips swinging haughtily. Elaine was now gripped by a strange curiosity, again wondering what Lassiter found so irresistible about her that would drive him to take such huge risks, to destroy other people's lives.

As she approached an alley, a big black sedan turned right in front of her, cutting off her path.

Cattoretti moved quickly, pushing Gypsy into the back seat. "Get in the front," he told Elaine.

"My name is Giorgio Cattoretti," Elaine heard him say from the back seat, as the car pulled away. "I apologize for snatching you off the street like this."

"Where is Gene?" a soft, German-accented voice said, almost a whisper. She sounded frightened. "I don't understand—what is happening?"

"Do not be alarmed," Cattoretti said reassuringly. "We will not hurt you. Gene is fine. You will see him very soon, I promise."

Elaine couldn't resist turning around to look.

When she saw Gypsy's face, she was flabbergasted.

The deep-set eyes, the heavy black eyebrows, the aquiline nose, the full, sensual lips...

A truly stunning creature.

What flabbergasted Elaine most was Gypsy's thick, neatly-trimmed black mustache and beard.

Gypsy was a man.

CHAPTER 3.10

Gene Lassiter had met Gypsy at a gay leather bar in Berlin.

The Ministry of Muscle was in the overtly-gay Schöneberg district, and appealed to the leather and rubber crowd. The bar's main room was an obstacle course—you had to duck to make your way through a maze of leather boots that hung down from the ceiling. The cruising area was around to the back, cordoned off by empty oil drums and heavy black anchor chain.

That was where Lassiter had first laid eyes on Gypsy. The moment he saw the young man, he stopped in his tracks. Gypsy was sitting in between two hardcore fetishists, one wearing a pair of black leather chaps, accentuated with a rudely jutting electric orange codpiece. The other was a "gummiboy," dressed head to toe in skintight rubber.

"*Entschuldigung*," Gypsy said to his two companions, in his soft, seductive voice. He rose, and noting Lassiter's relatively conservative appearance—ordinary slacks and a leather jacket—switched to English, "I simply *must* meet this handsome silver fox…"

"Silver fox" was code for an older man like Lassiter who went for young guys, and didn't mind paying for it.

An hour later they were both at Lassiter's hotel. Not the official hotel, where he was registered under his real name, but a seedy and exclusively gay establishment in Schöneberg not far from the Ministry of Muscle, where no passport or other ID was required.

That first night, Lassiter and Gypsy did things he had only fantasized about—Gypsy seemed to perfectly understand, and anticipate, all of Lassiter's most twisted sexual desires, and readily fulfilled them.

Now, Lassiter sat on the bed in the messy hotel room in Milan, staring at the email message that had come from Gypsy's account.

WE HAVE GYPSY. WILL EXCHANGE HIM FOR THE MONEY. G.C.

It was from Giorgio Cattoretti…

The old man was seized by panic. What might the Italian brute do to his beloved Gypsy!

Lassiter rose from the bed, shaking, and dragged the canvas bag over to the door.

He had to save Gypsy.

243

Thirty minutes later, Cattoretti's sedan turned down a road in a run-down area on the outskirts of Milan.   It ran alongside a narrow body of water, a small river or canal. The water looked as black as the night.

"These waterways are called *navigli*," Cattoretti commented. "They were designed by Leonardo da Vinci, in the 15th Century. They run all the way to Lake Como."

Everyone in the car was quiet—nobody was interested in a travelogue. They were about to meet Gene Lassiter to exchange Gypsy for the stolen money.

The car rolled to a stop. To the left was a huge, warehouse, the walls crumbling. It must have been hundreds of years old. To the right, the canal.

Elaine fidgeted while they waited. She didn't know what Cattoretti planned. She didn't quite trust him. But she was fairly sure he was not armed, and she didn't think Luigi was, either. If they had a trick up their sleeves, she didn't know what it might be.

After a few long minutes, a car turned onto the road from the far side of the warehouse. It slowly approached them, head-on. The road was only wide enough for one vehicle.   The automobile came to a stop about fifty feet in front of them. The headlights flashed on and off.

"That's him," Cattoretti said. He lowered the back window. "Throw the money out the passenger side!" he yelled.

"I want to see Gypsy!" Lassiter called back.

"You're trading me for money?" Gypsy gasped.   "Like a piece of *meat?*"

"Quiet!" Cattoretti said. To Luigi, he said, "*Accenda la luce all'interno.*"

The dome light came on.

"Let him see you," Cattoretti said to Gypsy.

The young man leaned forward, the light shining down on his hairy face.

"Now throw the money out on the ground!" Cattoretti yelled.

Lassiter shoved a bag out the passenger window. It tumbled down to the pavement.

"Back up!" Cattoretti shouted.

Lassiter's car slowly backed away.

"Ok, let's grab it," Cattoretti said to Luigi.

As the sedan slowly rolled forward, Cattoretti kept his eye on Lassiter's car and cracked his door. When they reached the bag, he cautiously pushed the door wide open and quickly pulled it into the back seat. He unzipped it and gave a smile of relief. It was packed with bundles of 500 Euro notes.

"There's a bomb in the bag!" Lassiter shouted.

Everyone froze.

Lassiter was holding something out the window of his car—it looked like a cellphone or a remote control device.

"Oh my god," Elaine gasped.

"*Merda*," Cattoretti said. "That stupid old fool. He's bluffing."

Elaine turned and looked at the bag in Cattoretti's lap, expecting it to blow them all to bits any second.

"Let Gypsy go or I'll kill you all!" Lassiter shouted.

Cattoretti stuck his arm out the window and made some kind of signal.

A shot rang out. Whatever Lassiter had been holding in his hand shattered to pieces, bits of it landing in the canal. He screamed. A second bullet struck him in the neck, his head snapping grotesquely to one side.

Elaine's Secret Service training kicked in. She assessed the situation in two seconds. *Sniper in the building.*

She threw her door open and sprinted towards Lassiter. "Hold your fire!" she screamed.

"Stop!" Cattoretti yelled, but she was already veering towards the car's passenger door.

She yanked it open. Lassiter was slumped over the steering wheel, blood trickling across the seat and the floorboard. His neck and chest were open. Two fingers on his left hand were missing. Elaine had been trained in Trauma Assessment. One cursory look told her he wouldn't live more than another minute or two.

She heard Cattoretti shout, "Stop! Come back!"

Elaine looked out the windshield. Gypsy had jumped out of the sedan and was running in the opposite direction, along the canal. Cattoretti dashed off after him.

"H-help me," Lassiter moaned, gurgling blood.

Elaine turned her attention back to the old man. She could see the life draining away from him. She gently put her arm around him, tears in her eyes. Even after all he had done to her, she felt compassion for the dying man.

"Why, Gene?" Elaine said. "Why?"

He looked up at her, his face ghostly pale. "The Russians...they blackmailed me." He coughed up more blood. "They...said they would...expose...Gypsy. Don't let them hurt...Gypsy."

He gave a violent spasm and became perfectly still, his mouth and eyes still open, staring at Elaine.

She slipped out of the car, her blouse and D&G blazer splashed with blood. She was trembling so much she could barely walk—she was in shock from seeing Lassiter's body ripped apart by bullets, the man bleeding to death in her arms. No amount of trauma assessment training had prepared her for that.

Cattoretti's sedan was just sitting there. The headlights were still on, the engine idling, all the doors open except the driver's. The interior light was on and she could see Luigi's face—he was looking around anxiously, like he didn't know what to do.

Cattoretti was nowhere in sight.

Elaine looked up and scanned the crumbling building, but did not see a sniper, or any movement at all. It was oddly quiet.

She had to get away from here. She climbed through the rubble of the decaying structure, stepping through the weeds and loose bricks. Passport or no passport, she had to get away from Giorgio Cattoretti. She had seen a different side of the man tonight—he was a cold-blooded killer.

She stumbled up the crumbling concrete steps to the first floor of the abandoned warehouse, panic-stricken, terrified that she would be next. When he found out she had betrayed him by not revealing all the errors in the counterfeits, he would surely get rid of her, and with vengeance.

Inside the dark building, there were loose planks and gaps everywhere she stepped, along with beer bottles and rubbish left behind by kids. The place stank of urine. She gasped when a shadowy blur waddled past her and disappeared behind a pile of bricks— it looked like a big, fat rat.

She stepped through a decrepit doorway and into a large room. She carefully picked her way across the floor in the near-darkness, being careful not to step into a hole. If she could make her way to the other end of the long building, maybe she could sneak away, run alongside of the canal until she was out of sight. But it was so dark inside she could barely see where she was going. And the farther in she went, the darker it got. She decided this wasn't a good idea.

At that moment, she heard the faint sound of a gunshot. She had been trained to identify weapons by the sounds of their discharges. This was not a sniper rifle, but a low-caliber pistol.

Gypsy has been shot, she thought.

Just as she turned around, she lost her footing. The next thing she knew one leg had plunged into space. She clawed at the floor, barely stopping herself from falling through the ragged opening.

Gasping, she pulled herself out, the edges scratching her shins and knees, and found her footing again. She continued on much more cautiously, testing each step forward with her toe before she put her weight down.

She stopped again—there was breathing behind her.

"Elaine?" a voice said.

It was Giorgio Cattoretti.

Maybe if she stayed still, he couldn't see her.

A second later, a hand took hold of her wrist. "You mustn't be afraid—it's all over now."

CHAPTER 3.11

A few minutes later, Elaine and Cattoretti were sitting in the back seat of the sedan, heading towards the castle. They had not spoken since they had gotten back in the car.

"I do not see why you are upset, *cara*," Cattoretti finally said. "The man destroyed your life. You said so yourself."

"You didn't have to kill him," Elaine said.

"He might have blown all of us to kingdom come."

"He was bluffing."

"I *thought* he was bluffing, but I could not be certain. How could I know? Would you rather that I risked all of our lives to find out?"

Elaine didn't respond. They drove for a moment in silence, then crossed one of the canals.

"What happened to Gypsy?" she said.

Cattoretti glanced at her, then shrugged. "He ran away."

"I thought I heard a pistol shot when I was in the warehouse."

Luigi glanced at his father through the rearview, then looked back at the road.

"I am not armed," Cattoretti said. "And neither is Luigi. You must have imagined it."

When they turned down the driveway that led to the castle, Elaine gazed out into the woods. Lassiter's last words were still reverberating in her ears.

The Russians...they blackmailed me. They...said they would...expose...Gypsy.

Now she was sure that Lassiter had lied to her about Nick. The old man had made the whole thing up just to lure her to Washington so she would complete his project.

Gazing into the woods, she wondered where Nick was now, and if he was happy.

CHAPTER 3.12

At that moment, Nick LaGrange was making his way down the ravine on the east side of Castello Fontanella, only a quarter mile from the driveway. He was wearing gray and black camouflaged fatigues and had a heavy knapsack on his back. His face was blackened with camouflage paint.

He had been investigating an Italian criminal named Giorgio Cattoretti for the past three weeks. It appeared that the genuine KBA Giori printing press that was behind the ever-improving-quality counterfeit banknotes might be located at this castle. Two days ago, he had gotten permission to go to Italy and check it out.

Getting close enough to the castle to see what was going on would not be an easy operation. In addition to the deep ravines that surrounded the structure on all four sides, there was also a moat and a 20-foot-high fortification wall. From satellite photos, it also appeared that the grounds around the castle, on the inside of the moat, were patrolled by guards with dogs.

It would not be easy, and he might end up dead. But if this was where the Giori machine was located, it was worth the risk.

When he stopped and rested for a moment, he glimpsed the headlights through the trees. A car was passing along the driveway that led to the castle, but it was too far away to see.

He wondered if Giorgio Cattoretti was in it.

Cattoretti told Luigi to stop the Rolls at the entrance to the East Tower.

He motioned to Elaine. "Tony will be upset if he sees you like this." She glanced down at her blood-splattered business suit. "Go clean yourself up and put those clothes in your wardrobe. I will take care of them later."

Cattoretti got out of the car and unlocked the door to the tower. Elaine went upstairs, alone.

She tried to convince herself that Cattoretti had done the right thing by killing Gene Lassiter, and that Gypsy was okay.

At midnight, Nick LaGrange lay on his stomach atop the fortification wall. There had only been one guard on duty, patrolling the grounds, and after swimming across the moat, Nick had managed to avoid him.

Now, he could see the windows in both towers, as well as the windows along the inner courtyard.

For the past few minutes, he had watched a slim, black-haired man in an apron washing dishes. Then the lights had gone off and another set of lights had come on, in the next room.

He was using a laser microphone to try and listen to conversations inside the castle, but the tiny panes on the windows were so thick the device was of little use. He kept hearing a faint clicking sound and then realized that one of the rooms must have contained a billiards table.

All in all, the castle seemed very quiet. If there was a counterfeiting operation going on at this location, he could find no evidence of it. Cattoretti owned a score of other businesses where the Giori press could be located, the nearest one—and most likely candidate—a printing company called DayPrinto, S.p.A.

If he couldn't learn anything here, he would see what he could observe there.

After Elaine changed out of the bloody clothes and showered, she put on a Fendi lounge suit and went downstairs. She found Cattoretti in the kitchen, talking to Tony. They were both drinking coffee. Cattoretti was telling him about the dinner they'd eaten at the restaurant. No one would have known that he had just been responsible for the death of one—and possibly two—people.

When Cattoretti saw Elaine, he motioned to Tony and said, "The chef at Il Luogo de Aimo e Nadia is the only chef in Milan that Tony holds in high regard."

"Who say I hold him in high-a regard?" Tony said. "The man puts liqueur in his *tiramisù*! Original recipe for *tiramisu* no have-a liqueur. Which make him a *dilettante*, like all the others." Tony looked at Elaine. "The problem is, we live too close-a to France." He paused. "What Tony no understand is why *signore* eat at restaurants when he has the best chef in all of Lombardy workin' right here in his own house!"

Cattoretti asked Elaine to go outside, to take a walk with him around the courtyard while he smoked a cigar. She had to take his hand to keep her balance on the uneven cobblestones.

"Are you cold, *cara?*" Cattoretti said.

"No," she said, but he gallantly took off his tux jacket and put it around her shoulders. He took her hand again as they walked. "I'm glad to see you in higher spirits."

It was true. Seeing Cattoretti and Tony together had raised her spirits a little. She didn't think the man could be all bad, not if he had someone like Tony working for him.

"I hope that you understand that everything I did tonight, I did for you," Cattoretti said. "I protected you, and I got the money back, money that you deserve."

"Yes," Elaine said, feeling guilty.

He shrugged, his cigar between his fingers. "It was a pity that Lassiter died, but it could not be helped. He was a small and selfish man, Elaine. Small men always get their just rewards. I think what he did to you was cowardly—there were any number of ways that he could have gotten the data key out of the United States. But he chose to use you to do it. Despicable and cowardly."

The words made Elaine feel better, but she also felt that Cattoretti was trying to manipulate her.

There was a sound from somewhere above them. It sounded like a pebble rattling in a gutter.

Cattoretti looked up sharply. One of the guard dogs started barking on the other side of the fortification wall.

"What was that?" Elaine said.

"Probably an animal. There is a lot of wildlife around this castle."

When Cattoretti finished his cigar, he walked Elaine up to her bedroom in the East Tower.

When they entered, he just stood there, gazing at her. There was a lustful glint in his eye.

"*Cara,*" he whispered, and reached up and tenderly touched her face. "You are so beautiful." He moved closer, gazing down at her lips. She could smell the cigar smoke on his clothes.

Her heart was pounding, but not from lust.

"This—this is too fast," she said. "You're a very attractive man, but we hardly know each other."

He ignored her, his lips suddenly pressing against hers. She fought it, but that only seemed to excite him. A prudent voice inside her head said, *You have no passport, and no money. In a matter of days this man will find out you lied to him about his fakes, and that they're worthless. You had better get him liking you a lot more than he does now, if you want to see your next birthday!*

He pushed her down on the bed, driving his body into hers. She could feel his erection pressing against her thigh as he probed her mouth with his tongue. His hands seemed to be everywhere, pulling her gown up, cupping her breasts, his fingers rubbing her nipples. She felt a dirty, almost pornographic sexual excitement, a part of her enjoying what he was doing to her.

Just let him have his way with you, the voice said.

Her eyes fluttered open for one second...and she saw a red light on the ceiling.

She gasped, roughly pushing Cattoretti away.

"What's wrong?" Cattoretti said, breathing hard.

"I..." Elaine tried not to look at the little dot of light. It was a laser beam, flashing on and off in what she thought was some kind of code. "I can't do this now, I'm not ready."

He frowned at her, then turned around and looked up at the ceiling.

At that instant, the little red dot winked out.

Elaine lay breathlessly on the bed, afraid it would appear again. She had recognized one word—it was Morse Code. The word that had hit her like a bolt of electricity. N-I-C-K.

He was outside somewhere. He had come after her!

Cattoretti was watching her eyes. The man had razor-sharp instincts.

"What is it, *cara?*" he said, looking back up at the ceiling.

Elaine sat up in the bed. "I'm—I'm just not ready for this."

"I see. And when do you think you will be ready?" The words were spoken in a tone that told her it wasn't a matter of "if," only of "when."

"I...I don't know. A woman can't give a schedule for these things."

He got up off the bed and straightened his jacket, looking edgy.

"Very well," he said. "Perhaps your feelings will change when we get to Vernazza."

"Vernazza?" Elaine said.

"Yes. Since your passport will not be ready for a few days, I thought we would take a little vacation there. I have a small villa by the sea. It is very secluded, very romantic." He smiled. "You will like it there."

Glancing once more at the ceiling, he said, "Goodnight, *cara*," and left, shutting the door behind him.

As soon as he was gone, Elaine went to the window and looked out. She could barely discern the courtyard and fortification walls—it was too dark to see anything else. She stood there a moment, then backed away, afraid that Cattoretti might see her.

She sat back down on the bed, goose bumps rising on her arms. Nick LaGrange was here! How had he found her? Was he here to rescue her?

About the time she started to wonder if she had imagined the little light on the ceiling, she heard a sound from the direction of the window.

Nick LaGrange was slowly making his way up the darkest side of the East Tower. He had thrown a grappling hook onto the roof and was climbing up the stone wall, afraid that the patrolling guard would see him.

He was still reeling from what he had witnessed out in the courtyard. If he hadn't seen it with his own eyes, he wouldn't have believed it.

His Elaine was *here*, at this very castle. And apparently good friends with Giorgio Cattoretti! *Very* good friends.

It had shocked him so much he had nearly lost his balance on the fortification wall, kicking stone against the gutter. For a few seconds, when the dog started barking, he thought somebody would spot him.

What disturbed Nick the most was when he saw that Cattoretti and Elaine were holding hands. He remembered the day he had met her in Bulgaria, when he had held Elaine's hand to play along with the Turkey Roll con. By the time they had gotten back to the office that day, he had fallen in love with her, though he hadn't realized it at the time. Seeing Cattoretti holding her hand made Nick smolder with jealousy. Why the hell had she abandoned him in Bulgaria after they had slept together for the first time? It had been emotionally devastating for Nick. He still had not figured it out.

He rested for a moment, catching his breath, and then began to climb again.

Elaine rose from the bed, breathlessly watching the window as she saw a gloved hand push the shutters open.

"Don't worry," a voice whispered from the darkness outside, "it's me, Nick."

He swung in through the window.

He was dressed head to toe in camouflage fatigues, his face blackened with paint. All kinds of technical gear was hanging off him. There was a harness around his chest, a steel cable dangling.

She wanted to rush into his arms...but then she saw the look on his face.

Nick glanced over at the dresser. The Chopard diamond necklace was spread out on top. He looked back at her.

Only now did Elaine realize how this appeared.

"This—this isn't what it looks like," she stammered.

"No? What is it, then?"

She felt defensive. "It's—it's called survival, Nick."

He glanced back at the necklace. "It looks like a lot more than 'survival' to me."

Now she realized that he might have seen her and Cattoretti walking hand in hand in the courtyard—she remembered the sound they had heard.

"Nick—"

"Why did you abandon me in Bulgaria?"

"Nick..." There were tears in her eyes. "I should have listened to you instead of that awful old man. I'm sorry, I—"

"Why didn't you respond to my letters?"

"Letters? What letters?"

"I traced you to that hotel you were staying at in Washington. I know for a fact they were delivered."

Everything was becoming clearer to her now. "Gene Lassiter, that bastard..."

"Gene—who?"

"Lassiter. He's the person I met in Germany, the one who told me you were under investigation. He told me you had been arrested, and had gone to jail."

"You believed him, instead of me?"

There was moisture in her eyes. "Nick...please."

He shrugged. "I'm just sloppy and lazy, that's all. I never got around to changing those rubles."

"I know, Nick, I made a stupid mistake. Can you forgive me?" A tear ran down her cheek. "I *love* you, Nick! I'm crazy about you!"

He noticed the little wind-up turkey sitting on the dresser. It lay on its side, one leg broken off. He cracked a smile. "You kept that dumb thing?"

"Of course I kept it!" Elaine said, tears now running down her cheeks.

He moved towards her, reaching out.

The door burst open.

Cattoretti was standing there in his tux, a pistol in his hand. His eyes cut at Nick, then at Elaine.

Nick reached for his gun.

Cattoretti fired. Elaine screamed. Nick staggered backwards. Cattoretti fired two more rounds.

Both hit Nick in the center of the chest. He hit the floor.

Wailing, Elaine rushed towards him, but Cattoretti grabbed her by the wrist.

"Who is he?" he shouted.

"Nick!" she cried, looking down at his lifeless body. "Nick!"

"Who is he?" Cattoretti demanded.

CHAPTER 3.13

The picturesque village of Vernazza was perched along the rugged coastline of the Italian Riviera.

It took a little over three hours to drive there from Fontanella. They left the next morning, immediately after breakfast.

Elaine was in such a deep state of shock and grief at Nick's death, she felt nothing. She had showered and dressed that morning like an automaton, her body going through the movements but her mind and emotions completely shut down. After Cattoretti had shot Nick, Luigi had dragged the body down to the dungeon.

When Tony prepared breakfast for her in the morning, Cattoretti was busy packing. She and Tony were alone in the Great Hall. Gone was the warm, jovial character that had welcomed her to the castle a few days ago. This version of Tony was a jittery, anxious little man who looked like he might fall apart at the slightest provocation. His face was pale, his black hair disheveled, and his hands were trembling.

When he reached to pour her coffee, he fumbled, and her cup crashed to the floor.

"*Merda!*" he muttered.

Elaine squatted and helped him pick up the pieces.

"Are you all right?" she said.

"No, Tony not all right. Tony *nervoso e spaventato!*" he declared. "I never seen nothin' lika-a in my life. I been a workin' for *Signore* Cattoretti for five-a years, and I never seen *nothin'* like-a that." He lowered his voice to a whisper and glanced at the doorway. "Two dead bodies in the dungeon! I never seen-a dead body before, *signora!* Never!"

"What do you mean, two dead bodies?"

"The man who-a broke in your room, and the other one."

"What other one?"

Tony made a wavy gesture with his fingers. "With the long black curly hair. He was in the trunk of the Rolls Royce, with big-a hole in his head!"

Gypsy, Elaine thought sickeningly. So Cattoretti had killed him, too. The thought that Nick's and Gypsy's bodies had been dumped together down in the basement of the castle was so repugnant she almost vomited.

"Tony gonna look for a new job," he whispered, looking at the door that led to the Great Hall. "Tony don't like this place no more."

Cattoretti drove Elaine to Vernazza in the Porsche. It was a three hour drive. They stopped for coffee in Tortona, a beautiful 2,000-year-old village, at a bar on the main *piazza.*

It was about 2 pm when they drove up the steep hillside road that led to Cattoretti's secluded seaside villa. He called it his "hideaway." It afforded a splendid view of the sea.

Elaine felt nothing. She occasionally found herself giggling, and at other times, hot tears silently coursed down her cheeks.

She only had one conscious thought. *Nick LaGrange was the only man who ever loved me.*

When they reached the villa at Vernazza, Cattoretti parked the car and carried their luggage inside.

Dazed, Elaine surveyed the living room. It was outfitted with modern furniture, in black leather, with a large desk that faced the Mediterranean.

Cattoretti unlocked a cabinet in the desk and deposited the Gucci bag there, relocking it. Elaine noticed the cabinet contained a set of file folders.

"I do a lot of private work here," he said, as if he felt the need to explain. "I often use this little villa as a retreat, a place to clear my mind."

He just stood there, smiling at her. She was wearing the black Prada dress he had given her the first day, and the Fendi heels.

He had been chattering on the entire trip as if nothing unusual had happened. She had barely heard anything he'd said, but she had gotten the gist of it. A Secret Service agent who she'd had a little fling with in Bulgaria had shown up at the castle, drawn his gun, and Cattoretti had killed him in self-defense. He was sorry that the man had died, but what did she expect him to do? Let the man kill him?

Of course Cattoretti did not know she knew about Gypsy, too. He had no excuses for that. Gypsy had been killed in cold blood.

"You look so beautiful in that outfit," he said softly, still gazing at her.

He slowly approached her, then embraced her and hungrily kissed her, running his tongue deeply into her mouth the way he had last night.

This time Elaine did not resist. There was no point in fighting him any longer. He was all she had now. She had nowhere to go, no one who cared about her, and no future with anyone but him.

During the trip today he told her he was going to set up a numbered Swiss bank account for her and deposit the eight million Euros there. That her passport would be there soon and she could go wherever she wanted.

He had no intention of doing any of that, she knew. He was going to turn her into one of his whores, nothing more. He would use her brain to improve the quality of his counterfeits, when he needed it, but other than that, she would be his slave, like everyone else around him.

Cattoretti was soon on top of her, grinding his body into hers, pounding away at her like an animal.

They spent most of the next two days in the villa's bedroom. Elaine was there, and she wasn't there. The earth spun on its axis. Night became day, and day became night again. Cattoretti was insatiable. He did things to her that no man had ever done. She let him satisfy all his cravings, no matter how depraved they seemed. He tied her up, he ejaculated on her face, he sodomized her.

Elaine succumbed to everything. Emotionally, she was numb. At times she felt like a mannequin that he twisted into various sensual poses to please him or give him better access to the parts of her he desired. Every now and then she would look down at his ankles and expect to see hooves attached, but there were only two ordinary feet there, with toes, just like everyone else's. He was a flesh and blood human being.

But what kind of human being?

Every now and then they "came up for air," as Cattoretti put it. They hiked up and down the cobblestone streets of the village, looking at the views, and the narrow houses that were painted in pink, blue and yellow pastels. They ate the local cuisine—*cappon magro*, a pyramid made of fresh vegetables and a half dozen different types of fish, and the *torta pasqualina*, a cake made of 18 layers of light pasta and stuffed with *ricotta* cheese.

Elaine became more animated. She smiled, she laughed, she did all the things that Cattoretti expected her to do.

She had ceased being Elaine Brogan. She was someone else, an actress in a movie. When they were in bed, Cattoretti told her about his days of working as an extra on films. That's what she felt like—an extra on a film. None of this was real, it was make believe.

As time passed, a thought began to nag her, one that she had almost forgotten about in her grief. *He'll find out about the IN GOD WE TRUST flaw. And when he does, he will kill me.*

She began to hear his voice in her head uttering the words he had spoken after they had gone to the opera.

You must reveal to me every defect you see in my money, Elaine. Every mistake. I would consider anything less than that a betrayal.

While they were in Vernazza, his cellphone rang often. If it happened while they were in bed, he wouldn't answer. Otherwise he would take the call out on the balcony, or in the lobby, if they were in a restaurant. Each time he took a call Elaine began to fear that he was receiving the news that the counterfeits were worthless, that the fakes wouldn't pass through bank verifying machines.

And she expected to see a gun pointed at her face.

But he would always come back after the phone calls with the same warm look on his face, and say, "I am sorry, *cara*. Business is such a bother."

Late in the afternoon of the fourth day, when they were walking along a path that overlooked the sea, he said, "Have you ever been to San Remo?"

"No," Elaine said.

"It has the largest casino in Italy. You would like it. A very colorful crowd gambles there."

Ten minutes later, they were driving up the coast, heading towards San Remo. It was almost sunset. The highway ran up and down the rugged cliffs along the shore. Soon, the sky exploded into a riot of orange and indigo and violet.

The Gucci bag was in the back seat. Inside was the fake money he had been carrying around, the money that was badly flawed, the money that wouldn't pass through even the older-model currency machines. The fake currency with the IN GOD WE TRUST phrase printed in the wrong place.

He had locked it away when they had arrived at the villa, but now he was taking it to the casino.

Did he plan on gambling with it?

The casino at San Remo was set up on a hill, amidst several expensive-looking hotels, restaurants, and cafes. As they approached it, Cattoretti slowed the Porsche a little, then brought the car to a stop just in front of the sidewalk that led up to the entrance.

He smiled, reached into his pocket, and pulled out an Italian passport. "Just as I promised," he said, handing it to her.

Elaine opened it. DE LA FONTAINE, MARIE it said, next to her photo. It was the same name she had used at the opera reception.

"I don't understand," she muttered. *Why is he giving me the passport now?* she thought.

He reached into the back seat and put the Gucci bag in Elaine's lap. "You are going inside the casino and change all of this into chips. I have some business to attend to. I'll join you in a little while. Gamble a little bit, enjoy yourself."

Elaine looked down at the bag. She was suddenly filled with terror. The first real feeling she'd had since Nick had died.

"But...what are you going to do?"

"I will have a coffee and a cigar over there," Cattoretti said, motioning to an outdoor cafe across the street. "I will join you at the tables in a little while. I have fallen behind on my business calls, and I need to catch up."

Elaine's throat was so dry she couldn't find her voice.

He gave her a puzzled look. "Is something wrong, *cara?*"

"I—I thought you weren't going to change any of the counterfeits in Italy."

He shrugged, glancing down at the bag. "It is only fifty thousand. This casino is owned by a French company—they send all their foreign notes to their main office, in Marseilles." He paused. "Anyway, this is a good opportunity to put all our hard work to the test, Elaine. I also happen to know that the currency exchange in this casino just updated the verifying equipment with the latest software updates."

"Oh." Elaine swallowed.

He put his arm on her shoulder. "*Cara*, you should have more confidence in yourself! You went over my counterfeits 'with a fine-tooth comb,' as you put it. You have nothing to fear." He patted her knee. "Now be a good girl and go change the money."

Taking the bag, she slowly opened the door and got out of the car.

Cattoretti leaned over, smiling up at her. "And try not to gamble it all away before I get there!"

As Elaine neared the casino entrance, she suddenly found her senses clear and sharp. She glanced over her shoulder. Cattoretti was already sitting at one of the outdoor tables at the cafe.

He smiled at her and waved, his phone already to his ear.

A uniformed man opened the glass door for Elaine and she went inside the lobby of the sprawling casino. She could hear the steady dinging and mechanical grinding of the slot machines.

She passed a security guard. He gave her a cursory glance as she walked by. The currency exchange was busy--there were a few people standing in line to change money into chips, or change chips back into money.

There were security cameras everywhere. Elaine glimpsed a sign on the wall.

- WARNING -
ANYONE CAUGHT TRYING TO PASS AS MUCH AS ONE COUNTERFEIT BANKNOTE ON THESE PREMISES WILL BE TURNED OVER TO THE POLICE

The warning was repeated in Italian and French.

Elaine's hands were already damp with sweat.

This was a test. Cattoretti wanted her to try changing the money, and take the fall if it was detected as counterfeit.

Then an even more terrifying thought hit her. Hadn't Lassiter told her that a few months ago, an Italian hooker had changed some of the fakes at this very casino and then disappeared?

Behind one of the counters, she saw a clerk feeding a stack of Euro notes into one of the high-speed verifying machines. There was no way she could convert the money here—the machines would set off alarms instantly.

Now fully out of the passive daze she'd been in for the last three days, she frantically glanced around the lobby—there had to be another way out of the building...but where would she go? All she had was a fake passport that Cattoretti had made for her and a bag full of worthless counterfeits.

She wandered into the crowded casino, past the slot machines and around the blackjack tables, her heart thudding harder with each passing moment. Her only hope was to pass the fake currency off onto someone else. But who? And how?

Scanning the crowd, she spotted a bleach-blonde weighed down by gaudy gold jewelry. She was with a man in a cowboy hat and string tie. They were at a craps table, gathering up their chips.

"Don't leave now!" one of the other players said. "You're on a hot streak."

"Darlin', we're quittin' while we're ahead," the woman said, greedily sweeping up the chips. There was a diamond on her finger the size of an acorn.

"I lost my shirt last night," the man with her muttered, sweeping the chips into his cowboy hat. "We're gittin' out while the gettin's good."

As they turned in Elaine's direction, she stepped around another craps table to intercept them.

"Ya'll are from Texas, I'll bet." Elaine said, with a big grin.

"We sure are!" the woman said. "Don't see too many Americans in this neck of the woods. We're from Galveston—where ya from?"

"Dallas," Elaine said, turning to keep up with them—they were walking hurriedly towards the currency exchange. "Listen, I can save ya'll a considerable amount of money on your winnin's, if you're interested..."

They slowed down.

"How that?" the man said guardedly.

"I can change your chips into U.S. dollars—you won't have to pay a bit of commission." Elaine glanced around to make sure no one was watching, then opened the Gucci bag so they could both see inside.

The man glanced at his wife, tempted.

"Chester, are you outta your mind?" the woman said. Glaring at Elaine, she said, "We weren't born yesterday, darlin'."

She grabbed her husband's arm and pulled him away.

Elaine walked around the casino, her mind racing. Only five minutes had passed since she had come in the door, but each subsequent minute seemed like a week. She shuddered to think what Cattoretti would do to her.

She could hear his voice when he had talked about Sforza:

It is said that he nailed one betrayer to his own coffin, still alive.

Elaine walked all the way to the back, where the restrooms were located. There was a rear door, an emergency fire exit, as required by law—but there were two armed security guards stationed there. Again—even if she could get past them, where could she go? She couldn't buy anything in Italy with any currency but Euros, she certainly couldn't chance using her credit cards.

Elaine went back to the front of the main hall, peering around the edge of the window frame.

Cattoretti was still sitting at the cafe across the street. He was too far away for her to make out the details of his face, but she could tell he was watching the entrance—she could see the flickering orange glow of his cigar each time he puffed it.

She went over to the craps tables and desperately looked around. There had to be some way out of this...but no one in their right mind would trust a stranger offering to change money. And if the guards saw her do that, they would throw her out, at the very least.

Then she remembered something: The Turkey Roll. A ploy along those lines might work.

She spotted a young, voluptuous blonde, about her age, who seemed upset about something. Beside her was a man with wire-frame glasses who looked old enough to be her grandfather. They were arguing about something.

Elaine moved a little closer so she could pick up the conversation.

"You say those chips *mine*," she said in a heavy Italian accent, "and then you say how I bet! I gamble how I want!"

"My dear, I'm just trying to keep you from losing." He spoke in a cultured British accent. "You need guidance."

"I no want your guidance!" she said haughtily. She slid her stack of chips farther away from him.

"Suit your bloody self." He picked up the dice and rolled. "Throw it all in the rubbish bin, I don't care. But you're not getting any more tonight."

"And neither are you," the girl muttered.

Elaine turned around and went straight to the women's restroom. There was an attendant inside, sitting at a table piled high with towels, reading a paperback book. Elaine went into one of the middle stalls. She locked the door, then hung the Gucci bag on the door hook. Making no sound, she slipped under the partition into the next stall, waited a few seconds, then flushed the toilet and emerged.

A minute later she was back out in the casino, stepping up behind the curvy Italian girl. Between her fingers was a sticky wad of chewing gum she'd picked out of an ash tray.

"Excuse me, you've got gum on the back of your dress," Elaine said.

The girl frowned. *"Merda,"* she said, reaching behind her back, trying to find it with her fingers. *"Questo vestito è molto costoso!"* She glanced over at her elderly male companion, who was now caught up in his own game, paying her no attention.

"That's a shame," Elaine said sympathetically. "I know how to get it off without spoiling the dress. Let's go to the ladies' room."

When they entered the restroom, Elaine said to the attendant. "Would you mind getting us some strong tape, please? From the kitchen, or the janitor?"

"Nastro d'argento," the girl said, translating.

"Si," the attendant said, and left the room.

"Tape will take it off like magic," Elaine assured the girl, who had turned and was looking at the sticky mess through the mirror.

"Excuse me a minute," Elaine said, and she went into the middle stall, shutting the door behind her. She slipped under the door and into the one where she'd left the Gucci bag, then back into the first one.

"Oh my god!" she cried.

"Cosa c'è?" the girl said.

Elaine came out of the stall with the bag in her hands, then quickly shut it. "Nothing...I...someone left this behind." She took a step towards the door. "I'm going to turn it in to security—"

"Wait," the girl said suspiciously, grabbing Elaine's wrist. "What is inside?"

"Nothing," Elaine said, averting her eyes.

The girl tried to pull the bag away. Elaine kept hold of it but made sure the girl got a glimpse of the money.

"*Madonna mia!*" she gasped.

"I found it," Elaine said, pulling it away. "It's mine!"

"*We* find!" the girl said, pulling it back. Her eyes were aflame with greed. "I call security!"

"Shhh," Elaine said, glancing nervously at the door, "Look, we'll split it? Fifty-fifty. Okay?"

At that moment, two other women came in the restroom.

Elaine and the girl went into one of the stalls and locked the door. Elaine quickly counted the money, the girl watching her every move.

"There's fifty thousand here," Elaine whispered. She nodded down at the girl's bag. "You give me twenty-five thousand worth in chips, and you can keep all of it."

It only took the girl a split second to decide the cash was better than the chips. She quickly counted out 25,000 worth of chips, and Elaine gave her the money in exchange.

As Elaine went out the restroom door she passed the attendant, who was carrying a roll of duct tape.

"Thank you," Elaine smiled, "but we got the problem solved."

A minute later, Elaine was at the roulette wheel furthest from the entrance, standing at a spot where she could both place bets and clearly see everyone who walked in the room.

All the chips were stacked in front of her, but she had not bet anything yet—she had merely been observing, waiting.

Cattoretti soon entered. He glanced around, looking for Elaine. She immediately shoved a €4,000 stack of chips forward onto the BLACK rectangle.

Cattoretti reached her just as the roulette wheel ball settled into one of the red slots.

"*Quattordici, rossa,*" the croupier said mechanically. He swept Elaine's chips away.

"I'm afraid my luck isn't very good tonight," she muttered.

"Oh, I would not say that." He looked down at the chips, then at the people surrounding the table, and finally up at her face. "I think your luck is holding out *very* well."

She glanced nervously at him. "What do you mean?"

He motioned to the chips. "You still have what—about half of the money you started with?"

"A little less."

"Roulette is a very seductive game. Many people would have lost it all by now." He glanced around at the others again, then extended his arm to her. "Come, *cara*. I will teach you how to play baccarat."

They gambled together for several more hours. Cattoretti had a couple of hot streaks. By 2 am, the chips had swelled to about €60,000 worth.

"Shall we go back to Vernazza now?" he said.

Elaine hesitated. She felt much safer here, around all these people, than at Cattoretti's hideaway. But she could think of no excuse to stay.

"Yes, I'm getting sleepy now."

During the winding drive back to Vernazza, Cattoretti did not utter a word. Elaine gazed out the window at the oncoming cars they passed out on the coastal highway, and became more and more anxious. If he knew that she had managed to change the money without using the currency exchange, he didn't show it. Yet there was something different about the way he was acting now. Something subtle. Something dangerous.

When they reached the villa, Cattoretti parked the car in the garage and they went inside.

He wasted no time in taking her to the bedroom. He was soon on top of her again, making love to her with a new ferocity that she had never seen before.

"You drive me wild," he said, panting, as he rolled her onto her stomach. He entered her from behind, driving himself inside her so deeply she thought she would pass out.

He was soon spent, collapsed on top of her, and softly snoring in her ear.

She lay there a long time before she very gently slipped out from under him, trying not to rouse him. He stopped snoring for a moment, then let out a long sigh and rolled over.

She was thinking about the locked cabinet in his desk, wondering if a gun was hidden there.

His face was only inches from his key ring, which lay on the nightstand.

She lay there another few minutes, debating, and decided it was too risky. They would jingle if she picked them up, and she already knew that he was a very light sleeper.

She slipped out of the bed, put on her robe, and went out into the hallway, gently closing the door behind her.

The stress of changing the money at the casino and outwitting Cattoretti had energized her, snapped her out of her daze. She was not going to let him dominate her, or get away with what he had done.

She went to the kitchen, poured a glass of orange juice, then casually wandered to the living room. She paused a moment at the door, listening. She could still faintly hear Cattoretti snoring.

She went to the desk and opened the top drawer. There were some paper clips of various sizes. She picked out one and knelt in front of the cabinet.

She had taken a lock-picking class at the Secret Service, and had spent one session on methods using "improvisational tools" like paper clips and bobby pins. Now she sorely regretted not paying more attention that day.

Elaine fumbled for a good ten minutes, cringing every time she made a loud scraping sound and pausing to make sure Cattoretti was still snoring.

Finally, the lock opened.

A quick survey of the cabinet revealed that there was no gun hidden there. Just a bunch of file folders.

She pulled one out and looked at the label.

Lassiter

She opened it. There were pages and pages of notes scrawled in Italian—in Cattoretti's distinctive handwriting.

Then back a few sheets, computer printouts, with photographs printed out four to a page, and notes scribbled in the margins: Gene Lassiter limping along 15th Street in D.C., his cane in his hand. Gene Lassiter eating dinner alone at a restaurant. Gene Lassiter opening the front door of his Georgetown home, this one taken through a telephoto lens.

Elaine turned the page.

The top of the paper was labeled, *Berlino, Germania.*

More photos. Lassiter and Gypsy, coming out of a seedy bar. Lassiter and Gypsy, walking hand in hand on some beach. Lassiter and Gypsy, together in a bedroom, naked and—

She quickly closed the folder.

When she picked up the next one, she had a strange, unsettling feeling. *Sofia, Bulgaria,* the label read.

She slowly opened it...there were photographs. Many photographs. Elaine and Nick having dinner at a restaurant. Elaine flagging down a taxi on Boulevard Todor Alexandrov, the main drag.

And Elaine and Nick going into the entrance of her apartment building.

The photos had to have been taken the night we slept together, Elaine thought dully.

Her head spun as she realized the implications. Cattoretti had been watching her back in Bulgaria. He had engineered everything! There were no "coincidences"—he had known exactly who she was all along. He had used unusual expertise to identify fake currency for his own purposes. Gene Lassiter had only been a puppet.

It was Giorgio Cattoretti who had ruined her life.

Elaine heard Cattoretti's cellphone start ringing from the bedroom.

She felt like jumping in five directions at once. She quickly put the file folders away and shut the cabinet door. Now Cattoretti was speaking in Italian on the phone, his deep voice sounding sleepy. Fumbling with the paper clip, Elaine tried to get the lock closed again, the metal raking noisily along the tumblers.

"*Cara?*" Cattoretti called.

Elaine ignored him, desperately trying to turn the lock. Finally, it rotated back into place.

"Elaine?" he called, louder. She could hear the squeak of bedsprings as he got up.

She quickly smoothed down her robe and picked up the glass of orange juice. She pretended to look out the window at the sea. It was dawn, and the sky was painted with violet and pink hues.

His footsteps were approaching the living room.

She glanced down at the desk.

The top drawer was still partially open!

She reached over to close it, and her eyes locked on something just inside the drawer. A letter opener. It was slim and silver, like a stiletto.

She quickly palmed it and shut the drawer.

"Ah, there you are," Cattoretti said.

She turned around, sipping the juice. "I couldn't sleep," she said.

He was standing there at the door, stark naked, his penis half-hard and throbbing.

When she looked into his eyes, her heart sank. He knew about the IN GOD WE TRUST flaw. Someone had just called him and told him about it.

She turned away and looked back out the picture window, at the early morning light show.

He walked behind her and slipped his arms around her, his manhood thumping against her bottom.

"It is beautiful, is it not?" he whispered into her ear. "Almost as beautiful as you are."

She sensed him cocking his head a little, looking down at the desk.

"You know," he said, "after that phone call, I am wide awake. How about we take a walk along the coastline?"

"It's cold outside," she said.

"I will keep you warm, *cara*. Come," he said, taking her hand. "It is time."

CHAPTER 3.14

They were moving along a path that ran alongside cliffs that overlooked the sea. They walked side by side, Cattoretti tightly gripping her by the hand.

When they reached a fork in the path, they veered off in the direction of Corniglia, the next closest village. The path widened a little—now there must have been a 200-foot drop down to the sea. Elaine could see the breakers smashing across the rocks below, feeling the thunderous impact in the earth beneath her feet.

Elaine walked mechanically along, possessed by a strange calmness.

He's going to kill me now, Elaine thought dully. *And there's nothing I can do about it.*

It seemed that her entire life had been composed of a series of events that all funneled her down this inevitable path. Dozens of vivid memories flooded her mind. Her father, his head hung in shame, standing on the other side of the prison glass. Luna Faye, rising up from the training mat, wiping the blood from her mouth, grinning. *Well done, girl. Looks like, there's hope for you after all.* And her loyal friend Dmitry, jumping the pedestrian bridge in his taxi, risking his life for her.

And Nick, making passionate love to her…the one and only time they had slept together, in her apartment in Bulgaria.

She walked on, up the cliffs, almost unaware that Giorgio Cattoretti was still holding her hand.

They reached a crest in the hill. Cattoretti slowed, moving towards a rock ledge. The air was filled with brine, and she could hear the waves crashing down against the boulders below.

"Isn't the view amazing?" he said, putting his arm around her.

She said nothing.

He moved between Elaine and the hill, forcing her to take a step closer to the edge, which was a sheer drop down to the sea.

"How did you do it?" he said softly, looking into her eyes.

"How did I do what?" Her voice sounded small over the crashing waves.

"Change the money." He paused, his dark eyes boring into her. "I know about the flaw, Elaine."

She didn't answer—she glanced down at the thrashing water.

"I gave you everything," he said, his voice rising. "Everything! And what do you do to show your appreciation? You betray me."

"You destroyed my life. I know everything you did to me."

He looked surprised by this. "What 'life'? You had no life before I found you in Bulgaria."

He was breathing hard now. She found herself looking into the eyes of another Giorgio Cattoretti, a man she had never met. This was the one who had served time at Attica, had been deported from the United States, and had arranged the brutal murder of everyone who had ever crossed him, and had built an empire through 25 years of theft, bribery and extortion.

Both his hands shot out together, directly at her chest. She reacted as she had been trained, blocking the forward energy and grasping both his hands and driving them backwards, trying to break his wrists.

He screamed, bringing his knee up into her thigh, knocking her off balance. The next thing she knew both his hands were around her throat. He had pushed her back a little more over the cliff edge—her left foot was kicking wildly over empty space. Now she held onto to him, determined to carry him over the edge with her.

Elaine felt her face turning purple, his thumbs pressing into her windpipe. She let go of him. In a flash, she reached behind her back and grabbed the letter opener, which she had slipped into the elastic clip in her bra.

She plunged it into his left eye.

He let out a blood-curdling scream, staggering backwards. He yanked out the blade, bellowing like a bear, and flung it down, holding his palm over his eye socket. Blood spurted between his fingers. He began swinging wildly with his free hand, trying to force her over the edge of the cliff. Elaine backed away, then slipped and fell. She clawed at the loose dirt and plant roots, trying not to slip any farther. Cattoretti tried to stomp on her hands.

She grabbed his ankle and yanked hard. He fell over on his side, kicking at her, and they both nearly went over.

"You goddam bitch!" he spat, groaning in pain.

They were both on their feet again, circling each other on the edge of the cliff, Cattoretti still holding one hand over his bleeding eye—he was in agony. He kicked her hard in the shin. She whirled around and tried to kick him in the head, but he ducked and her foot only grazed him.

MIKE WELLS

He looked down and saw the bloody letter opener a few feet away.

When he bent to reach for it, Elaine whirled around again and kicked him square in the chest.

His body flew through the air and disappeared over the cliff edge, a look of horror on his face.

Elaine kicked him with such force that she lost her balance, and she fell again, this time slipping even farther down the precipice. She clawed at the loose rock and dirt, but only found herself sliding farther towards the rocks below.

"Help!" she wailed, above the pounding surf. "Help me, please!"

The slightest movement made things worse. Even her heaving chest caused her to slide. She dug her fingernails into the dirt, closing her eyes as loose earth and pebbles fell in her face—she could hear the hungry waves smashing beneath her.

"Help me, please!" she gasped again, her voice growing weaker. She wanted to live.

There were footfalls along the path. Someone was coming.

"Hold on!" a voice shouted. "Don't move!"

Elaine hugged the cliff edge and pressed her face into the dirt, making as much contact as she could with the ground, trying not to slip any farther.

A pair of strong male hands reached down and took hold of both her wrists.

"I've got you!"

The voice was familiar...but it couldn't be.

She looked up, and she found herself staring into the face of the most handsome man she'd ever laid eyes on.

Nick carefully pulled her up, little by little. Finally, her knees found purchase on some rock edges, and she scrambled back up onto the path and out of danger.

Elaine hugged Nick with all her might. "I thought you were dead!"

He hugged her back. "I was wearing a Kevlar vest. You didn't notice?"

"No," she said, hugging him tighter. "I was too happy to see you."

"It's not the first time I've stayed alive by playing dead. What happened to Cattoretti?"

Elaine motioned over the cliff—she couldn't look. She gazed up into Nick's eyes. "How did you get out of the dungeon? How did you find

272

me?"

"Tony let me out. He told me you were at a villa somewhere in the Riviera, but he didn't know exactly where." Nick smiled. "He said, 'Tony don't like this place no more,' and that he was leaving."

Elaine laughed, wiping her tears. "Oh, Nick, I love you so much! I'm never letting you go."

"I'm never letting you go, either." He slipped his arm around her waist and peered briefly down at the waves crashing over the rocks. "Come on, let's go synchronize our DOPS."

EPILOGUE

Elaine Brogan and Nick LaGrange live in an old country house in the Provence region of France. They have two children.

Their housekeeper and cook, Tony, engages in never-ending battles with the local *dilettantes* about the inferior quality of French cuisine and the French people's "odd ways."

A Moscow taxi driver named Dmitry found a briefcase in his trunk with $50,000 in it. There was a note that said, "Thanks—your friend forever, Janet."

Interpol and the Secret Service located Cattoretti's printing press and destroyed it. Luigi and a number of Cattoretti's staff were sent to prison.

At present, Giorgio Cattoretti's body has not been found.

ABOUT THE AUTHOR

Mike Wells is an American bestselling author of over twenty "unputdownable" thriller and suspense novels, including Lust, Money & Murder and Passion, Power & Sin. He is also known for his young adult books, such as The Mysterious Disappearance of Kurt Kramer, The Wrong Side of the Tracks, and Wild Child, which are used by English teachers in high schools and colleges worldwide. Formerly a screenwriter, Wells has a fast-paced, cinematic writing style. His work is often compared to that of the late Sidney Sheldon, with strong and inspiring female heroes, tightly-written scenes, engaging action/dialogue, and numerous plot twists. He currently lives in Europe and has taught in the Creative Writing program at the University of Oxford. For a complete list of his books, tips for writers, and to sign up to his VIP Reader List, please visit his website at www.mikewellsbooks.com.

ACKNOWLEDGEMENTS

As this is my first foray into the world of independent book publishing, I would like to thank those who have helped me with my writing career along the way.

A few who have given much-needed general encouragement are Tom Patterson, Gina Ledbetter, Carol Bartels, Randy Frost, and Edie Joslin.

Fellow writers who I've learned a lot from include Elaine Floyd, Ellen LaPenna, George Williams, Emily Trenholm, Lisa Ernst, Farsheed Ferdowsi, the late Gary Provost, and my wonderful sister, Regina Wells.

My mother and stepfather, Betsy and Jack Hancock, have always been a great source of support, and my writing will always pale in comparison to my mother's.

Those who helped proofread and gave feedback on early versions of this particular manuscript deserve a big thanks: Myriam Boscarolli, Luba Pravotorova, Natalie Lundsteen, Olga Maday, and Dax Tucker.

Of course, my wife has always been my greatest source of inspiration and support. Poor Anya has spent countless hours reading drafts, editing storylines, and generally listening to me whine and complain. Anya, you are the greatest!

NOVELS BY MIKE WELLS

Baby Talk

Blind Scorpion (with Farsheed Ferdowsi)

The Drive-By Wife

Forbidden (series, with Devika Fernando)

Lust, Money & Murder (series)

The Mysterious Disappearance of Kurt Kramer

Passion, Power & Sin (series)

Secrets of the Elusive Lover

With Mother's Approval (series, with Robert Rand)

The Wrong Side of the Tracks

Wild Child (series)

Made in the USA
Monee, IL
01 March 2020